DISEASED INTENTIONS

DANIEL MUNRO

In celebration of
Hunter Stanley James Hutson-Bickley
Welcome to the world lil man!

AÉROPORT RENNES BRETAGNE (EUROPEAN ALLIANCE P.O.W FACILITY)

The wooden panelled walls glowed a dark brown and orange, as though the desktop lamp was trying to mirror a secluded cabin's log fire. The added illusion of warmth was welcome in the cold environment of the airport's prohibited staff corridor. No one knew what was happening behind the closed door of Tech Supervisor Gabriel Monreal's private quarters.

He hated spending any prolonged amount of time there, but constantly reminded himself it was only temporary for the two missions he was to oversee. The European Alliance would never know what was going to happen, and it was right under their noses.

Project Zodiac and Operation Rat Nest.

The technology he held in his palm would aid in the success of each project, and he didn't want to know how their inside men had created an untraceable bug, and more so, how they managed to get it to him while being stationed nearly four hundred miles away in Brugge. The apprehension smothered him like a duvet on fire as he plugged the thumb-drive into the laptop, and he wasted no time clicking the pop-up in the bottom right of the screen. The Catfish Program had installed to his device within seconds and camouflaged itself within the

European Alliances firewall. He was now in full control of not just the airport's security system, but every other terminal and device connected in the Western Europe strongholds.

He sat back and poured himself a scotch, glancing around the room that was not his own. The former occupant had been clean and well-disciplined with his hygiene, and to somewhat of a degree, he respected that. There was the vaguest amount of guilt lingering within him for making this person the patsy of the upcoming operations, but those feelings flittered away when he remembered that this was needed to get everything back to normal.

Until the time to execute Project Zodiac came, he couldn't tamper with the systems too much. The Catfish Program was to be used sparingly, just like his time in this room. It wasn't just a patsy he needed, but a room that was close to the POW corridor.

"I won't let you down, Admiral," he whispered, sipping the harsh alcohol and letting it flow through his veins while he basked in his new purpose. His loyalty was to the recent calling he'd been offered, and any of his friends who didn't believe in it were now secondary to him. No matter the amount of respect or trust between them, they were disposable if they attempted to halt what needed to be done.

The first of what would become many encrypted messages pinged in the bottom left corner of the screen. He led the cursor to the notification and clicked.

•*Kurusotovia45 ready for human testing + syringes obtained.*
  •*Deliver to Project Zodiac upon confirming.*
  •*Cargo ship docked in Portsmouth for Operation Rats Nest.*

The first set of human subjects volunteered three days ago, and the conclusion said the serum was safe to take. Human meat would no longer be the vital requirement to sustain the effects of Kurustovia45.

"When this is over," he said to himself as he stood and adjusted his uniform in the wardrobe mirror, "there will be no more wars. No more terrorism." He lifted the tumbler of scotch and emptied the contents down his throat. "Just full, humane control."

His two volunteers had proved that, and now some new, unaware human subjects were needed before they started clearing out the pests —the disposable rodents who stained Admiral's vision of the future.

Penbrook Vineyard may be flourishing, but they were going to be used as an example. They were, indeed, secondary to the cause.

1

Ryan clasped his hands together and let out a long breath, releasing the aching tension that constricted his stomach so tight he wanted to vomit. The walls of the medical room felt like they were collapsing down on him, burying him in his own darkness as he sank deeper into a leather side chair. He caught Mikey's eye as he looked up, covering him with another wave of sadness. It was the overbearing truth of what he wasn't revealing during these therapy sessions, and he hated not being able to tell his friend of what was eating away at him.

Mikey sat back against his chair's support. A generous tan covered his olive skin, a glaring contrast to the all-white uniform he wore when on shift in the medical corridor. His pen scribbled down everything that Ryan selectively admitted over the past half an hour. "Carry on," he urged with a nod, his slick, jet-black hair remaining in place. Even with time and the stresses that had befallen them, he still looked in his twenties.

"Do you think this'll actually help?" Ryan asked, wiping his clammy hands on his white vest. He didn't know if the sweat was from nervousness or a product of the heatwave. His blond dreadlocks clung to the moisture on his back. *I don't have to fight anymore*, he reminded himself, as he often did since that heart-wrenching day at the graves.

"Everything I've been learning about psychology suggests it is helping," Mikey said as he pointed to the stack of books on the shelf against the far wall. "As long as you're telling me everything that's on your mind."

"Okay then." Ryan rolled his green eyes and tried to appear bored, instead of revealing how terrified of himself he truly was. "What do you want me to talk about now?"

"Anything."

"Broad subject."

"Well," Mikey huffed with a look of disappointment, watching the final grain of sand empty into the bottom compartment of the egg timer, "your time is up."

"Already?"

"Yep. That was the deal. Thirty minutes a week."

"Thank fuck," Ryan said, standing and stretching his arms. "How are these sessions for you?"

"I feel like I'm learning when to ask you the right questions and what to extrapolate from the answers."

"Big word for you."

"They're big books." Mikey chuckled. "What are your plans for the morning?"

"To finish planting the new greenery—and get to know Drinker a bit better." Ryan yawned, pushing his dreadlocks off his shoulders. "Damn, this heat is killing me."

"As Harper said, we can thank China for the new climate."

"Yeah, Harper," Ryan said with a frown.

"You're still pissed off at him," Mikey noted. "It's understandable given the recent demands he's passed onto us. Keep your brain focused on work and our trip into town today. Plus, you've got a stag party to be ready for tonight."

"A joint hen party."

"Either way, it's a party for you and Cassy. Make sure that bitchy look has fucked off your face by tonight."

"Prick." Ryan smirked at Mikey. His best friend could always get him to look on the brighter side, even if it meant burying the self-loathing even deeper.

Mikey turned to the door. "I'll see you in the cafeteria at lunch."

Ryan turned his thoughts to his morning shift. The extra work he'd taken on was a personal choice, and it served one purpose: keeping his mind from descending into guilt-filled depression.

————

Autumn had never felt so non-existent as the sun's rays burned down over Maidville, more intense than the year before. Ryan had only ever felt temperatures this extreme while on summer vacations to Florida, never in England. The sweltering heat was only matched by the unforgiving dryness that ripped at his throat.

He worked through the late morning to plant the newly-cultured orange trees along the northern side of the vineyard's grounds with the help of the community's newest member, Chris Drinker.

The Glaswegian warmed up to everyone during his three visits from the European Alliance ground force, which internally encouraged him to leave the temporary service he'd enrolled in for the previous five years. Drinker wasn't officially a soldier. When the bombing of Europe's major cities and The Fast War had begun, Drinker was on holiday in Marbella, southern Spain. He avoided the bloodbath in the more heavily populated areas and followed the coast to Gibraltar, eventually crossing paths with Lieutenant Harper and his unit. He stayed with them until the inland invasion receded, and once he'd demonstrated a willingness to help, they took him under their wing. Harper gave him a uniform and weapons training, made him into an honouree private, and allowed Drinker to partake in various low-level search missions. After seeing the community of Penbrook and how they lived, the urge to return to normality became too strong.

The newer orange trees that Ryan and Drinker were planting were gifts from the European Alliance. An attempt to take the sting out of an order that Penbrook Vineyard had received the previous week. An order that left them defenceless, removing their perimeter traps.

"You were actually a chef?" Drinker said with a laugh. His black goatee was soaked with sweat and his spiked hair wilted. Perspiration was visible through his black T-shirt and urban camo pants. "I can't imagine you losing your shit in the kitchen."

"Did it since I was thirteen." Ryan grinned at the response, leaning on the shovel and wiping his forehead against the back of his hand. "Me and my sister got moved around from foster home to foster home. When we finally got put with a family that didn't give up on us, I started washing pots at my foster dad's local pub. One thing led to another, and it became my career."

Drinker nodded, sipping from a bottle of grapewater. "Sounds like a rough start for you and your sister," he said. "Did cooking help?"

"Kept my hands and brain busy." Ryan snorted and then said, "I actually found a calmness in the kitchen's madness."

"Most of the lads I knew in that trade turned out to be raging alcoholics."

"Luckily, I managed to avoid that."

"And you actually got famous from cooking?" Drinker asked, carrying on with the questions.

"Only locally." Ryan shrugged.

"Any other famous people from round here?"

"Err..." Ryan scratched his head, trying to remember. "Couple of actors and musicians. We even had the 'Bully Killer' live round here. Well, that's what the police suspected."

"That fucking batshit ham-doughnut who was torturing people?" Drinker remembered seeing the news broadcasts before the war.

"Yeah. Some people praised him. Said he was the right form of vigilante."

"That's crazy."

"Yeah, I thought so too." Ryan took a drink of his grapewater. "I've seen crazier since then."

There was a pause between the pair. Their first meeting was a scene that most horror movies would fail to replicate.

"I'm sorry we didn't get there sooner," Drinker said, breaking the tension.

"Don't apologize." Ryan stood back after patting the dry soil down with the back of his shovel, then looked over the young, orange tree.

"It wasn't your fault. Anyway, I can't think about that now." He untied his dreadlocks and said, "Got a big party tonight."

"Aye, you have! First stag-do I've seen since I was club rep." Drinker slapped his thigh enthusiastically, then poured a bucket of water on the tree's base.

"You were a club rep?" Ryan roared with laughter, using the shovel to hold him upright as his legs gave way.

"If there's one thing I know, it's drinking. How'd you think I got the name?"

At least two minutes passed before Ryan regained control, pulling himself up from his knees and wiping a tear away. "Makes sense, I suppose." He didn't realise how much he needed the laugh.

They walked back to the winery, passing Sanjay and Rani who were bringing in the first batch of harvested grapes from the western vines behind the building.

"Harper will be back in time for the evening party," Drinker reported, waving to the Pakistani couple.

"Anymore bullshit laws he wants to inflict on us?" Ryan responded without trying to hide the disdain. They pulled the fire exit open and entered the largest medical room. The shade felt soothing compared to the harsh morning sun.

"He didn't make the rules regarding your self-defence traps," Drinker pointed out, pulling the next door open to the ugly yellow and blue medical corridor. "It's the alliance's stand on those kinds of weapons."

"I know," Ryan sighed. "We've just got so used to them being our first line of defence."

For the past four years, the maze that encircled their grounds had been armed with hundreds of randomly hidden acidic-salt traps. They were deadly efficient and brutal to see when in full effect. Ryan had witnessed many intruders lose their lives in the slowest and most agonising way possible, only justifying it by saying their signs outside clearly read: "Do Not Enter."

Those traps violated the new accord being drawn up by a government that was desperately trying to kickstart a new civilisation, and Ryan had the headache of having to come up with an alternative method to protect the vineyard. The maze still stood strong at a hundred metres thick on all sides, but they needed more. In this world, a warning system was the difference between life and death. Though the war had ended, danger was still lurking outside the vineyard. Be as it may that they were no longer nearby, maybe even oceans away, they were still out there.

Mikey stepped out from the same medical room they held the therapy session in. "Everything okay, guys?" he asked. "Does our new recruit know he's getting a tour of our hometown when we go wedding ring shopping later?"

"Obviously." Ryan pushed the doors open to the cafeteria. "Hope you're working on your best man speech for the big day."

"I've finished it. Just picking some music for the evening now." Mikey followed them to the hot counter. "So far, I've got Slipknot, Korn, and Children of Bodom."

"I don't want any of your heavy metal shit for my wedding party!"

"It's real music!"

Drinker laughed behind the pair's squabble. Ryan and Mikey bantered the way they once used to. It felt like ages since they acted like friends and not a doctor/patient relationship.

The three men filled their bowls with berry porridge, sitting at the table nearest the stairwell, and started listing off the equipment necessary for the day's trip.

"How many of those hand-held radios do you have?" Drinker asked, scraping the last of his bowl.

"Three." Mikey unclipped his from his waist and placed it on the table. "Ryan and I have one each. The other stays with whoever is on top-floor lookout. They're solar charged, so battery life isn't an issue."

"Range?"

"Roughly fifty miles," Ryan answered. "That's our safety net if we ever venture further out."

"Aye," Drinker nodded as he looked over Mikey's device. "I'll see if Harper can get you anything more high-tech for longer distance excursions."

"One day at a time." Ryan laughed, though his smile dropped as he brought himself back to the moment. "We do what we need to do today. We may have been given the all-clear that we're safe, but we stay vigilant when we're outside our grounds."

It wasn't just Drinker's first look around Maidville town centre. It was Ryan and Mikey's first venture outside the vineyard since retrieving Doc and Sam's remains.

Ryan waited for the others to finish and head upstairs to get changed, leaving him on his own at the table. The conversations and footsteps around him drowned out as the burning anxiety rose from inside, engulfing every rational thought he had for this simple mission today.

What if they're still out there?

2

C anopies had been erected down the main driveway for the upcoming wedding, with fairy-lights rigged through the sycamore trees that ran down both sides. Ryan and Cassy wanted to celebrate the beginning of married life near the animals, who all occupied the front right side of the grounds. They initially planned for the ceremony to be performed out back by the graves, but after a long debate, death wasn't the right environment for it. Wherever they got married, their lost friends would be watching and celebrating with them. Chairs and decorations remained inside until the wedding day, just in case another random storm formed during the week.

Cassy had kept her dress a secret from Ryan by hiding it in Mikey and Jen's room. She planned to use Ryan's trip into Maidville to perform a literal dress rehearsal to make sure it fit and also testing for the perfection of hair and makeup.

Most of the community took a rare day off from their usual jobs of soap production and corn oil processing, opting to help organise the cafeteria's furniture for the conjoined stag and hen party, while others helped in the downstairs kitchen to prepare for the evening buffet.

Mikey walked out of the winery's front entrance and under the canopy, carrying his G36C assault rifle across his chest. Despite the scorching heatwave, they still opted for black sportswear for outside excursions. Like always, he made sure his equally jet-black hair was side parted perfectly.

He noticed some light footsteps running on the tarmac and getting closer, with a giggling that grew louder. Maisie, Ryan's adoptive daughter, appeared. She sported a bright smile in pretty much any situation, and Mikey knew he would be bombarded with questions.

"Uncle Mikey!" Maisie shouted excitedly, her blue eyes wide with mischief, and her ice-blonde hair bouncing frantically.

"Oh God." He rubbed the bridge of his nose, repressing a grin. "Hi."

She skidded to halt in front of him, jittering on the spot like she'd had an espresso sneaked into her breakfast. "We just fed the chickens! Where are you going?" she asked, looking over Mikey's attire.

"We're going out today," Ryan interrupted, walking over the footbridge. "Gotta get some final bits for the wedding."

"Can I come, Daddy?"

"Nope." He approached and scuffed her hair. "You need to go inside and help your mum with the wedding plans. I'm not allowed because I'm a man!"

Maisie giggled again.

"Go on." Mikey nodded towards the doors. "We'll see you when we get back."

"Bye, Daddy!" Maisie hugged Ryan's leg before running inside. Drinker just managed to dodge her as she ran through the front doors.

"Women doing the clothes fitting while the men go out? You know, if social media was still a thing, you'd be cancelled tomorrow," the Scotsman joked, a constant habit that everyone liked about him. "It's been years since I've seen children able to run around freely. I'll never take that for granted again."

Ryan and Mikey nodded in understanding. They didn't know much of what Drinker had seen over the years, but from the small details they were given, their own settlement was the most civilised that he had come across. Drinker's second visit to the vineyard had reminded him what being a civilian was like. After seeing the elation on everyone's faces when the end of the war had been announced, the urge to leave became too great.

Lieutenant Harper, though reluctant to lose him, was understanding.

"Do you know Cassy's ring size?" Mikey asked.

"That size." Ryan held up a bit of string that he'd looped around her finger.

"So romantic."

"The way your missus has been talking, you're next," Ryan teased.

"Fuck off!"

The party of three walked up the driveway and entered the maze, taking their time before reaching section D9.

"At least we can maintain the bushes better when the traps are gone," Mikey said out loud, observing how wild the pathways had gotten in the two months since they last left the vineyard.

"How in the name of fuckery do you navigate this whole maze?" Drinker asked, looking at the towering walls of fauna around them.

"It's split into twenty-six sections clockwise. A-Z." Mikey explained. "Then ten sections deep. We just had to memorise the only route that didn't have a trap in its pathway."

"Fucking impressive."

Ryan reached into the wall of D9 and pulled on the trip wire, setting off the emergency trap in section C10. "Weird knowing that's the last time it'll be used," he whispered behind the sharp hiss that shot the corrosive mixture into C10. "Might wanna cover your nose." He turned to Drinker and said, "This shit stinks."

They waited for the mixture to dissipate, then stepped out onto the carriageway, performing a quick scan of the car park and sewage plant opposite. Everything looked quiet and lifeless, the way it should've been. They knew that back in the winery's top floor, their look out, Dominic, had a rifle aimed at Maidhill, and would radio if he spotted anything. With the sun beating down, they made their way up the road and into town, ready to get the final pieces for the party and wedding.

———

The jewellery shop was opposite the church on Maidville high street. Like all the buildings in the area, it had avoided significantly more damage compared to the surrounding towns, which had been subjected to heavy petrol bombing during The Fast War. However, many still wore the scars of rogue Molotovs, bullets, rockets, and other explosives. Moss had grown wild in the erratic weather conditions, coating most of the town's brickwork and roads. Various weeds coated the cars from inside and out, growing over to the pathways and security railings.

Within the store, jewellery lay everywhere under the smashed furniture and glass. Brambles rose from the wooden floorboards, wrapping around the dust-covered furniture and beams.

"Got it!" Ryan shouted from behind the serving counter. "It's perfect." He stood with a look of pride on his face, waving for Mikey to join him. Drinker stood on guard by the front door, never lowering his weapon.

"She'll love it," Mikey said, inspecting the ring before handing it back.

Ryan looked over the ring again, faded white gold with three small diamonds atop, sparkling like Cassy's big eyes. He could already see her smile when presenting it to her at the ceremony. He selected his own wedding ring out of the few available that fit. Having a ring of his own didn't bother him, but it would make Cassy happy, and that's all that mattered.

Stepping out of the broken doorway, they walked to the concrete flower show that was the high street and began to head home. Drinker led in front, sweeping each corner and every building efficiently, getting used to what would be his surroundings from now on. Ryan didn't approve of him wearing sunglasses while going out, but they were the last thing Drinker owned from before the war, and he wasn't going to deny a man from holding on to any good memories.

Like Drinker wearing glasses, a lot of Ryan's paranoia and strict security protocols were marginally eased since the announcement of no threats nearby. The overnight trench shifts were axed, leaving one person in the second reception and one on the top floor restaurant throughout the night.

"Feel a bit better now that we've been into town?" Mikey asked, breaking the silence as they approached the roundabout on the town's border.

"What do you mean?" Ryan replied while watching Drinker in front, impressed with his attention to detail.

"You looked like hell during therapy this morning, like you were holding something back."

"I wasn't, but I am happy I found a decent ring for Cassy."

"Good." Mikey shouldered his bag higher as they pushed through the car barricade.

Ryan raised his weapon, aiming straight ahead to the old hotel, shaking off the visions of blood and flesh. *I don't have to fight anymore.*

Mikey noticed his movements. "Still having nightmares?"

"It's not therapy now, Mikey," Ryan said, turning towards the carriageway. "It's party night. As you said, I need to be in the right mood."

"Fine."

"Anyway, you need to organise the stripper situation for tonight."

"Strippers?"

"It is a stag-do. And seeing as the only three women who can dance is my future wife, my sister, and your missus, I guess that kinda narrows it down. Tell Jen I'll pay double."

"Fuck off!" Mikey cackled. "You know Jen would kick your arse if she ever heard you say that."

"She can spank it if she wants..." Ryan's voice trailed, realising Drinker hadn't joined in with the banter, which was something he'd usually make sure to be part of.

The pair looked forward to their lead man. He stood with his gun aimed directly at the petrol station to the left. His free arm was in the air, fist clenched. They raised their own weapons in the same direction, not seeing what he was seeing.

Everything was silent. No movement.

"What is it?" Ryan whispered as they carefully treaded up beside him.

"The first pump on the right side," Drinker reported quietly. "The few times we drove down here, I never spotted it."

Ryan looked over. The pump looked as battered as before, with the hose still rusting against the tarmac. "I don't see anything."

"Look at the support foundation."

Ryan's eyes moved to the faded white support.

There they were. A pair of eyes staring back—or what he thought was a pair of eyes. It was glasses, held in place by a knife pierced into the support. He couldn't remember if it had been there when he bought back his friend's remains, but given the state of distraught he was in, it was understandable that he'd have missed it. On the other hand, this could've been something new.

Ryan went to burst forward before Mikey grabbed his arm.

"It could be a trap," Mikey whispered harshly.

"Watch my fucking back then," Ryan rasped. "Drinker, watch the surrounding area. Mikey, look back towards the roundabout, see if anyone's watching."

"Check," Drinker confirmed.

"Fuck!" Mikey protested, though swinging his rifle round and following the order.

Ryan's body screamed to run but was subconsciously reminded that his last emotional impulse had cost two of his friends their lives. Cautiously, he paced to the petrol station with his gun tight to his shoulder, flicking the safety off and listening out for anything louder than his heartbeat. The closer he got, the more he made of the display. The knife held a zip-up plastic sleeve in place with what appeared to be a note inside. Unaware of his own actions, Ryan picked up the pace before halting, chills running through his core.

He had seen these glasses before and knew the pair of eyes that should be looking back at him.

Doc.

In a maniacal panic, Ryan performed a clockwise scan, expecting to see Connor laughing back at him, watching the torment with that distorted grin. There was nothing. Mikey and Drinker looked back at him with dread, knowing that Ryan had just seen a ghost. They carefully checked their flanks, never lowering their weapons, and joined him by the pump.

"What the fuck did you just see?" Mikey demanded to know.

"Those glasses." Ryan nodded behind him with a shiver. "They're Doc's."

Mikey didn't say anything, and Drinker didn't need to ask.

Ryan turned, strode to the pump and pulled the glasses down, carefully folding them and putting them into his hoodie pocket. He then pulled the knife out, recognising the wooden handle immediately. It was Sam's pocketknife. Ryan slipped it into his hoodie next to the glasses before opening the plastic sleeve and pulling the letter out, his skin crawling as he knew exactly who had written it.

Dear Hippy Cunt,

Whatever happens to me today, whether I live, die, or get to fuck your little girlfriend in front of the decaying bodies of your people, know this:

We will never stop.

I'll be seeing you again.

I mean, if the taste beneath your skin is as good as your friend's, how could I say no?

Your good friend,
Connor

3

For the first time in a while, Ryan was grateful to be alone in the family bedroom. He locked the door behind him, resting his forehead against the wood and letting out a heavy breath that became a restrained scream.

"Connor isn't here," he reassured himself. His hands shook before cramping up. The familiar feeling of a stress vomit wanted to show itself. "He's not here."

I don't have to fucking fight anymore.

He'd ordered Drinker to contact Harper as soon as they returned but requested they keep this incident between the three of them. He couldn't put a downer on tonight's celebrations or let the discovered items scar their way into people's minds, especially his sister, Steph.

She'd completely devoted herself to understanding Doc's work, performing the tasks that only he had the knowledge of and doing it well, with only the aid of his notes that were left behind. Ryan knew she missed her partner more than any words could describe, so she put everything into keeping his memory alive.

Before stepping away from the door, he remembered the night Steph had told him about her relationship with Doc. 'My old sous chef is banging my sister!' he remembered joking before hugging her tight.

My old sous chef. Doc.

Shaking away his memories, Ryan drew the desk key from his pocket. Once opening the drawer, he unloaded the pistol and gently placed it down, then reached into his hoodie pocket and removed all three of the salvaged items. His fingers tensed when he felt the paper brush against his palm, causing his hand to shake again. Once the knife, glasses, and note rested on top of the firearm, he firmly closed the drawer and locked it.

"Fuck," he growled through gritted teeth while pulling his hoodie off and turning towards the bathroom. He wanted a shower straight away to scrub off the itchy feeling that covered his skin. It wasn't sweat, but he felt dirty all over. "Connor isn't here. He's in France, in jail, under constant surveillance." He repeated the words over and over as he leaned into the shower and switched it on. His eyes caught something in the bedroom that pulled him back to the real world.

In the midst of his haunted confusion, he'd forgotten to take his G36C back up to the weapon storage—something that he'd always made sure to do immediately when returning from an excursion.

"Come on, get a grip," he encouraged himself, picking the assault rifle up from off the bed. "Imagine if Cassy saw this or if Maisie found it."

His thoughts trailed to his wife-to-be, knowing she was trying on her dress for their big day. He didn't have a clue what it looked like, but he could picture her wide smile and glowing eyes. Then he pictured Maisie harassing her with questions as the dress was being altered, causing him to chuckle out loud.

This love briefly overpowered any damage that the note caused. It had been written and left for Ryan to find with an intent to harm, but he wasn't going to let that happen. When the time was right, he'd hand Doc's glasses to Steph. That time would have to wait.

———

The top floor restaurant was spotless, as always. Even the stairwell was regularly mopped, more so than when Sam oversaw security shifts. It was a nice touch, but Ryan secretly missed the random water bottles and food waste left from whenever Sam had been on shift. More to the point, he missed Sam. He missed them all. Fergie, Cooper, Doc, Sam, and Hamsa.

Ryan found Dominic sitting in the single chair, overlooking the front of the vineyard's grounds, staring intently at Maidhill.

"How'd the shopping go, *boss?*" the bulky, dark-skinned frame asked without turning.

"For fuck's sake," Ryan groaned. "I swear I'll suck your dick if you stop calling me that."

"I'm married." Dominic turned with an immature smile on his face. "What do you think Sandra and my kids would say about your offer?"

"Was worth a shot."

"Well, you missed... *boss.*"

"Fucker," Ryan scoffed. "Shopping went well," he said to change the subject.

"Find the perfect ring?"

"One that'll do."

"Lucky Cassy," Dominic said sarcastically before standing and pointing to the back of the restaurant. "I got those spare mop buckets you asked for."

Ryan looked round the stairwell, seeing the broken equipment by the back wall. "They definitely not in use?"

"Nope. We have one for the stairwell, another for the cafeteria, and a few spare in case those break."

"Good."

"What do you need the broken ones for?" Dominic asked.

"Target practice." Ryan turned towards his former galley-style kitchen, which now served as the gun storage. "You, me, Mikey, Rich, and Steph are pretty decent with the L96 rifles, but none of us are anywhere near as good as Sam was."

"I know." Dominic nodded before returning to the chair. "I'll never understand how he pulled off that shot against the other sniper."

Ryan agreed mentally, pushing the door open into the kitchen. He pulled the magazine out of the G36C and placed the unloaded rifle next to the others on the nearest rack. He knelt and opened what used to be the waist-high fridge, placing the magazine next to four extras, which were located in front of multiple ice cream tubs filled with extra ammo.

As he stood up, he reached high to the right, putting his hands on the barrel of Sam's old hunting rifle. His lost friend loved that gun like it was his partner, it never leaving his side. The only time Sam had faced danger and not decided to take it, it cost him his life.

That wasn't true. Ryan's angry outburst cost Sam his life.

It wasn't your fault. He shook his head vigorously. The guilt for that day was beyond intense, and there was no easy way of shaking it off. He just had to live with it.

However, a completely different kind of remorse had left him. The guilt for melting hundreds of men, women, and children outside their grounds at the turn of the year. The manipulatable slaves called 'Termites', who at the time were breaking their way through the walls of the maze to get into the vineyard's grounds. He knew that he'd done what was necessary to save everyone's lives, but it taunted him for months, even making him question if he was human enough to be a good dad.

Later, after being forced to watch more of the Termites eat two of his friends in front of him, he didn't care about what he'd done anymore. He'd happily do it again. Men, women, or even children... he'd kill them in whatever way was necessary. He hated them.

He guessed that was the truth he'd been hiding from Mikey during therapy, and it terrified him to say it out loud to anyone, especially his best friend. How could he openly admit that he felt at peace with the horror he'd committed that day? He didn't even know if that was the real thing that was eating at him. Whatever was boiling inside spread through him like a plague.

He lifted his eyes towards the gun he'd used to ignite the lamppost bombs that fateful night. The personalised SIG716. He'd only used it once, and it held the highest death count of any of the weapons they had. Carefully pulling the weapon down by the foregrip and pulling it into firing position, he remembered the enormous pressure he felt to fire at the hidden bombs. The bullets had exited the chamber and burst along the barrel, leaving a unique screech as they left the modified suppressor. It was a sound Ryan would never forget and one he started to enjoy the memory of.

If Connor were to come back, that would be the noise he'd hear.

There and then, Ryan made his mind up. This SIG716 was now his weapon of choice.

I've promised myself I won't become that person again. But if you ever come near my family, I'll make an exception for you.

————

A small community meeting took place during the afternoon before the joint party was to start, helping Ryan take his mind off the letter. Food supplies were better than forecasted given the extreme heatwave, though the two-showers-a-week rule was still going to be held in effect to conserve whatever water was needed for the crops. The beetroot, spinach, corn, and rye wheat had been ninety percent harvested, with only a few shifts left to bring in what remained.

Steph had raised the point that maybe they could start constructing green houses along the northern wall now that they had the means and supplies from the European Alliance to expand their variety of crops. Ryan had to remind everyone that newer orange trees were merely a gift to take the sting out of the recent requests that had been thrust upon Penbrook.

The world may have been starting to open for them, but until this new world felt like home, they had to remain as self-sufficient as possible. The meeting closed with an agreement to only ask for outside help in the most drastic of circumstances.

Ryan leaned against the open reception door, looking at the gradually darkening sky behind Maidhill as the all-too-familiar streaks of red, orange, yellow, and purple shone from the sunset behind.

"How are you feeling?" Mikey prodded, approaching from behind.

"Doing my best to block out this afternoon." Ryan turned, greeted by a glass of red wine that Mikey handed to him. "Thank you."

"Drinker will keep it quiet, but he thinks you should tell everyone."

"I will, but not tonight, and not till after the wedding probably."

"For your sake?"

"No," Ryan said sharply. "For Cassy. For Steph. For everyone. The wedding isn't just mine and Cassy's day. It's everyone's."

"I know, mate," Mikey agreed. "I just don't want it to burden you on your big day."

"You worry too much."

"And you hide too much."

"Twat," Ryan moaned loudly like a teenager who had just been asked to tidy their room.

"Prick," Mikey returned, imitating the tone.

They chimed their wine glasses in a moment of mutual understanding. They had definitely spoken worse to each other over the course of their lives.

High heels clicked off the reception floor and interrupted their bromance moment. Cassy appeared with a mischievous smile, which matched her vibrant red dress. Her large brown eyes always found a way to melt Ryan's heart, putting him in a better mood than he should've been. "Are you two going to have to get divorced before I can marry him?" she asked.

"Probably." Ryan chuckled and said, "What can I do for you, fair lady?"

"Number one. Don't ever call me that again." She stepped forward to add, "And two. Our daughter seems to have learned the C word from you. I need you to come in and tell her not to say it."

"What makes you think she got it from me?"

Cassy stared Ryan down with an unimpressed look. "Really?"

"Okay. I'll be in once Harper lands." He pulled a cigarette from his pocket. "He's doing us a favour by providing security for the night so meeting him on arrival is the least I could do. If Maisie says it again, send her to our room, and I'll deal with it when I get in."

"Okay, baby." She kissed him on the cheek before turning to go back inside. "Try not to go too hard on Harper when he lands," she called over her shoulder.

Mikey swiftly downed his glass of wine before lighting his own cigarette. "I wouldn't blame you if you did go hard on him."

"It wouldn't solve anything," Ryan admitted.

"You're right, but those traps are our first line of defence, and it's clear we're a constant target now."

"Connor isn't coming back."

"I know he isn't." Mikey said, flicking the ash off his cigarette. "But once we remove our traps—at Harper's boss's request, I might add—we're open to the world."

4

The single Blackbird helicopter thundered as it descended onto Penbrook, silhouetted as it passed the evening sun before touching down in the northwest corner of the grounds. The European Alliance had only just started to feel secure with sending out the unarmed MH-6 Little-Bird choppers without an escort, but given just how desolate and free of conflict the UK had been since the Russian/Islamic Coalitions retreat, it was a huge time saver compared to sending units via the sea.

Ryan had already made his way to the prearranged landing spot upon identifying the airborne transport, leaving Mikey at the front doors. He felt naked without a weapon, just one of the many discomforts that the new world was responsible for.

The thumping draught from the rotary blades had initially felt cool against the lingering heat, then proceeded to kick up dirt and hurl it in Ryan's direction. *Now I know why Drinker wears glasses,* he thought while dusting off the front of his hoodie.

The engine powered down, and the high-pitched whining receded to a whirring growl. The right-side passenger door swung open, and Lieutenant Harper stepped out while taking his aviators off, greeting Ryan with a warm smile, which he softly returned. Harper wore a grey combat sweater, matching cargo pants and boots, with his sidearm in a holster on the right hip. His ginger hair hadn't been cut since they met, and it flopped onto one side, naturally parting on the right, with his bushy beard sticking out, though well-trimmed.

"Bit hot for a sweater, isn't it?" Ryan called.

"Have to make the big-wigs back in France think I'm upholding their standards." Harper turned and pulled a duffel bag from the floor of the passenger section. "They don't know we're doing security duty tonight."

"It's appreciated."

"Least we could do." Harper approached and shook Ryan's hand. His New Jersey accent sounded tired from the journey. "Given our last meeting."

"Again, it's appreciated."

"How's Chris settling in?"

"To be honest, that's the first time someone has referred to Drinker as Chris," Ryan said. "But he's settling in well. We took him for his first tour of the town today."

"I heard." Harper nodded and added, "I also heard about your find."

"I know. I asked Drinker to tell you."

"Why would you tell us before you tell your own people?"

"So you're aware that there's clearly a target on our backs." Ryan rubbed his forehead before continuing. "And it's going to make our job of removing the traps that much harder."

"Can we talk about this at another point?" Harper pleaded. "I've come one day earlier than planned so you can enjoy your night. I want to keep it that way."

"Fine," Ryan grumbled in frustration. "Sorry. I've had a horrible day."

"I know."

"And sorry I had to make you land over here. We've got the canopy put up round the front. Didn't wanna risk it blowing down."

"You don't have to apologise for that. Plus, it gives my men a chance to see a bit more of your grounds. Help them understand what they're defending tonight." Harper turned to the helicopter. "You've already met my pilot and co-pilot?" He pointed to the twins. Both were smaller in stature, with dark, curly hair and trimmed beards. "Alessandro and Francesco,"

Both men approached, shaking Ryan's hand. "Thank you for having us," they said in their thick, Italian accents.

"Thank you for coming and doing us this favour," Ryan said, returning the greeting. "Come on. I'll show you to your rooms and give you a tour of the lookout points."

———

The music thumped around the cafeteria as the evening celebrations swung into full gear. The couple-to-be stood by the stairwell and watched the party from their vantage point.

Ryan held Cassy close, inhaling the basil shampoo lingering from her hair. "Enjoying the evening so far?" he whispered.

"It's been amazing." She kissed his cheek. "How come you're not drunk yet?"

"Mikey's been told to leave me alone until half past nine."

"Jen's orders?"

"Yep. After that, he's not going to leave me alone," Ryan said, spotting Steph by the hot counter with a rare smile on her face as she cradled her green eyed nephew, Alfie—Cassy and Ryan's youngest.

"I'll have to hold you hostage until then," Cassy cheekily said as she took a mouthful of wine.

"Fine by me."

"How's our security for the night?"

"Harper knows his way around the top floor. His two companions seem to have their heads screwed on." Ryan took a small sip of his own wine. "Alessandro asked if we could trade one of our Glocks for his."

"Oh? Why?"

"Ours were the newer batch apparently. Something to do with the safety and loading mechanisms. Bit of a collector's item."

"What did you say?" Cassy's eyes sharpened, knowing he wouldn't give away any weaponry for free.

"I said it depends on what he gets us for our wedding," he joked, placing his glass firmly on the table. "Anyway, I can't get too drunk tonight. Harper wants to see me in the morning. If he has more bad news, I don't know how I'll react when hungover."

"It can't always be bad news. We have to start looking forward," Cassy said in encouragement as she lifted his hand to her lips for a kiss.

"I know, and I will." Ryan had no idea if any of that promise was a lie, and he wouldn't know until he'd spoken privately with Harper.

———

"What time is it?" Harper asked from behind the restaurant bar.

"Midnight, sir," Alessandro reported from the front window.

"Does Francesco have a damn stomach bug or something?"

"He always takes his time when going to the toilet, sir," the Italian chuckled. "Our mother used to hate waiting for him to get ready for school."

"I hear ya," Harper said, laughing back. "I had the same problem with my eldest."

He walked around the front of the bar and towards the back window, catching his reflection. The man staring back at him was grateful that he still had his family, just like the people he was protecting now. He needed to keep this community safe if there was to ever be a future for Europe. It was going to work anyway he could make it, including being honest with Ryan. There hadn't been a good time to tell him about the secret of his past. It was a fifty-fifty situation. Tell Ryan now and risk damaging their relationship or don't tell and let him find out eventually, of which the consequences would have longer-lasting damage.

———

The smell of scrambled eggs caused Ryan's stomach to turn as he sat at the end of a table with a slice of soda bread, trying to soak up the alcohol he swore he wouldn't indulge in. *God dammit, Mikey.*

"Morning, *boss.*" Dominic's voice sounded less playful than normal. "Have you heard the bad news?"

"No?" Ryan asked, looking up straight away. "What's happened?"

"Rich is looking really ill. He woke up looking like a sack of shit today."

"Hangover?"

"If it is, it's the world's worst looking hangover," Dominic said as he pulled the chair out opposite Ryan. "Cold fever. Migraine. Vomiting. Shakes."

"Was he that bad last night?" Ryan asked, trying to remember if anyone was in a worse state than him.

"Don't think so. He went to bed earlier than everyone else. Disappeared before midnight."

"Hmm." Ryan stood, picking up his plate. "I've gotta go see Harper. Can you tell Rich to head to Medical Room one if he can? I'll get Mikey to give him a look over."

"Sure," Dominic nodded and said. "Thank you."

While finishing his toast, he headed into the cafeteria kitchen and rinsed his plate clean. He stepped out of the old delivery entrance, pulled a cigarette out and lit it before leaning back against the brickwork. Between getting married, having to take the traps down and Connor's note, he had enough to worry about. He hoped Rich wasn't too ill. He also hoped whatever Harper wanted to talk privately about wouldn't add yet another layer of shit to their lives.

5

The conversation between Ryan and Harper was light as they walked through the maze, eventually stepping out onto the deformed tarmac of the dual carriageway. Though the heat continued throughout the afternoon, a chill managed to burrow down Ryan's spine as they reached the train tracks that tunnelled underneath the road. Not more than fifteen feet below lay the final resting place of Captain Morgan Jeffries, the man who waged war on Penbrook.

A man known to his followers as Father.

"I've got something to tell you," Harper admitted as he looked over the wall, seeing Father's decayed corpse laying sprawled across hundreds of other scattered remains. "I knew him before all this. Jeffries, that is."

Ryan froze, locking his eyes on the lieutenant. "Y-you... you knew him?" he stuttered. Blood began pumping through his veins with hate.

"Yes," Harper exhaled sharply. "There hasn't felt like a right time to tell you. You'd never let us near you if I'd said anything the first time we spoke."

"You're fucking right I wouldn't!"

"Please, Ryan. Don't take it personally."

"Personally?" Ryan shouted. "You never actually saw what he threatened my family with."

"You're right. I didn't see any of that because I had nothing to do with that side of him. While he was becoming whatever he eventually became, I was defending the eastern front against the outland invasion," Harper barked back. "I just want to say goodbye to the good man I once knew."

The thought of Father being referred to anything more than a demon pierced through Ryan, lighting up the anger he'd been repressing. He marched over and stood toe-to-toe with Harper. "Good man? I'm still mourning the death of my friends. We found a note that pretty much says our community is under constant threat from his followers, and now you're telling me that the man who started this all... is a good man?"

Harper stepped back, never once removing his gaze, and straightened his jumper. "I appreciate your hatred for this man, but never square up to me like that again."

"Fucking what?"

"I said, never square up to me like that again. I'm still a Lieutenant of the European Alliance, and if you impose any threat on me, I will deal with the situation accordingly."

"You'll fucking arrest me?" Ryan sneered.

"If I have to." Harper stood strong with an officer's bearings, "I didn't have to tell you about this at all, but the dependency of our survival needs to be built on trust, so I told you when I thought it was the best time."

Ryan weighed the situation as Father's cold, dark eyes flashed across his vision. The sick chuckle and calm decorum he had when talking about the people he held captive. The passe way the monster described killing Hamsa's family with his bare hands. Ryan couldn't fathom how someone as diplomatic as Harper could've associated with someone as inhumane as that man.

That's what Harper was though, diplomatic, and had been since they met two months prior. He was nothing like Father. Everything about his actions had been for the greater good. He wanted life and civilisation to succeed, whereas Father wanted to control it.

"Fine. Say goodbye." Ryan felt himself slowly calming down. He hated Father getting the silent respect of a former friend, but if it kept the tension between the two to a minimum, then he'd grit his teeth and swallow his pride for now. "Just never refer to him as a 'good man' again. Ever."

Harper stood by the edge of the road, looking over the rotted remains of his former colleague. He emptied a hip flask over the side, went to salute but managed to pull himself back and began walking back to the vineyard.

The sound of helicopter blades travelled over the derelict field. Alessandro and Francesco were to perform a quick thermal scan of the local area before their evening mission to Milton Keynes. The town eighty-five miles north of Penbrook had been the base of operations for Admiral and Father and believed to be where they held all the Termites and human cattle. It had been three weeks since the European Alliance sent a small recon team to sweep the area and see what more they could uncover about Admiral, but all they had found was a football stadium that had been converted into a farm. A human farm. A place they herded anyone who didn't share their worldview and deemed them to be nothing more than protein.

"I don't expect you to ever fully trust me, now that I've told you," Harper admitted as they approached the opening to C10.

No fucking shit. Ryan had a million questions to ask about Harper's relationship with Father but knew that it wasn't the time. He had to absorb the news before going any further into that rabbit hole. "Why'd you need our trust so much?" he asked, distracting himself from the theoretical elephant in his head. "I mean us, here, specifically."

"What you have here... it's what the world needs to see. We can rebuild. Even your signs say so."

"We wrote those signs before people wanted to enslave or eat us."

"Those people aren't here now," Harper said sharply. "They're not here."

"Not right now, they're not." Ryan corrected. "Connor will come back if he's ever freed, and you still haven't found that Admiral, have you? How is our place a good sign for the world if we're a target?"

"We're going to aid you should they ever return. You know that. I thought you'd be more optimistic about the future."

"Maybe I once was..."

Harper's radio interrupted. "Sir, I think you and Ryan had better get back inside," Francesco warned.

"What's going on?" Harper asked.

"We've picked up thermal signature northwest of here. Roughly half a mile away. It's moving... fast."

6

The cafeteria was full. Everyone wanted to know the extent of what had everybody on edge throughout the afternoon and whether Ryan was okay. Dominic remained upstairs on lookout.

Mikey stood on the podium and raised his hand for silence. "Please, everyone. Ryan will be in soon."

"What did they see earlier?" Sandra asked from the table to the left.

The kitchen doors opened at the back of the room. Ryan held out his hands in a calming gesture as he met Mikey on the podium.

"False alarm," Ryan announced. "It was a fucking giraffe. It's likely one of the many animals that escaped from zoos." He looked over the crowd. "But we can't risk this being a one-off. We haven't had any wild animals near here for years, birds included. If other animals, such as predators, are feeling comfortable getting closer to our town, that puts our animals and us at risk."

"What do you think we should we do?" Mikey grunted.

"Bring in all our animals immediately. We'll have to keep them inside until we've secured our border. We still have to take down our traps."

A wave of moans filled the room. The disdain of having to remove their first line of defence was clear.

"I don't like it any more than you do, but at the same time, no animal deserves to run into any of our traps if they try to get in," Ryan said factually. "And yet, we have to protect ourselves. We have to figure out this situation as soon as possible. I don't fancy having a fucking lion interrupt my wedding next week."

The last part was meant for humour, and it seemed to have been received as such. A lion would've been a problem, but it wasn't the biggest problem out there.

"All crop and vine picking shifts are to be carried out with an armed patrol until then," Mikey told the crowd. "Let's get our animals in by tonight. All those who can spare their time off, hugely appreciated."

The cafeteria began emptying. Mikey tugged on Ryan's shoulder, pulling him towards the back end of the podium. "Need to talk to you," he said.

"Fuck sake, what now?"

Mikey was taken aback by the harshness. "Fucking hell. What's pissed on your chips?"

"Nothing," Ryan lied.

"Don't lie to me. What's happened? What did Harper say to you earlier?"

Ryan didn't know what to say. He was still processing the Harper's admission. Right now, wild animals were the least of his worries.

"I'll let Harper tell you when he gets back," Ryan said, evading the issue, feeling like a coward. "What did you want to talk about?"

"What are you hiding?" Mikey asked again.

"Forget it for now. What did you want to talk about?"

"Fine, it's Rich."

"Is he okay?" Ryan immediately looked at the medical corridor.

"Yes," Mikey assured, pulling Ryan back. "He seems to have made a full recovery from how he was this morning."

"So, it was just a hangover?"

"Well, this is what I wanted to talk about. He only drank two glasses last night and he blacked out. The last thing he remembers is going downstairs to grab another box of wine, and that's where his memory blanks out. He woke up on the other side of the basement, out of sight from anyone."

"Didn't think he was a lightweight," Ryan thought out loud.

"He's not," Mikey corrected. "What the fuck is wrong with you?"

"Sorry. I'm glad he's okay. Can you clear him for work?"

"He's good to go."

"Okay. I'll be upstairs if you need me. I'm going to get a crack on with the new perimeter plans." Ryan turned sharply and headed for the stairwell. Mikey could only watch with alarm, knowing something had knocked his friend off kilter. Whatever it was, he knew it couldn't be good.

————

"Fuck!" Ryan slammed the door to his nightshift room, holding back from punching it. He slumped in the armchair, leaning forward and holding his head in his hands.

Harper knew Father... Worked with him... Probably shared good memories, drinks, shook hands... Knew of each other's families and hometowns... He pictured the pair laughing and smiling, sharing good times.

Without warning, his breakfast started to shoot up his throat. Ryan turned quickly for the sink, spraying the broken-down soda bread around the bowl. He ran the tap and cupped his hands, rinsing his mouth.

"Shit," he wheezed, spitting out the last of the acidic taste. "What do I do about this?" He didn't know who he was asking, but the answer wasn't going to come from the four walls surrounding him. Everything weighed down on him, and he felt his brain beginning to lose grip of reality. *I won't go back to being that person.* It was times like this where he could've used Doc's rational thinking, something Ryan lacked when news like this was presented.

"Ah!" He sat back in the chair, trying to keep his thoughts from cycling out of control. "What the fuck do I do? What the fuck do I do?"

He noticed the repetition in his thoughts and that his breaths were becoming shorter and faster. He had to get out of the room and get back to something productive. He wiped the towel across his face and checked himself in the mirror, seeing if he'd missed any spots of vomit from his chin.

"Do the maze plans like you said you would," he urged himself. "Get a grip, man."

He tossed the towel on the chair and opened the door, only to find Steph waiting for him in the corridor. Her blue tracksuit covered in soil smudges, and her blonde hair was tied back, signalling she'd been threshing the rice today, one of Rich's jobs that she'd covered for in the morning.

The siblings normally had pale skin, but hers was lighter than ever. She hadn't seen much sun since Doc was murdered. Her matching green eyes focused hard on Ryan, like she was about to give him the sister bollocking he was used to through their childhood.

"I saw the conversation you had with Mikey," she said, pushing herself off the wall, arms crossed. "What's wrong? You're supposed to be upstairs."

"I had to take a quick five minutes here."

"For what? To let out some anger? Or for an anxiety puke? Judging by the look of you, and the smell, I'm going to say both."

"I forgot you grew up with that smell." Ryan gave in, stepping out and closing the door. He heard some of the families making their way around the corner. "But I can't tell you here." He directed her to the stairwell.

"You've had to take on a lot, since it's only you and Mikey in charge now," Steph said from behind. "You're a superhero to a lot of people, but you're only human."

"It is taking its toll. Which is why I don't know what I can trust at the moment."

"Trust?" She picked up on the word as they ascended the stairs, stopping briefly to replace one of the candles that was missing. "Cassy told me that Harper wanted to speak to you. I know you had a brief scare with the giraffe, but I know that's not what has got you worked up. What did he say?"

"Fuck sake." Ryan knelt to the candle box on the stairs, picked one out, and positioned it in the wall fitting. Two small sparks later and it was lit. "He told me something about his past."

"We all have a past." Steph sounded more like Doc with each day. Blunt and rational.

"Not like his."

They entered the restaurant, with Ryan immediately heading for the lookout point. Steph walked behind the bar, pouring herself a beet-root juice from the decanter. "So, are you going to tell me?" She leaned against the metal counter.

Ryan sat in the chair by the eastern window, pulling Sam's rifle away from the wall and sitting it across his lap. "Harper..." he paused, not wanting to believe it, "...he used to work with Father."

He heard Steph push away from the bar before she walked over and sat in the chair to his left. She set the glass down and held his hand. "Served with him?"

"Yes."

"And now you don't know what to do with that information?" She truly knew Ryan better than anyone.

"Why should I know? We were told that the war was over, so why is everything getting more fucking complicated?"

"Such as?"

"Having to take down the traps, a fucking giraffe heading towards us, and our correspondent to a new government once held hands with a fucking monster," he snapped, ripping his hand away from hers and pulling the rifle into firing position, scanning for anything across the road.

"You feel like we're always at war," she stated. "Like we're constantly under attack."

"That's because we are."

"What's bought this on? You were moving on from what happened, and so was I. We all were."

He wanted to tell her about the note and Doc's glasses. He couldn't.

"Taking down the traps, whether we like it or not, is for the best. You know that," Steph continued. "As for the giraffe? Well, we've been lucky with the wildlife as it is, but it was always going to catch up with us. You were right about bringing the animals in until we secured our borders."

"And Harper?" Ryan looked away from the scope, wanting an answer.

"Harper? Well, the man looked out for all of us last night while we got drunk. He even lied to the chain of command in Rennes so he could do us this favour. If he was even remotely close to being like that monster that took us to war, you'd be dead right now."

If there was ever a moment since Doc passed that Ryan needed this to-the-point logic, it was now.

"Don't get me wrong, I'm not fully sold on him," Steph pondered honestly, "but he deserves a bit more credit than being compared to Father." She finished her thoughts, then took a mouthful of beetroot juice.

"God dammit." Ryan lowered the rifle, knowing his sister was making sense of the situation. "So I should just sweep it under the rug?"

"No." She stood then said, "You should focus on the current tasks in hand, like securing our perimeter. If Harper is hiding something, it'll come out eventually, but he's just like us."

"Like us?"

"He's a family man. He wants what's best for his children."

The words hit home for Ryan, and although they hadn't had much interaction over the recent months, Steph was still as good as she always was at keeping her brother in check.

———

The multi-coloured sky shone through the few restaurant windows that weren't boarded up. Not much time remained before the sun finished setting and darkness took over.

It'd been months since Ryan had to do an all-night shift, and he was on his third cup of quadruple-sugared tea as he sat alone upstairs. The ginger cat rubbed up against his leg, purring loudly,

"What's up, Munky?" He tickled the top of the cat's head. "Annoyed you can't go outside?"

The cat's affection was always well-timed, giving Ryan some thinking space as he sat at a table with the vineyard's hand drawn blueprints rolled out over the surface. His beloved sidearm lay next to a nearly empty bowl, with a few berries remaining from the evening snacking.

Every time he saw Doc's notes on the corner of the maze's map, it pulled at his heart.

He missed Doc terribly. His sharp, puzzle-solving brain. The monotone voice that very rarely displayed emotion unless he was fixing something or calming a situation down.

"Puzzleboy," Ryan whispered with a smile, running his left hand over Doc's scribbles. "How would you solve this conundrum?"

Footsteps echoed up the stairwell—a certain rhythm that was starting to become familiar. "Animals are all in their respective places," Drinker reported as he entered, holding his hand out. "Harper asked me to give you this before he left."

Ryan lifted his head, presented with something that looked like a smartphone. "What is it?"

"High frequency digital radio, like the one I have. I'll bring the spare charger up later."

"How does it work?"

"Pretty much the same as any smartphone." Drinker shrugged his broad shoulders. He hadn't lost any of his muscle tone, even without the rigorous lifestyle of serving under the European Alliance. "Just dial in the code you want and bingo. Harper's number is already saved."

"Thank you." Ryan took the phone and looked it over, locating the lock-screen button on the right side of the device.

"Mikey said he'll be up soon," Drinker added. "Give you some help with this perimeter problem. I can help if you want. My shift is over."

"Only if you're up for it?"

"Aye, I'm not drunk yet."

"Good," Ryan sniggered. "If you could grab a few grapewater's from downstairs, that'll be appreciated."

"Will do. I promise I won't get bored without wine," Drinker joked as he left to head downstairs.

Bored.

Ryan heard that word again but in Doc's voice. His brain began playing the same trick it always played on him. Telling him he had just figured something out but not revealing it out right. Violently swinging his head back towards the window, he stared at the maze, trying to find whatever message the voice was to explain.

"What are you trying to tell me?" He scanned the front of their land. *Bored?*

His eyes shot to the southern and eastern interiors. The last development on the maze had been the reinforcing of the inner walls, designed to protect from any spears coming from the outside.

Bored. Board. Boarded up.

"That's fucking it!" Ryan exclaimed loudly, catching Munky off guard as he hurried back to the table. The cat quickly scrambled downstairs.

There was more than enough timber left over from January's project to start sealing up the northern and western interiors. The outside walls, however, were going to require a lot more.

Glancing over the blueprints, he read the length of the maze's perimeter. Eight hundred metres in length each.

"Three point two kilometres." He rubbed the bridge of his nose. "Where the fuck are we going to find that amount of material?"

Ryan leaned behind the bar, grabbing more detailed maps of the area and laying them over the blueprints of the maze. With Mikey and Drinker both coming to help later, maybe they had a chance of locating enough abandoned construction sites to find the right amount of supplies. Boarding the entire exterior was going to be a daunting task, but right now, it was better than nothing.

———

Henry, the rooster, let his morning call roar from inside the medical corridor. All the chickens had been separated into the least used treatment rooms, which would need a hard, deep clean once they were let back outside.

Ryan had checked on all the animals during the night, even

surprised to see that one of the female deer had given birth in the water purifying corridor, which would also need heavy sanitisation.

He was already feeling better about the vineyard's security after a long night of drafting the plans to start boarding. The uncertainty towards Harper had begun to wane. It could be a while before he accepted that he used to work with Father, but the man was trying his best to make things right. The extra gesture of giving Ryan a smart-radio took the sting out of yesterday's revelation, knowing he had twenty-four-seven open communication with Harper. He'd just have to make sure he didn't call during the lieutenant's personal time, as the man didn't see his own family as much as Ryan saw his.

Maybe Harper was right. They could build a future.

Ryan would find out more once Harper returned from Milton Keynes. He had messaged Ryan during the night to let Penbrook know they would be landing on the grounds at six-thirty in the morning.

While managing to keep himself awake, he showered vigorously and changed into his all-black excursion attire before heading upstairs to the restaurant. He watched as the Little-Bird helicopter returned from Milton Keynes, waiting for it to land before he headed to the basement to relieve his nephew, Lyndon, who had been on overnight duty in the second reception and would no doubt share the same drained eyes.

As he stepped into the basement, a flicker of a dying candle caught his attention, placed in the middle of the table outside the broken cell door. Wax leaked over the side of the saucer as what remained of the wick flickered, vaguely illuminating the crate of wine that Rich left on the table before he had passed out. Ryan picked a bottle from the plastic storage crate, looking it over like it was a present from a relative at Christmas time.

"I suppose I should," he muttered to himself and slid it into his hoodie pocket. As he walked away from the table, he lost his footing and slipped hard on his back.

"Motherfucker!" he yelled in pain, pulling himself into a sitting position. He looked at the sole of his right foot and found folded layers of toilet paper stuck to the bottom. With disgust, he peeled it off and threw it in the bin by the door.

He pushed the door open into the second reception, told Lyndon to finish up his shift before heading back up to the ground floor, and opened the main doors. The air was brisk, and a few dark clouds were visible on the southern horizon. After living his whole life in England, Ryan never thought he'd welcome the sight of rain. He glanced at the smart-radio device. Six-thirty. Harper was punctual to his word. All three men looked exhausted as they approached; Ryan was surprised they had chosen to fly without rest.

"Morning, gentlemen." He raised his eyebrows in concern. "Long day?"

"Morning, Ryan." Harper forced a smile. "Thank you for having us back. Are the rooms we slept in still available?"

"Of course. Having a nap?"

"No. Just a shower, please."

"Help yourself," Ryan said as he led them inside. "Your rooms are still open." He directed his voice to the pilots then faced Harper. "I need to speak with you, if that's okay?"

"Thank you," the twins said and disappeared inside.

"I need to talk to you too." Harper yawned as he rubbed his eyes.

"Is it serious?"

"Not really. Just something I think you should know."

"Okay." Ryan pointed him inside.

They sat in the cafeteria. Harper placed his duffel bag on the table. "Do you want to go first?"

"Okay." Ryan poured himself a cup of tea, offering Harper one, but he declined it. "We're going to board up the interior and exterior of our mazes. We'll make gated doors at each exit and rig them with something that alerts us should someone try and take the incorrect route through."

"That's good to hear. I like that. Non-lethal, I assume?"

"Non-lethal," Ryan confirmed. "Maybe fire extinguishers, or something along those lines."

"Can you start taking the traps down?" Harper sounded eager.

"Once we've boarded the interior, which we start today," Ryan said, standing strong on their stance but giving Harper what the European

Alliance had wanted to hear for the past few weeks. "Once the inner walls are done, then we'll start disarming."

"Excellent." Harper pulled the chair out. "I have my first report in front of the governing board today. That's some good news I can pass onto them."

"Governing board?"

"All the bigwigs from each respective country. They're proposing to begin rebuilding the continent once the new European border has been agreed upon. Knowing that communities are starting to follow regulations is a big step, and hopefully, they'll talk directly to me more instead of using their shitty telegrams."

"I don't miss having bosses," Ryan said with an understanding smile. "What's your news?"

"Well... first. The recon team working in Admiral's former Milton Keynes stronghold has confirmed there are no combatants in the area. There was a fear they could've taken refuge and set up newer operations in basements or underground car parks to avoid being detected by the drones thermal scanning," Harper explained, leaning elbow first on the table. "Admiral and his followers have completely evacuated, as we expected."

"That is good to hear. What's the second bit of news?"

"When I have my meeting with the governing board, I'll be proposing something that should guarantee you more security and would hopefully propel plans for a functioning society."

"Such as?" Ryan asked, pushing against the vague answer.

"I can't confirm now."

"Classified?"

"Classified," Harper replied.

"I'm starting to hate that word." Ryan rubbed his temples. "Mikey said he'd meet me down here soon. He's got some requests regarding medical supplies."

"Okay. I'm just going to use the restroom." Harper stood. "Hopefully, he'll be here when I get back."

"He will. He's just as punctual as you."

"Good," Harper smirked. "I can't promise we can get everything on his list, but I'll do my best."

"I know."

Ryan watched the lieutenant walk towards the customer toilets by the stairwell before pulling the bottle of wine from his pocket. *Stress relief.* Harper was truly trying to help Penbrook, and Ryan could see it now. He knew that Harper had his family stationed in Rennes. It couldn't have been fun watching your children growing up in a heavily militarised area, then coming to Penbrook and seeing everyone live free.

He wondered what he'd prefer for Maisie and Alfie. Living under constant surveillance but with guaranteed security, or free but in more potential danger? If Ryan could guarantee their safety, he'd live freely, given the choice. That's what he'd been doing since it all started.

At that very moment, it all clicked. That's what Harper saw in Ryan. This is what he wanted for his family. No person should be denied letting their children live.

"I know what to do with you," Ryan said directly to the bottle of wine as he pulled it out his hoodie pocket and placed it on the table, reaching over to the nearest note pad and pen.

Though Harper was a man of orders and Ryan was a man of principle, they had one common trait. They wanted the best for their families.

7

A faint drizzle pattered over the city of Rennes, Northwest France, as council members made their way into the European Alliance headquarters. The city centre's opera house glowed despite the miserable weather. The double-floored arched façade had been repainted cream after the war, with the window framework covered in black. Anyone could be forgiven for thinking the home of the continent's highest-ranking officials was actually a Tudor-style town hall.

It was a little after eleven-thirty when Harper's helicopter landed in the city's open plaza, which had been transformed into helipads. The area remained heavily guarded twenty-four hours a day with foot patrols and dogs.

The surrounding buildings were equally protected and fortified, serving as sleeping quarters for the elected officials and highest-ranking military personnel who were to begin forming the newer European government. They had one goal: securing Rennes as the new capital of France and beginning the process of rebuilding the continent. Many of the city centre apartments held the families of such people, where they could live their lives in comfort while having full access to the local parks.

The city's hospitals, schools, farmlands, and sports centres now served as refugee camps. Survivors from all countries held on for life until the border between the new Europe and the Russian/Islamic coalition had been agreed upon. That was the case in all the few strongholds they held across cities in France, Belgium, and Holland.

All farming and agriculture took place outside the northwest of the city, stretching between the towns of Montgermont and Saint-Gilles, producing enough food and occupational employment to the population of Rennes.

The most feared part of Rennes lay at the southwestern outskirts, Aeroport Rennes Bretagne. It housed all the European Alliances armed forces who were currently not on battle rotation, and was a mix of nationalities and ideals, never mind the drug problem that ravaged one-third of the soldiers. Fights regularly broke out through different political beliefs, resulting in whoever had thrown hands spending a night in the POW corridor. A corridor where there was only one full-time tenant. Sergeant Connor Lovell.

———

Harper left his duffel bag in the Little-Bird and hurried to the opera house, leaving Alessandro and Francesco to begin their afternoon standby shift on the helipad. He quickly relieved himself in the restroom, then checked himself in the mirror, brushing his red hair neatly and making sure his combat uniform wasn't too creased. The brief sleep on the helicopter had left him with dark bags under his eyes, but it was impossible to look perfect given the long overseas shift he'd performed. They could've picked a better time to hear his official report of England.

It was the first time he'd been called up to give a briefing in front of the council. There were a lot of important decisions that hung in the balance, and his word could very well define the beginning of the new world.

The future of what was left of Europe rested on this moment.

Shortly after he freshened up, Harper found himself standing in the centre of the opera house's stage, looking out into the modified committee hall. Every face concentrated on him.

The two tiers of audience chairs were long gone and had been replaced with a semi-circular ring of tables, six across and three deep. Spotlights shone down along the rim of the top balcony, and the cream walls glowed against the magnificent rouge carpet. The J-J Lemordant artwork that coated the dome ceiling held its own spectacular awe, representing a Breton farandole leading to the sky. The light mixtures of pastel reds, greens, yellows, and blues against the pale sky was a sight any true art lover would behold.

"Members of the committee and future European Government, I would like to start by saying thank you for giving me the opportunity to stand in front of you." Harper gripped the podium, clearing his throat and composing himself. "As you know," he continued, "I was sent on a covert mission to England three months ago to bring in Captain Jeffries and Admiral Caven of Task Force 205 for multiple counts of mutiny and war crimes. During my unit's time there, we carried out thermal scanning of their last known location, a town north of London called Milton Keynes. On our initial sweep, we found nothing other than the remains of their operational base and mixed wildlife. There was no indication at the time, or has been since, that the rogue group of that size remained in the vicinity." He cleared his throat again.

"From there, we began a town-to-town search, heading south towards London. During this time, we found the remains of freshly consumed carcasses. Human carcasses."

The silence hung in the air. That was the first time cannibalism was confirmed by a direct witness.

"The modified strain of Kurustovia45, created by the Russian/Islamic Coalition, had been utilized by Captain Jeffries' unit. They were using it on prisoners of war..." Harper paused, then said, "...and were using any survivors they came across as both the antidote and their food supply."

"Who was this confirmed by?" French Immigration Minister Thierry Thuram called out, sitting at the table directly in the middle front row.

"Penbrook Vineyard. Southeast England. That's the group you've heard plenty about."

"The ones with the acidic traps in their perimeter?"

"That's correct."

"And you can trust the word of traumatised civilians who resorted to barbaric methods to keep people away from them?" Thuram asked sceptically, looking over the top of his thick glasses.

"I do," Harper said, staring directly at the minister.

"You don't think it's unethical to associate with them?"

"No."

"Why not?"

"Because when we found the leader of the vineyard, he'd been bound to a chair and forced to watch two of his friends be eaten in front of him." He held eye contact with Thuram, watching the unimpressed look fade as the reality slammed down hard. Harper repressed a shudder. Not just remembering the scene that he'd found but the smell of charred flesh that had stuck to his clothes and hair for weeks. "Barbaric or not, during the time of war, their traps were justified."

"Those traps are a violation of our accord," Thuram reminded the assembly.

"Which is why they're removing them. At the council's request, sir." Harper held the stare until a new voice entered the conversation.

"Is this *Penbrook Vineyard* where you detained Sergeant Connor Lovell?" Danish Health Minister Naomi Eriksen asked without a hint of emotion while flicking through her notes.

"Yes."

"How did you find this... vineyard?" she asked. "I mean, how did you know they were there?"

"One of our radio communications was intercepted by the survivors at Penbrook." Harper cleared his throat again, thankful that the conversation had moved on. "They had retrieved some military grade radios after their first encounter with Captain Jeffries."

"First?"

"It was a standoff that lasted through the entire winter. Captain Jeffries was going to take their home and use it for his people's new base of operations."

"And according to what we've attained from your notes and words from General Woodburn—with the expectation of Sergeant Lovell—these survivors killed Captain Jeffries' rogue unit?"

"Yes. That's true."

"That's quite the story." She looked over the rim of her glasses. "But you know why we summoned you for this meeting, don't you, Lieutenant?"

"I do, ma'am."

"So, tell us what you think about the proposed relocation plan. And how will pockets of survivors, like this vineyard group, react to it?"

———

Harper inhaled deeply as soon as he stepped outside, welcoming the much-needed fresh air. His position on the opera house stage became unbearably stuffy as the meeting continued through the whole afternoon and into the hours of the late evening. He rubbed his face, feeling how clammy his skin had gotten under the lights. He was definitely having a bath once he reached his private room.

He strolled across the plaza to the stationary helicopter, donning his sunglasses to shield his eyes from the spotlights. Alessandro and Francesco were polishing the outside windows of the Little Bird. Harper greeted them, then opened the right side passenger door.

"I thought you sold that perfectly," a voice from behind said.

Harper knew that voice like it was his father's. He pulled his duffel bag out the helicopter, turning to see his mentor approaching with a warm smile.

General Woodburn had just turned sixty but didn't look a day over forty. His brown side swept hair had minimal greys. Soothing dark blue eyes, only countered by his dazzling smile. The man was a walking picture of the American dream. Even his mid-west Wisconsin accent held a southern charm that wasn't normally associated with that area.

"General," Harper saluted. "How are you, sir?"

"At ease." General Woodburn opened his arms and hugged his fellow countryman. "We can drop the formalities until the Alliance Army has finally been established. We both know our ranks don't even mean anything until they've pulled their thumb out their asses and settled on where our future lies in the newer military."

"Understood, sir."

"I do, however, think the relocation program you just laid on the table for them is a brilliant idea."

"Of course, it is." Harper smirked and said, "It was your idea."

"I'm full of them, old friend." Woodburn grinned, exposing his perfect teeth. "Has Ryan started to comply with last week's orders?"

"Yes, sir. He's found alternatives for his peoples' safety."

"He sounds like a stand-up guy and a resilient son of a bitch."

"He is," Harper said with a chuckle before turning sombre. "But we may have lost some of his trust. I told him about my former relationship with Captain Jeffries. In all honesty, I don't blame Ryan, considering I once worked with the man who put his community in danger."

"We both did. A lot of good men did," Woodburn reminded.

They walked to their golf-cart transport. Harper yearned for a decent night's sleep after the early morning commute and day-long conference.

"Does Ryan know about the relocation program?" Woodburn asked.

"No, sir. That was kept confidential, as you requested. I respect Ryan, but my loyalty runs through you."

"That's why I send you out on these missions. You have my permission to tell him once it's been confirmed by the council."

"You think I should tell him before the program is in effect?" Harper asked, surprised by the openness.

"Absolutely. If you surprise him with something like that before he has a chance to voice his concerns, it could turn into the fucking wild west."

———

Harper threw his bag on his bed, letting out a long sigh. Looking around his on-duty room, he felt relieved that it was all over. He stripped down, opened the door to his en-suite bathroom and turned the tap on to a large, free-standing bath, thankful to have the privilege of being able to soak. Not that he minded the showers at the vineyard, he was just more of a bath kind of guy. He set the alarm on his smart-radio for seven a.m., which was considered a lay-in for him. A day off duty was always welcomed, especially as it gave him time to see his family on the north side of Rennes, and he would spend all day with his wife and two children. No doubt the time would fly, and before he knew it, and he'd be waking up at five a.m. the day after, ready to report for duty. The fact that he had two weeks leave coming up made working a tad more bearable.

A knock on the door pulled him out of his thoughts. Wrapping a towel around his waist, he opened the door.

"Just here for your dirty travel washing, sir." Alessandro stood in the hall with an open laundry trolley.

Harper collected his clothes from the floor and placed them in the basket. "Thank you, Corporal."

"You're welcome, sir. Enjoy your day off."

"You too, Alessandro."

Harper closed the door and returned to his bag, looking for his smart-radio charger. He felt around, knocking something hard that chimed off his wedding ring. He pulled a cylindrical object out—a bottle of wine with a note attached to it.

Hopefully, this'll help after your meeting.
    Don't drink this all at once. It's stronger than regular wine.
    The recipe is 'classified'.
    Thank you for the radio.
    See you soon.
    Ryan

A gift and welcomed token, despite what he admitted to Ryan the day before. He had earned more of his trust.

8

Whether it was coming from the toilet or the sink, the random dripping was adding to his rapidly deteriorating mental state. Every splash on the tiled floor chipped away at his brain. If only he could just see the fucking splashing, it would take the edge off.

Sitting in the dark. Sitting in the fucking dark. He wound himself up again, springing forward off the shitty single mattress and throwing his fist to wherever the noise was coming from. The chains jolted his forearm to a halt, sending a jarring sensation through his shoulder, deep into the socket.

"Fuck!" he screamed, before the pain instantly vanished behind the numbing rage.

Another drip.

It had been days, maybe even a week, since the anonymous contact had provided him with the protein, and now his inhibitions were beginning to fail. His heart raced as his thoughts took over. He had to get out of here.

It wasn't being held captive that he despised. It was being prevented from killing that self-righteous, smug asshole—that wet flannel of a man who could only kill people with bombs. Ryan.

Fuck, he didn't even have the balls to kill me, he laughed to himself. Another drip.

This world would never get back to how it was with someone like him in charge. That hippy cunt.

His breathing took a life of its own, switching between short, rapid breaths to long and deep ones. His palms burned as the sweat itched away at his skin, forearms shaking with the adrenaline pumping.

Another drip.

The visions began their usual cycle. His unit lying dead. The flash of the fireball that launched him through the air and into the river off the road. The smile of Ryan. That fucking invisible dripping noise.

Drip. Drip. Drip.

The cell door creaked loudly, springing him out of his thoughts. A crack of light poured through, causing his eyes to protest straightaway. He held his shaking hand out, trying to block the torturous beam.

"I haven't got long," the fake English accent whispered. "Here."

A syringe rolled in. He picked it up and injected it between the little and ring fingers on his right hand. Within a minute, his breathing calmed, the screaming in his head stopped, and his hands were under his control.

"That was too fucking close," he wheezed, spitting out the sticky white substance that had been secreted under his tongue. "What's the update?"

"Admiral is a fortnight away from green-lighting Project Zodiac." The figure stepped in front of the opening, keeping themselves fully silhouetted as always. "I can't stay. Roll it back."

With steadier hands, he rolled the syringe back towards the door. The light exposed where the drips were landing on the broken tiled floor.

Fucking sink. "I can't wait to see the look on Ryan's face before I cut it off." He sat back on the mattress, letting himself relax as the Kurustovia45 watered down the cortisol that had been threatening to overload his self-control. "You're still not going to tell me who you are, are you?"

"I can't for now. For my own good," the unknown helper said.

"In case I slip up during interrogations?" he rasped.

"You know that's why." He slowly closed the door. "I'll see you soon, Connor."

9

"That's probably the hardest graft we've ever done," Mikey wheezed, pulling the gardening gloves off and leaning on the footbridge railing. Ryan passed him a bottle of grape-water and looked out to the inner perimeter. Every exit point and western inner wall were now closed off. The timber had been dug five-feet into the soil and compacted in with mortar, standing well over ten-feet above ground level.

"Is everybody in?" Ryan asked, huffing from the day's hard push.

"Everyone's counted for, and dinner will be ready in five minutes," Mikey said, wiping his forehead and drinking from the bottle.

They locked the front doors and headed up the stairwell to the top floor.

Drinker sat by the eastern window. "Evening gentlemen," he called out.

Ryan tapped him on the shoulder. "Go get some food if you want. Mikey can take over for now."

"Aye. As long as the dinner lady doesn't make another fucking joke about giving me pasta," Drinker whined as he stood. "She keeps saying I look like those Italians' dad," he grumbled some more as he left to go downstairs. "I'm fucking younger than them!"

Mikey sniggered as he sat in the warm chair, pulling the L96 sniper rifle into position and scanning the carriageway. "It's a good thing that Sandra is winding people up again. She's been reserved since... you know."

"I agree," Ryan acknowledged, knowing what his friend was getting at. He lowered his SIG716 to the floor and looked over a map of Southeast England that he'd left from the day before. "Now, time to solve this ball-ache," he called to Mikey. "If we go from each confirmed construction to the next, we're running the risk of burning through at least eighty percent of our stored corn oil."

"Not necessarily," Mikey corrected. "Jen mentioned that before the war, a lot of construction companies switched to electric vehicles. They ran on some kind of new technology that had long life energy storage. We could use those to bring the materials back."

"Can we guarantee they'd still work?"

"You'll have to ask her. She said she'd join us up here when everyone's in."

"So, what sites are we aiming for then? Large scale developments? Apartments? Schools?"

"No!" Jen shouted as she trundled up the stairs, puffing heavily with each step. Four months into pregnancy and she was already struggling with the stairs, though her Dominican toned skin was already glowing. "Those kinds of sites would've been left to the weather and all the elements of the war. That'd leave way too much work to fix the trucks."

"Hi Jen." Ryan looked up as she entered. "How you feeling?"

"I'm good," she smiled as she walked to Mikey and kissed the top of his head. Her dark, frizzy hair bounced on her shoulders. "And construction sites wouldn't be good as the other potential spots."

"Such as?"

"Storage warehouses. Most are situated on the outskirts of towns. Should've avoided much combat during the war. That's our best bet for materials and the trucks to bring them back."

"Wish I'd thought of that," Ryan admitted. "Though, I don't like the idea of you going outside to get one of these trucks up and running."

"Because I'm pregnant?"

"You know that's exactly why."

"I do appreciate your concern," she said while pulling out the chair next to him. "But I'm the only mechanic here. I have to be out there to ensure we can transport the materials back."

She was right. He knew it, which created another personal issue he was going to have to swallow his pride for. If Jen were going out on this one, then the father of her child, Mikey, would inevitably be going on this mission for medical support, which meant Ryan would have to stay behind to keep an eye on Penbrook.

Ryan looked where the tiny baby bump was beginning to show. "I'll stay behind. Mikey needs to be with you." He grabbed one of the hand-held radios and placed it in front of her. "Take one of these with you. There'll be two people here ready for any communication while you're out."

"That's probably the most mature reaction I've seen from you," she joked. "And, you know that everyone would feel safer with you here."

"Have you been taking lessons from Cassy on how to talk to me?" Ryan raised his eyebrows, daring her to answer.

"She's given me pointers," Jen said with a shrug.

"Well, it's working." Ryan moved the map closer to Jen. "Where do you think you should start looking for materials?"

"Let's start in this district. If the lorries had been fitted with the new AX-50 batteries, they won't degrade for twenty years. I can rig a few together for enough charge to get them back here."

"Sounds good." Ryan smiled, glad to have Jen onboard and working with them. Without her knowledge, the task they faced would be astronomical.

———

Ryan got into bed with a mixture of feelings that he struggled to process. Cassy's warm smile calmed his heart rate as he pulled the covers over.

"Are you happy with Jen's ideas?" she asked as she cuddled up to him.

"More than happy," he replied. "If it all goes well, she'll have saved us a lot of fuel and time searching."

"You're not happy about staying behind, are you?"

"Of course not."

"You know they'll be fine. Mikey, Rich, and Drinker have got Jen to keep them safe," Cassy teased. "Pregnant or not."

"She is a hardass. I'll give her that." He laughed as he stroked her arm. "I've been thinking about bringing her onboard with me and Mikey. It's getting hard for just me and him to oversee this place."

"I think that's a good idea." She kissed his shoulder and asked, "Anyone else?"

"I'll have to think about it." He cuddled up to her. "I've got some free time while the crew is out material hunting. I'll be in a better place to think about it then."

"You have seemed a bit brighter the past two days."

"Is that a good thing?"

"People here react to it," she explained. "You've made them feel safe, even after telling them to remove the traps. The work everyone did today is because they see that you believe in it."

He kissed her cheek. "Maybe the future doesn't have to be ugly anymore."

"I'd like to think so. I'd like to think that one day we could be angry at Maisie for coming back late one day after going to see her friends."

"Or boyfriend?"

"I feel sorry for the boy she has to introduce to you," Cassy said, nearly snorting.

"Depends on what his intentions are," Ryan dismissed. "I know plenty of places I can bury him."

She giggled again and turned, looking him in the eyes. "Imagine that. Being able to go places again."

"Cinema? Restaurants?" Ryan asked sceptically. "It'll be a long time before that."

"Why? You can just put a DVD player in a theatre for the cinema. Meanwhile, other people come and eat here."

"Let's not get ahead of ourselves, but yeah, I'd love that to actually be a thing."

He turned and blew out the candle on his bedside table. Alfie stirred briefly in the cot on Cassy's side of the bed as the room fell into darkness. He hugged her tightly and began to wonder what the future held for everyone.

Positivity kept them alive but being naive could get everyone killed.

10

Harper's work alarm called out at five a.m. He was already awake, doing his morning routine of push-ups, sit-ups, burpees, and a five-minute plank. He kissed his family goodbye while they slept and jogged through the city to his private quarters. He helped himself to a glass of orange juice in the mess hall and had a quick chat with one of the guard dog handlers. After taking a bath, he pulled on his grey combat sweater and cargo pants before checking his watch.

Seven-twenty.

Enough time to make a call to Ryan. He took the smart-radio off charge and punched in the private code. The call went through instantly.

"Hello?" Ryan sounded out of breath.

"Are you okay, Ryan?" Harper noticed his breathing straight away.

"Yeah. Early morning graft. Everything okay?"

"Yes. I just wanted to say thank you for the wine."

"Ah, it's all good," Ryan said. "I didn't know if your meeting with the bigwigs would require some medicine after."

"Well, thank you," Harper said and laughed. "I have some news next time I come back. Good news."

"Oh really? Care to share now? Or is it classified?"

"Very funny. I'll contact you when I know when my next journey to you will be."

"Okay, Lieutenant. Stay safe."

"You too." Harper ended the call, placing the device in his back pocket before picking up his travel bag. The last part of his morning ritual was to slot his M17 pistol in the holster before leaving his room, ready to do his duty.

———

"Bourguignon for breakfast again?" he questioned as he walked back into the mess hall, though he welcomed the meat-based food. He was still getting used to the vegetarian diet that the vineyard lived by.

"I already got you a bowl." General Woodburn pointed across the table. "Good as always."

"They do breed a good cow in France." Harper pulled out the chair and sat opposite, taking a spoon to the meal and devouring it. "What is today's task? Has anyone located the computer guy?"

"Computer guy?"

"I heard from ground command that one of the programmers has been M.I.A for a week now. The guy with the mermaid tattoo on his neck."

"Oh, Tech Supervisor Monreal?" Woodburn remembered. "No, he hasn't been located, but rest assured he will be doing some serious time when he's brought back." He finished his bowl, resting the spoon on a napkin next to it. "There is a different person of interest I need you to bring in. We need you to head out to Hel to pick up a soldier who's under the suspicion of supplying narcotics."

Hel was a town at the tip of a peninsula, fifty miles north of the Polish port city of Gdansk. That was the furthest eastern point where the European Alliance had a stronghold. Many of the soldiers serving there referred to it as *Hell Point*.

"Who's the soldier?" Harper asked.

"Sergeant Kieran Rook, former medic of the marine corps," Woodburn said while picking his teeth. "He's now one of the spotters on the front line."

"Why's he under suspicion?"

"He returned to Hel two days ago after a week of leave," Woodburn explained. "The same day fifty-four syringes went missing from our medical supply. He was the only person with medical access that departed that day, and Hel has a giant drug problem."

"Is it a formal arrest?" Harper wanted to know if any force would be required.

"No. Just bring him in for questioning."

"Understood, sir."

———

Harper's helicopter landed back in Rennes just after noon the next day, with a ground crew waiting for them by the helipad. The journey took ten refuelling's all around, with a three-hour rest at Hel before the return trip.

Sergeant Rook came as ordered and under no protest. Once they returned, he was led away by the waiting ground crew and taken to the airport, where they would hold him until the morning.

General Woodburn met Harper outside the opera house. "Good work, my friend."

"I thought this wasn't a formal arrest?" Harper asked.

"It's not. We're merely holding him as a formality. Sergeant Rook is a devoted soldier. He understands."

"General! Lieutenant!" Francesco called from the helipad. "Come quick. You must see this."

Both men jogged over as the blades powered down. Francesco led them to the open passenger hatch on the left side, pointing to the floor in front of where Sergeant Rook had been sitting.

"Look." Francesco pointed inside.

Harper and Woodburn leaned in, looking at where the flashlight was shining. There was a piece of clear synthetic material with black markings pressed against the metal flooring, like it had been crushed by a foot.

Alessandro picked it up with his cleaning clothe and handed it to the General.

"Was Sergeant Rook sitting on this side?" Woodburn asked, holding the shrapnel up to the light.

"Yes, sir," Alessandro nodded.

"Well, this doesn't look good for him." Harper sighed deeply, shaking his head.

It was part of a crushed syringe.

11

Much needed rain drizzled down gently as Ryan exited the maze and walked onto the carriageway. A soft wind wrapped through the trees of Maidhill's western slope and into his face.

He looked over the warped tarmac, remembering the absolute destruction and fatalities that the bombs had caused back in January. A scene he had created. His eyes panned over to the lampposts where the explosive contents had been hidden. The bases had been ripped open by the force of Doc's concoction of death. The metal frames were bent and melted, only to solidify shortly after, leaving a molten slag that arched over the far side of the road.

Ryan thought about the number of lives that had been taken on that small stretch of road. The doomsday cult of three summers ago, an untold number of Father's people.

"Mikey, how's the next warehouse looking?" Ryan asked into the hand-held radio, taking his mind off the souls that haunted the road.

"Fucking goldmine, bro!" Mikey answered, a bit more excited than Ryan was expecting. "If I'm ever stupid enough to say I'm the clever one in our relationship, you have my undying permission to let Jen kick me in the balls."

"Want to go into any more details?"

"About being kicked in the balls?"

"About what you've found, you thick twat!" Ryan sniggered, shaking his head. "Where are you and what materials can you bring back?"

"Oh." Mikey paused. "We're outside Redhill. There's a construction warehouse hidden off the A23. It was fully stocked before the war. Remember there were plans to renovate the multi-storey car park at Gatwick?"

"Yeah?"

"Well, we are at the firm that was supplying it, and get this..." Mikey trailed off then said, "It's the same contractors as down in Lewes. They have a warehouse there if we ever need more."

"That's fucking brilliant!" Ryan blurted, not realising how happy he was with some news that was finally good for once. "How can you get the goods back here?"

"Easy. There are two eighteen wheelers here. Jen checked them over while we loaded the cargo."

"And you couldn't have told me this sooner?"

"We've been loading over three kilometres worth of timber, you impatient prick," Mikey huffed. "Kinda been busy."

"Get back to it then, twat," Ryan laughed.

"I'll let you know when we're on the way back. Jen will be in one of the HGV's with me. Rich will drive the other, and Drinker will be in the Land Rover. The man's pretty excited as he never drove legally in Britain."

Ryan didn't want to know any more than that. "Alright mate, see you soon." He turned back and waved to the restaurant window, clicking the radio receiver again. "Dominic? Did you hear all that?"

"I did. I'll pass on the great news to everyone later. Just so you know, Lyndon's on his way through the maze," Dominic reported back. "He should be with you soon."

"Nice one. We'll head straight up once he gets here. Keep us covered."

"You got it, *boss*."

Ryan smirked and clipped the hand-held radio to his waistband, then knelt and grabbed the stack of broken mop buckets by his feet.

The carriageway's scene of destruction no longer held any power over him now compared to this very recent elation.

"Dominic really loves calling you *boss*, doesn't he?" Lyndon asked as he stepped out of section C10. Over the summer, he'd grown nearly as tall as his uncle, and his equally long dreadlocks had turned slightly darker than Ryan's.

"That was quick," Ryan noted, impressed with his nephew. "And stealthy."

Many of the events of the previous year had aged Lyndon. He'd gone from looking barely pubescent to almost a fully-grown man. The sixteen-year-old's eyes had darkened, and he didn't seem so timid to the outside world.

"Practice makes perfect." Lyndon grinned, pulling out a role of fluorescent tape from his hoodie pocket. "Anyway, I got what you asked for."

"Good lad. Can you carry these for me?" Ryan handed him the mop buckets. "Have you got your pistol on you?"

"Tucked down the back of my pants," Lyndon answered, tapping his hip.

"Safety is on?"

"I have no plans in shooting my own arse off."

"Good." Ryan nodded before pulling the SIG716 into firing position. "Come on. I'll show you what we're doing today."

Uncle and nephew made their way across the bubbled tarmac, stepping over the mid-road barrier towards the sewage work car park. Lyndon had never been up the west slope of Maidhill, whereas Ryan wished he hadn't. At least this time it was by choice and not necessity.

Rain dripped from the leaves above, soaking into the ground that was still hard after the month-long heatwave and covered with dried nettles and thorn vines. Ryan had seven wooden stakes slotted through his back pack's straps, which got caught on the occasional branch or bush as they pushed up the bike trails.

"Think this'll turn into a storm?" Lyndon asked, already out of breath.

"Hopefully not," Ryan said with eyes fixed through the ACOG scope. "I'd rather no storm while we board up the maze."

Upon reaching the top, Ryan eyed the wall of nettles that covered Maidhill's vast peak. The two pathways, though slightly overgrown now, were still accessible into what was once the grounds of a family mansion. Ryan had set the large building on fire after the conflict at the turn of the year. Father and his men had used the mansion as a stronghold through the winter and planned to butcher everyone at Penbrook after capturing them and bringing them back there. Ryan had seen the butchery equipment and mass amount of human meat they already had stored, and even though he hadn't acknowledged it since, the sight had probably made his decision to set off the lamppost bombs a touch easier.

Ryan turned his head to the southern slope, catching a small glimpse of the area where Father had been executed. Sam pulled off that shot from all the way back in the restaurant window—over seven hundred metres away. The very same firing position where he'd outwitted another sniper who was hidden somewhere close to where Ryan now stood.

That's what this small venture was all about. Ryan wanted to set up targets on the western slope, giving him something to practice his shot against from back in the vineyard grounds. He took two of the mop buckets from Lyndon and walked into the open field, pushing his way through the tall grass and waving his hand back towards the vineyard.

"I see you, *boss*," Dominic reported through the radio.

I'm having a word with your wife when I get back, Ryan thought, waving Lyndon over. "Can you wrap these two with the tape, please?" he asked, pointing to the mop bucket.

Lyndon did as asked while Ryan stabbed one of the stakes into the ground before walking further down the slope and piercing the ground with the second one.

Lyndon followed and placed one of the mop buckets on each. "Think you'll be able to hit these?"

"As you said earlier, practice makes perfect," Ryan replied like a cocky teenager.

The hand-held radio crackled again. "Anyone there?" Mikey's voice sounded faint.

"Here," Dominic answered first.

"Me too," Ryan said, joining in on the three-way conversation.

"Cool. We're heading back now. We'll be about an hour. Jen is now driving one of the trucks, and I'm in the other. Drinker is in the Land Rover with Rich."

"Jen's driving on her own?" Ryan asked sharply.

"I'll explain why when we get back." Mikey kept his tone calm, but Ryan didn't like the sound of it. "Are you and Lyndon still out?"

"Yes."

"I need you guys to start pushing the car barricade apart. These trucks are fucking massive. They won't fit through the current opening."

"Okay. Dominic, stay on watch till we get back," Ryan ordered. "We'll finish setting up the mop buckets, then head up to the barricade."

"Got it," Dominic answered.

"Thank you," Mikey added.

Ryan clipped the radio to his waistband before looking back over to the vineyard. *Why is Jen driving? What's happened?*

"Ryan?" Lyndon's voice pulled him out of his internal confusion. "Want to finish up here?"

Lost in his thoughts, he hadn't noticed the rain coming down harder. "Yeah."

Lyndon wrapped the rest of the mop buckets with the high-visibility tape while Ryan pitted stakes randomly across the western slope, trying to keep some hidden in the treeline. Once the mop buckets were in place, they headed down the slope and reappeared in the car park.

"I see you guys," Dominic announced via the radio.

Ryan stuck his thumb in the air to signal he'd heard. "You can get your gun out now," he said bluntly to Lyndon.

"What?"

"Your gun. We're heading up to the roundabout. You need to start protecting yourself when you're outside."

"I thought we were clear of trouble?" Lyndon asked while reaching for his pistol.

"We might be, but you can never afford to let your guard down,"

Ryan warned, not sure if that advice was aimed at himself or his nephew. As happy as he was that things might start getting better, or back to what it was before, being prepared was what kept everyone alive for the past six years.

————

The rain had eased off by the time nightfall arrived, and the grey clouds had moved north and out of sight. A half-moon shone over the vineyard, displaying just how empty the grounds had become without the animals' presence out front.

Mikey's convoy arrived shortly after dinner. They parked the eighteen-wheelers outside the southeast corner of their grounds. Upon entering the building, Mikey requested to do the night shift with Ryan, while a concerned expression spread across his face. More notably, Rich had gone straight to bed. His skin was paler than when he had left the morning before.

"How's Jen?" Ryan asked urgently as he heard Mikey coming up the stairs.

"She's fine. Just gone to bed now." Mikey said as he pulled the chair out. "It's Rich. It looks like he's getting sick again."

"What happened?" Ryan looked up, placing Sam's rifle on the table.

"Sweats. His hands wouldn't stop shaking. Severe anxiety. He doesn't know why."

"Is it contagious?"

"I don't think so." Mikey rubbed his forehead. "No one else is showing symptoms. It's likely heatstroke. He does spend a lot of time outside, and that heatwave was intense."

Ryan couldn't deny it. They had all felt the effects of the unusually burning sun. "What's your suggestion for Rich?" he asked while pouring himself another tea.

"We'll have to keep him inside," Mikey suggested. "He can't be involved in any of the maze's reinforcement. We could end up burning him out."

"You'll burnout too. You've had a long couple of days."

"So have you. That's another reason why I came up. We can make sure we're both rested and trade sleeping shifts tonight."

"I would tell you not to worry about me," Ryan said and took a sip of tea, "but that wouldn't work, would it?"

"Has it ever?" Mikey grinned. "I'll take the first watch." He pointed to the sleeping bag by the back wall. "I'll wake you up in a few hours."

"Fucker." Ryan hated being made to rest, whether he knew it was for the best or not. The scale of the perimeter project told his mind to get some sleep, but his heart was concentrated on something else. *What's happening to Rich?*

12

After five gruelling days of extensive labour, the southern, eastern, and western exteriors were boarded up, with gated doors fitted on all exit points. Sudden bursts of rain and the odd flashes of lightning had slowed the progression of sealing the remaining exterior, but they planned to have the northern wall finished within the upcoming days.

The lorries had been moved to the car park opposite the vineyard. No one had any suggestions on what to do with them and using them in the roundabout barricades seemed such a waste.

Huge puddles engulfed the vineyard grounds, soaking Ryan and Mikey's feet as they trundled through the maze, disarming the traps one at a time. Only thirty-five remained, but the process was as slow as it was dangerous, requiring a fishing rod attached to the tripwires to set them off from a safe distance.

Mikey attached the hook to the tripwire at Y4. "Ready?" he asked, backing into Y5.

"Yeah," Ryan replied, pulling his hoodie collar over his nose.

Mikey slowly wound in the fishing-line, meeting resistance until he gave it a forceful pull. The tripwire sprung away, and the gas screeched before exploding through the compressed-corrosive mixture. Even though they made sure they were always a safe distance, the sulphuric mix stank like a vinegary-egg mayonnaise, tainting the air.

"Where's next?" Ryan coughed, squinting over his collar.

"Err... A4," Mikey said, flicking through his notes.

They walked left through the next opening. The pathway between Y5 and A4 stretched over one-hundred and fifty metres with multiple exits leading to other routes.

"Oh, I forgot to tell you," Ryan glanced at Mikey. "Harper said he'll be coming back in three days. That's when he'll share this 'good news' with us."

"Why three days?" Mikey moaned. "If it's that great, why not just tell us now?"

"Says he's got something else to take care of first."

"Did he say what?"

"Nope. Classified," Ryan said dryly.

———

The interrogation room in Rennes Aeroport was no bigger than three-squared metres. The cube-like room had blackened walls and ceiling, matted grey flooring, a singular table with two chairs on either side, and a single lightbulb hanging from above. The reflective wall on the right side served as a one-way mirror for the observation room next door.

Sergeant Kieran Rook sat in the chair opposite the door, still sporting the same uniform he wore during the arrest. Though he was given shower privileges and fed well, the 'one-night-stay' had turned into a weeklong occupation of cell five.

He was a little over six-foot, extremely muscular, and well-postured. Long, rust-coloured hair tied into a bun and a scruffy beard that was a shade darker surrounded his face. A webbed scar ran from his left eye to around the back to his neck. The missing ear was a daily reminder of shrapnel nearly taking his life during the siege of Brugge. Even with only fifty percent hearing, he was still considered the most efficient lookout at Hell Point.

Harper opened the door, and Rook stood and saluted.

"At ease." Harper sat in the chair. "How are you this morning, Sergeant?"

"Good, thank you, sir."

"It always catches me off guard how calm you look."

"I'm trained to look calm." A wry smile formed in the corner of Rook's lips, "But I have nothing to hide, sir."

"Everything is pointing towards you, including the remains of a syringe found where you were sitting on your extradition."

"I've told you, sir. I have no idea how it got there. I'm not a user."

"That doesn't mean you're not a supplier," Harper suggested, trying to assess the reaction.

"Ask anyone at Hell Point. They'll tell you I'm not into that," Rook replied factually.

"No doubt they would. However, a fair percentage of them are users. Of course they'd deny it."

"You're right. They are users." Rook leaned in to say, "And I have to work with them. I'm constantly on the lookout for an enemy force that nearly ended the world or retrieving dead bodies that have washed up from the Baltic Sea. So why the fuck would I want to aid those around me in getting high when I need them to watch my fucking back? Sir."

Harper didn't enjoy being sworn at by a subordinate, but Rook had been known for his exceptional courage and duty. This man was no liar.

"Watch your tone with me, Sergeant," Harper said coldly, asserting himself.

"Sorry. Sir." He sat back. "Has there been any consideration for alternative scenarios? I'm not the only person who had access to the med-bay on the day the syringes went missing."

"We're aware of that. Yet you were the only person with syringe remains on their uniform."

"I could've stood on something at any point," Rook suggested. "Or maybe I'm being set up."

"How would anyone benefit from setting you up?"

The door opened slowly as General Woodburn stepped inside.

Both men stood from their chairs and saluted. "At ease," Woodburn said. "I can't believe I'm still having to say that."

"We're technically on duty," Harper pointed out.

"And we're still technically unranked." Woodburn placed a folder on the table. "Rook, I for one don't believe that you're involved in any smuggling, but the governing board is out for blood to tighten the ship before the new armed forces are aligned." He sighed. "I've spoken to them directly and pleaded your case, and I've tried to give you the best outcome until this situation is resolved."

"Thank you, sir," Rook said, looking at the folder on the table. Woodburn said goodbye and shut the door as he left.

Harper flicked through the folder, running his eyes across Woodburn's statements. He took his time, scratching his beard with confusion as he came across something. "Damn it," he whispered out loud.

"Sir?"

"The governing board have pretty much come to their conclusion with you," Harper said. "I don't actually believe it!"

"No trial? I'm considered guilty?" Rook questioned.

"No. It seems when General Woodburn stood in front of the council..." Harper paused, "...they said if you were found guilty, you'll be discharged permanently. Your sentence would be carried out in the cells... here."

"They can't do that. What do they think they're doing?" Rook demanded. "Treating me like I'm some kind of convict?"

"To make an example of you. Any soldier involved in narcotics while the war effort is still happening is considered detrimental to the future cause," Harper answered. "Woodburn just told you that he doesn't think you're involved, but he also knows that everything we found would tell any judge or jury that you are. So, he's suggested an alternative."

"Alternative?" Rook screwed his face with bewilderment. "What?"

"A temporary suspension. Offsite. While the investigation continues and until your innocence has been proved."

"Offsite? Where am I supposed to go? Live with the refugees in La Bertaiche?"

"No," Harper shook his head, trying to understand what he was reading. "England."

"England?" Rook dropped his head in defeat. "Why?"

Harper closed the file and held his hands together, pondering what Woodburn was thinking with this plan. This could have adverse effects on everything he'd worked on.

"I can't give you the details for that now, Sergeant," he said coolly. "But unless you can give us another reason for the syringes, this is your best outcome for the time being."

Harper knew the ultimatum was unfair. The governing board and council were taking the harshest possible approach with this, leaving Rook in an impossible position.

"I don't know anything, sir."

Harper nodded his head resentfully, knowing the front line would lose an irreplaceable professional. "I'll walk you to your cell."

Both men stood, exiting the claustrophobic surroundings and walked into the guards' room outside the cell's corridor. Two plump guards sat at the desk. One stood and swiped his key card, opening the heavy door into the bright corridor.

"I'll fill you in on the details when we transport you," Harper explained as he unlocked Cell Five's door. "For what it's worth, I hope this is solved as soon as possible."

"Thank you, sir." Rook entered the cell and turned. "One question, if I may?"

"Yes?"

"I've only heard of one settlement in England. Are you taking me to the vineyard?"

Chains rattled in the cell opposite them, like the occupant had shifted their position on cue. Harper noticed it, turning his head towards the door. He was one of the few people who knew who was inside, and this conversation would no doubt peak the inmate's interest.

Harper turned back to Rook. "Classified," he said softly, closing the cell door and locking it.

Looks like I need to make another phone call.

―――――

The smart-radio vibrated in Ryan's back pocket as he marched down to A4. "Harper?" he answered.

Harper got straight to the point. "Hi, Ryan. Listen, there's been a change of plan. I'll be back tomorrow, if that isn't a problem?"

Ryan picked up on the directness of the request. "Tomorrow? Should be good. What's changed?"

"Something that I can't explain over the radio."

"Doesn't sound promising, Lieutenant," Ryan huffed. "Are we in danger?"

"No. Nothing like that," Harper reassured. "It's classified."

Well, there's a fucking surprise. "Okay." Ryan turned to Mikey, who was rolling his eyes. "I will make sure the three bedrooms are ready for you."

"We'll need four... please?" Harper didn't sound like his usual, confident self.

"Four? Who's the extra? Are they safe?"

"I wouldn't bring them if they weren't."

"Who are they?" Ryan requested.

"A Marine Corp medic. I wouldn't bring them if they were a danger to you. I wouldn't put you in a position where I'd lose trust." Harper went on the defensive, saying, "If they're a problem for you, I will take them away at once."

Mikey walked to Ryan and tapped him on the shoulder. "Either we accept that this is classified or we turn him away now."

"What the fuck do you want me to say?" Ryan growled, keeping his hand over the microphone.

"You've had more interaction with him than I have. I trust your judgement."

"Thanks," Ryan puffed mockingly, returning the conversation to the smart radio. "Okay. I'll have another room prepared for you."

"Thank you," Harper replied. "We'll be with you tomorrow afternoon."

"See you then." Ryan disconnected the call, slipping the device back into his pocket. They continued walking up the long stretch. Section A4 was on the next right turning.

"You're starting to trust Harper more?" Mikey asked, but it felt more like a statement.

"I trust him more than the people giving him orders," Ryan answered.

"I don't think he's the kind of person who would put us in danger."

A scream cut them short. Both men looked at each other with wide eyes. Ryan felt his heart begin to thud uncontrollably. A second scream rang out, transitioning into a roar.

"Go!" Ryan barked, already reaching for his Glock and picking up the pace. Fear took control as they weaved through the clear route, making sure they took each correct turn while moving as fast as possible. They reached section X1, throwing open the newly fitted gate and coming out behind the beetroot patches. Rani and Sanjay looked back with an expression that caught Ryan off guard. They weren't scared. They were confused.

"What was that noise?" Mikey asked them, not lowering his pistol.

"Over there." Rani pointed towards the main driveway.

They hurried until they met the driveway, spotting Rich stumbling along the cracked tarmac, holding his head. He was topless, wearing only black jogging bottoms. He let out another roar, sounding increasingly enraged. As Ryan got closer, he saw nail marks over his shaved head. *What the fuck?* Suddenly, Rich reached for his scalp again and dug into his flesh uncontrollably.

"Rich? What's wrong?" Ryan called, lowering his gun.

"I can't stop thinking about it!" Rich shouted, turning round to reveal bulging eyes. His teeth ground together. "I should've killed Sam."

"What?" Mikey gasped at the statement.

"It was his fault Fergie died. Same as he did to Cooper." Rich fell to his knees. "No, it wasn't Sam's fault." His tone switched dramatically. "I don't know why I feel like this," he babbled, almost incoherently.

"Feel like what?" Ryan asked as they slowly approached.

Mikey knelt beside him. "Rich. Look at me, please."

Rich looked up. His eyes displayed unnerving hate and sadness at the same time. "I know it wasn't Sam's fault, but I can't stop thinking about it."

Mikey felt Rich's forehead. "You're burning up bad. I need to take you to the medical room. Can you come back with me?"

"Will you stop this?" Rich begged.

"That's what I'm here for, buddy. I think this fever is making you delusional. It's playing games with your brain."

Mikey picked him up under his arm and led him towards the main building. Rich began to sob on his shoulder, crying that he knew it wasn't real. Ryan could only watch as they made their way down the drive before disappearing through the front doors.

His condition was serious. Rich never acted like that.

————

"Afternoon, everyone." Ryan stood at the podium, overlooking the community. "Got two bits of news for you, and the first one does concern one of our own." He took a mouthful of grapewater. "Rich's illness seems to have taken a more serious turn on him. Fortunately, it doesn't look like it's transmittable. However, I ask you kindly to alert Mikey, Steph, or Lyndon straight away if you have any of his symptoms."

Everyone nodded.

"The second bit of news. Lieutenant Harper is coming tomorrow, and he's apparently got some good news with him for once. He'll have his two pilots and an extra with him this time, so can we make sure we show them the same hospitality we always have, please? Thank you."

Ryan stepped off the back end of the podium, walking around to the main reception.

"Was Rich really that bad?" Cassy asked as she caught up with him.

"It was... different, for Rich, anyway." He put his arm around her and directed Cassy to the front doors.

"I hope it's just heatstroke." She hugged him as he leant against the railing of the footbridge. "Are you going to bed soon? You've had a lot of long shifts recently."

"I will, definitely." Ryan stopped talking as the day shift team passed them over the footbridge, heading towards the northern wall to begin the final piece of the new exterior. "I need to be clear-headed when Harper tells us whatever this news is, and for our conversation."

"Conversation?" Cassy knew he wanted to say something but not in front of everyone else.

"After Harper lands, I want to meet the new guest straightaway," Ryan explained. "He wouldn't tell me why he's bringing someone new to our home."

"I thought you were past not trusting him?"

"I am... But I feel like there's an ulterior motive." Ryan knew it was time to start trusting his instinct again. Promises of a better future could wait for now. This new guest felt like Harper wasn't even sure about bringing them to the vineyard.

13

"So?" Harper asked Ryan nervously. "What do you think?"

Ryan turned back from the bar with a pot of tea, picked up two mugs and walked to the table by the window. "It's a bit sudden," he mentioned with agitation. "It's actually very sudden. I don't think I can make this decision with just Mikey's approval. This has to be okay with everyone. What's the deal with this Rook fellow?"

"I'll explain when he comes up to see you, but I can vouch for his service record and ethics."

"I don't doubt that you have faith in him. But you and the Council in Rennes are asking a fucking big favour, Lieutenant."

"I know." Harper knew all too well what the vineyard stood for and what they'd overcome. "It would mean a lot if you could meet us halfway."

Ryan poured a cup and handed it to Harper, who took it and turned to the window. He spotted Drinker showing Francesco and Alessandro the structural work that had been done to the maze since their last visit, and the pilots were visibly impressed with the results of the week-long project. Harper looked over the most recent renovations. "I've got to say, that's a fucking incredible effort."

"Everyone worked hard to get the walls up," Ryan said as he poured himself a cup.

"How many more traps to disarm?"

"About six left. Mikey and Dominic will finish that before we board up the northern wall."

Footsteps echoed up the stairwell before the new guy entered the restaurant. Standing before them was Sergeant Kieran Rook. He wore the same grey sweater as Harper but requested to keep his urban camo pants and black service boots. Ryan noticed his missing ear and webbed scarring.

"Thank you for the room and the shower." He nodded at Ryan. "This is one hell of a set up you have here. Better than anything I've seen in rural Europe."

Ryan smiled and pointed to the seat opposite him. "Your Lieutenant wants me to offer you a home here, like we've done with Drinker."

"Yes." Rook sat in the empty chair.

"With Drinker, that was only possible because I got to know him, and he wanted to be a civilian again. From what I understand, you're a career guy, a loyal soldier. So, I need to know the real reason you want to join our community,"

Harper cleared his throat, pulling up a chair next to Rook, taking over the conversation. "Sergeant Rook has been placed on temporary suspension until a case against him has been resolved," he informed Ryan.

"What kind of case?"

"Classified."

Are you fucking joking? Ryan couldn't hold back his expression even if he wanted to. "No, it's not," he said, dismissing Harper's words. "Not when my people are involved."

"You know I can't tell you," Harper replied sternly.

"And then you know I can't take him in."

"For God's sake, Ryan. Don't put me in this position," Harper protested.

"Then don't put us in that position," Ryan fired back. "We won't let in someone who's potentially shady. For all we know, this guy could be suspended for suspected war crimes!"

"I'm accused of smuggling narcotics," Rook said bluntly before cutting off Harper. "And now I've just committed another offence by telling you classified information."

Ryan pondered before nodding for Rook to continue.

"Where I'm stationed on the front line, there's a big intravenous drug problem among some of the soldiers. The last time I was on leave in Rennes, a bunch of syringes went missing the same day I flew back to duty."

"You're going to tell me you're not guilty, aren't you?" Ryan said, leaning forward.

"I put my life on the line where I work. Like you, I've sacrificed enough of myself to defend what I fight for." Rook pointed to his missing ear. "There's no way I'd help colleagues feed their habit when they're supposed to watch my back."

Well at least I'm getting some truth from this guy. Ryan sat back and glanced at Harper. "Why would you not tell me that?"

"Our senior officer spoke to the court on my behalf," Rook said, interrupting again. "They were going to lock me up like some kind of petty criminal. General Woodburn, my superior, pleaded my case and suggested I stay here, saying you'd keep an eye on me and do what was necessary if I acted out of line."

"They agreed," Harper added, "considering how much they admire you, given what they've heard."

"Admire?" Ryan quizzed.

"They don't just know this place exists. They know about the enemies you've fought off and how you did it."

"How do they know?"

"I told them," Harper said while sitting back.

"You told them?" Ryan snarled.

"It's my fucking duty!"

Ryan eyed him, contemplating punching him in the face before calming down.

"Sorry, Ryan. This is your home, and I thank you for having us,"

Harper said, taking a diplomatic approach. "I'm just trying to do what's right."

Ryan could see Harper was genuine, truly believing in this soldier's innocence.

Another set of hands is always welcome, and Drinker has settled in well. Ryan looked between the two soldiers opposite him. *Harper hasn't let us down before.* But this was different. It felt forced. *I can't make this decision on my own.*

"If we let you stay," Ryan said, focusing on Rook, "you're only allowed to be armed when we say so."

"Understood," Rook agreed.

"You only go where we say you can."

"Understood."

"And if you do anything to threaten the safety of my people, I'll kill you. Soldier or no soldier, I don't care. The welfare of everyone here comes first."

"Understood." The corner of Rooks mouth lifted. "You are as fearless as I've heard."

———

The cafeteria hosted its second community meeting in two days. Ryan took the podium with Harper, ready to address the crowd.

"Afternoon, everyone. Before I let Lieutenant Harper take over, I have something to share with you." Ryan untied his dreadlocks and rubbed his eyes. "We've been asked to take in another soldier temporarily. I was told this individual is reliable, though the reason for his stay involves a legal case against him. His name is Sergeant Kieran Rook." Ryan paused and glanced at Harper before continuing. "This is our choice. I can't make this decision on my own. If anyone has any concerns, rejections or questions, please voice them now, and we'll come to an agreement between us all."

Jen raised her hand straight away. "What's the legal case he's involved in?"

"Drug smuggling," Ryan answered loudly. "It's an ongoing investigation. Harper would like him to stay here until he's proven innocent."

"Does Harper believe he's innocent?" Teddy asked from the right. A rarity as he was usually someone who went along with whatever.

"He does, and Harper wants Rook to say here during the investigation to spare him from having to stay in the P.O.W cells in Rennes. Apparently, it's not a place an innocent soldier deserves to stay."

"Do you believe Harper?" Steph asked coldly.

The question hung in the air longer than Ryan noticed. He didn't know where the pressure came from to answer this out loud. "I do," he replied eventually. "Whether we like everything Harper has said or not, he's always told the truth, and he's never put us in a position of peril. We were given time to take the traps down and defend ourselves—he never demanded it from us."

The concern in the room eased. Everyone agreed between themselves, knowing Harper had never bought anything on them by force.

"Any other questions?" Ryan asked, looking around the room. No one raised their hand. Everyone seemed satisfied. "Okay then. I ask you to treat Sergeant Rook with the usual warmth you show everyone. You all know Harper by now. He's got a bit of news for us, so please give him your full attention." He stepped off and headed to the back of the cafeteria to lean against the hot counter.

"Thank you, Ryan." Harper then addressed the community. "Hello, everybody. Thank you for having us back here. It's always appreciated. And I must say a huge well done to all of you for the project of securing your perimeter."

A few people cheered and clapped, and the coming together and strength of this community clearly made Harper happy to be working with them.

"As you remember, on one of my first visits, I bought news from the governing body for the European Alliance, which instructed me to tell you to remove your self-defence traps. Obviously, this wasn't the best news and put you in potential danger, but you pulled together as an outstanding community," he praised. "This time I bring you different news. Better news."

Harper paused, giving himself time to deliver the next part properly,

"Secondary thermal scans of England have confirmed no threats.

The remainder of the group that attacked you have fled the country. After reporting this to the council in Rennes, a vote has been passed to bring refugees from the European war over here."

No one said a word, not even Ryan who stood with his mouth slightly open. The so-called good news had been received more as a shock.

"The goal is to begin rebuilding civilisations and cultures while we negotiate borders with the new Russia and the Middle East. I assure you that the refugees are not hostile. We've been watching over them in all our strong points of Rennes, Caen, Amiens, Bruges, Cologne, and Rotterdam."

"Will you be sending any military escorts or aid over with them?" Mikey asked as he joined Ryan at the back.

"At first, yes. The timing and plans for all of this is still being discussed. We'll be surveying which towns are best to start rebuilding. Infrastructure will be put in place before the relocating starts."

Everyone remained silent.

"I see that this has come as a shock, but we're going to make sure this works. Thank you again for having us and thank you for your time." Harper nodded and stepped down, walking over to Ryan and Mikey. "That wasn't as cheery as I anticipated."

"Probably something to do with the thousands of strangers you're sending our way," Ryan replied, his hand over his mouth.

"I think everyone is just going to need time to absorb it," Mikey added, then looked at Harper. "We've lived alone for so long, doing what we can within these grounds. Soon, we could have neighbouring towns? How do you process something like that?"

"Did you think you'd ever hear that again?" Harper asked optimistically.

"No. None of us did." Ryan pushed himself off the counter. "There's every chance this'll all be fine. There's also every chance this could go south in a bad way."

"I thought you two wanted this?" Harper pushed.

"We did. We do..." Mikey answered. "But it's a different thing to imagine it for so long..."

"To being told that it's actually happening," Ryan said, finishing his friend's sentence.

————

Ryan found himself denied of sleep as he lay next to Cassy. The thought of a populated town close by was wreaking havoc on his own insecurities. After hours of trying to get some sleep, Henry's morning call forced him to get up and start the new day.

He took a very grumpy morning shower, helped Maisie get ready for the day and took her down for breakfast, then dropped her at morning school. Drinker and Lyndon were beginning to move the animals back outside, and Rook had joined in on the task—with Ryan's permission. Harper's two pilots kindly restocked the medical supplies in the room next to where Rich was being observed.

"Have you seen Mikey?" Jen asked Ryan by the stairwell. "He hasn't come back from night duty."

"That's weird." He looked around the cafeteria. "I'll check in second reception, see if your man has fallen asleep."

"Thanks, muppet," Jen laughed. "Can you tell him I'll meet him in the water room, please?"

"No worries." He headed down through the basement and opened the door to the second reception. Mikey was indeed asleep. Ryan cleared his throat to wake him up.

"What time is it?" Mikey groaned, sweating profusely and holding his hands to his eyes.

"Eight thirty. You okay?"

"Think I've got a migraine," Mikey said, touching his temples.

"Take some painkillers. We should have plenty now. Alessandro and Francesco topped up the spare medical room." Ryan tossed him the key to the cupboard.

"Yeah, they came down and told me last night."

"Also, Jen said she'll meet you in the water corridor."

"Okay. Thanks." Mikey stood and left the room.

Ryan watched him disappear into the basement. He looked around the dingy second reception before picking up both the empty water bottles from the table. "My best friend is a messy fucker," he complained to himself, wiping the table of cigarette ash and picking a couple of scrunched up tissues from off the floor, putting them in the bin. "One messy fucker."

———

The afternoon's graft on the northern wall exterior had kept Ryan's brain focused, so much to the point that he'd forgotten about the relocation plan for the refugees. He was working relentlessly with a few of the families that he didn't see that often. The lack of interaction wasn't personal. It was due to his security shifts and being upstairs a lot of the time that tended to keep him away from many of the core community.

He caught up with Teddy and Johanna while they boarded up the exits along the T to Z sections. Their son was at the toddler stage and regularly destroying their bedroom as any two-to-three-year-old boy would. They were going to select a date for his birthday, as one wasn't confirmed when he was born. They knew his birthdate was in autumn, but Sam hadn't started making the calendars until over a year later. The couple looked excited to celebrate something yearly for their son, and Ryan couldn't have felt happier for them.

Once they finished the Z-section exit, they headed back inside and left their tools in the cafeteria. Ryan headed upstairs with a rare smile on his face. What could've been perceived as a dull afternoon shift of hard labour, catching up with a portion of the community he rarely had time to interact with, was actually the medicine he needed to bring him back down to earth. He'd locked himself away from them just to do his duty of protecting them instead of engaging with them. He'd forgotten that other people had their own aspirations. Their own families. Their own futures. Maybe more people living nearby was the best for things to move forward.

A few voices came from the top floor restaurant as Ryan entered, finding Drinker with Alessandro.

"Evening, gentlemen," Ryan announced himself as he walked in. "Everything okay?"

Drinker looked up from the inventory pad. "Alessandro was just wondering if he could exchange one of our Glocks. He said that it was okay with you. I just wanted to make sure before I altered the stocklist."

"Oh, yeah, it's cool. I meant to sort that out last time you were here. One second, Alessandro," Ryan said as he walked into the galley kitchen, returning with one of their pistols. "What's the fascination with this?" he asked, setting the weapon on the table.

"This model was going to be a permanent replacement," the pilot said, brushing back his thick, curly hair. "They were being tested among the UK's antiterrorism units before the war."

"Limited edition then?" Ryan raised his eyebrows.

"Very much so."

"What's the difference between the original to this?"

"The safety device. On mine, it's located in the trigger mechanism," Alessandro explained as he placed his on the table. "Yours has the traditional flick switch found on most sidearms."

"I see." Ryan took the pilot's pistol. "Well, consider it a trade then." He shook the Italian's hand.

"Thank you." Alessandro smiled. "I'll see you gentlemen soon. I have to prepare for our morning flight now. Thank you again."

"You're welcome." Ryan turned to Drinker. "You can change that in the inventory now."

"Aye, that's something I wanted to speak to you about." Drinker looked over the listings of weaponry. "There's no recollection of this rifle in your inventory." He pointed to Sam's rifle by the window.

"Yeah. It was Sam's. He didn't want to keep a record of it. He had it before the war. I'm pretty sure it was illegal."

"Ah, I see." Drinker laughed and shook his head.

"Ryan! Ryan!" Lyndon called before stumbling into the room, panic painted across his face. "I need you to help me with Rich."

Ryan hurtled down the stairs, bursting through the cafeteria and into the medical corridor. Rich's manic yelling echoed off the walls and pierced Ryan's ears as he entered Medical Room One. Rich was strapped to the bed with zip ties, his limbs shaking violently.

"Lock me away!" Rich screamed. "I need to hurt."

"Hurt who?" Ryan ran to the side of the bed.

"I can't stop!"

"Stop what?"

"Stop thinking about it. Killing Sam," Rich roared.

Lyndon entered the room. "He asked me to tie him down when it started. I didn't know what to do."

"What to do?" Rich laughed, but something was off about it. "You should've killed Connor. Your uncle couldn't."

"What?" Ryan snapped.

"I didn't mean it. Sorry." Rich now sobbed, switching between maniacal and upset.

"What's going on? Why are you thinking like this?" Ryan demanded, trying to make sense of the chaotic mood swings.

"I don't know." Rich squinted away in disgust before a crazed look filled his eyes and glared back at Ryan. "I just know people need to die."

Without the slightest warning, Rich's left arm broke free, snapping the zip tie clean off and grabbing Ryan by the back of his head, thrusting him towards his own forehead. He laughed again—a nightmarish cackle.

"You will all..." Rich's voice cut off as Lyndon covered the man's mouth with ether. With one final burst of energy, Rich pushed Ryan hard against the wall before falling unconscious. Lyndon looked in horror as his uncle's head smacked against the wall and the air shot out his lungs.

"Fuck!" Ryan yelled, holding the back of his head while slowly picking himself up. His shoulders and back screamed, but he couldn't acknowledge it as he looked at Rich. He wasn't just dumbfounded that Rich's skinny frame could exert that strength, but more so his behaviour. That wasn't Rich. Something was changing him. Ryan bent down and picked up the broken zip tie.

"Are... you okay?" Lyndon stammered.

Until last year, Ryan had never seen that kind of power before. He didn't know it existed in people. It wasn't human. Nothing about the people who had that strength were human.

Hopefully, this was just a bad dream, and Ryan would wake up next to Cassy. If not, he'd have to start finding out why Rich was acting like a Termite.

14

R yan leant elbow first against the restaurant bar with his forehead buried in his left palm, gazing sparingly at a half-empty bottle of white wine. Rich had been put under anaesthesia—a decision that was probably best for everyone and only possible now with some of the newer supplies from Rennes. The biggest problem they faced was that if Rich was inflicted with Kurustovia45, there was only one known suppressant for the side effects. Human meat.

It felt like a race against time. Not even Mikey with all his years of medical training knew how to combat this illness. Everyone was to stay away as Rich was being examined, in a desperate hope that what Ryan and Lyndon saw was a misunderstanding and Mikey could find another explanation.

Rook had suggested that he help Mikey, but Harper refused, telling him to keep his head low and stay away from the situation. If anything was to go wrong in Rook's presence, the fallout could be disastrous.

How has this happened? What have we missed? In defeat, Ryan sank the rest of the glass, hoping the answer would come from a rare drunken moment of self-loathing. In his few encounters with alcohol, he knew the answer was never there, but it would help numb all the screaming doubts that purged his confidence. He didn't notice the evening drift away, swarmed in a brief, substance-based relief as the golden-red sunset disappeared from the restaurant's back windows.

"Mikey has some theories," Harper said as he walked in, lighting a candle and placing it on the bar.

"Such as?" Ryan questioned without looking up, reaching over the bar and grabbing another bottle of wine.

"Rabies." Harper pulled out the nearest stool.

"Rabies?" Ryan scoffed, unscrewing the lid and drinking straight from the bottle. "Can rabies cause extra strength?"

"It can cause delusions, which can affect strength. Ever seen anyone running away from a bull? They can jump a fence higher than they could've ever imagined. It's unreal to see what's possible when the body and brain are in survival mode."

"Rich wasn't running away from a bull."

"I know." Harper took the bottle and poured himself a glass. "He snapped a zip tie, that's all. It wasn't a pair of steel handcuffs. We don't even know if your nephew fastened it tightly. He said he was in a panic before he came up to get you."

"Maybe," Ryan sighed, keeping his head down.

"You're always the person who looks for every possibility. That's what helped you keep everyone alive."

"It wasn't just me," Ryan mumbled. "We had Doc back then, too."

"Again, I know." Harper took a sip of wine. "But you always explored every option. Don't jump to assumptions on this. It can't always be that bad."

"Can't it?" Ryan asked, finally looking up and taking the bottle back. "Things were supposed to get better after the war. Now Rich is going mental, we're not as secure as we were before, and the person who ate my friends in front of me has left me a love note saying he'll be back to finish the job."

Harper placed his glass down, folding his hands and holding eye contact. "Have you heard of a town called Hoyoqueda?" he asked gently.

"No," Ryan answered, confused by the change of topic.

"It's about forty miles west of Madrid."

"So?"

"My unit passed through that town at the beginning of The Fast War on our way to reunite with the front lines against the outland invasion. Hoyoqueda is not too dissimilar to here. Nice scenery, a vineyard, football team, schools... picturesque, you might say," Harper explained. "And as you did here, they survived the inland invasion, preserving the town as well as they could, combining with police and armed forces to take down the R.I.C in the area."

"R.I.C?"

"Russian/Islamic Coalition."

"Oh, well. Good for them." Ryan burped, uninterested.

"Years passed," Harper continued, ignoring the bitter response. "I was serving on the frontline until the R.I.C started retreating this January."

"Because of the Yellowstone bombs?"

"That's correct." Harper nodded. "From January, my new role was to help stabilise what was left, and my first assignment before coming to the UK was in Spain."

"Let me guess. You went back to visit this... Hoyoqueda?" Ryan asked, wondering where the conversation was going. "Were they still alive?"

"They had all the hallmarks of people who were alive..." Harper sighed heavily, drinking the rest of his wine and dropping his head, "... but they weren't."

"What do you mean?"

"A town no different to yours, and not under threat from Admiral or Father, had collapsed. Morally and socially. They gave into the fear, becoming the opposite of you."

Ryan cocked his head. "Opposite?"

Harper took the bottle back and poured another glass. Ryan spotted his hands ever so slightly trembling and his eyes beginning to water. Harper leaned his elbow on the bar. A tear dropped down his nose and off the tip. The lieutenant wiped it away and cleared his throat. "They had segregated all the non-Spanish residents into a school, forcing them to live off whatever they could grow in the sports fields. Anyone trying to leave the school was executed on sight. They were completely locked down, only giving a water supply every two weeks."

"Jesus," Ryan gasped, feeling the urge for a cigarette. "All the non-Spanish?"

"Not all of them, no." Harper looked away, wiping his nose on a handkerchief. He began shaking. "Anyone with Islamic or Russian Heritage... I've never seen a torture like it."

"What the fuck did you see?"

"A flag. A giant, Spanish flag. It covered the whole of the library's three-story wall. It was made from human skin."

Ryan's mouth dropped. He didn't want to picture it, but his brain betrayed him. He knew how it was made.

"The red part of the flag was the inside of Muslims' skins. The yellow was the Russians', dyed in urine." Harper downed his glass. "They weren't just alive when it happened. They were all in a circle, forced to watch it happen to each other. Once the skin was removed, they were given one minute to free themselves from the racks they were strapped to. If they didn't, they were burned alive."

The burning candle seemed benign compared to the visions that flooded Ryan. He could almost hear the screams. "And the whole town was in on this?" He wanted to deny what he was hearing.

"From what we heard, it started with one person. A woman. Extremely conservative." Harper folded the handkerchief and placed it in his pocket. "She staged multiple fake assaults against her. All 'Muslim and Russian perpetrators,' of course. She guaranteed the town a fighting chance of survival if they purged the town of all foreign invaders that abused her and their country."

"No one stood up to her?"

"A few voted against it, but she had too much of a following by that point. Anyone who protested found themselves banished to the school lockdown."

"What did you do when you found out?" Ryan asked, downing his full glass.

"We were ordered to detain them. They resisted. Once the fighting broke out, they knew they'd lose." Harper lowered his head again.

"They set fire to the school with everyone locked inside, then committed mass suicide."

A faint gust of wind howled gently through the window. The room dropped into a candlelit silence. Even for someone like Ryan, who'd thought he'd seen every kind of hell, it still sent chills into his bones. "Why are you telling me this?"

"I'm telling you because that town faced the same war you did, yet didn't face any of the ulterior threats you encountered," Harper said, becoming slightly calmer. "You never once thought about singling anyone out. You never gave up your humanity, and you focused on surviving. Everything you've done has been with empathy and sympathy, even regret, in some cases."

"So?"

"So, yes, you did get requested to remove your self-defence. Yes, you did find a note from an evil specimen who wants to hurt you. And yes, your man is showing signs of hysteria downstairs... but you've never given up before. Never." Harper took the wine bottle and poured it into the sink on the other side of the bar. "Your people need you. So don't even think about giving up now."

Ryan watched the contents of the bottle empty out, feeling a shame blending into horror as he pictured what Harper had just described. The world had fallen into madness and given people free rein to perform acts that would never have crossed their minds before. In an unexplainable way, he felt truly grateful for what he had here.

However, Rich's condition was real, and with the wedding in two days, it wasn't going to feel right without him there. The young man had lost his entire family in this vineyard, and all he had left was everybody here.

"I've got to speak with my wife-to-be." Ryan pushed himself away from the bar and off the stool. "We'll have to postpone the wedding until Rich is better."

"Are you sure that's the best course of action?"

"You told me not to give up. So, I'm not giving up on him. He never gave up on us."

"I didn't think you'd take my advice that quickly," Harper admitted.

"With a story like that, how could you expect me not to listen?"

Ryan reached for some grapewater on the nearest table and downed it. "I guess all this change has been playing games with me."

"I know it's been hard, but your people are lucky to have you."

"Sure." Ryan smiled weakly, annoyed with himself for turning to the drink. "You'll be happy to know I'm entrusting Rook to do a nightshift up here with Drinker."

"When did you make that decision?" Harper asked, happy with the change in tone towards the sergeant.

"Just now. Maybe I'm drunk. Maybe I'm moving forward. Maybe I want two people with military training on security. Who knows?" Ryan pulled a cigarette out of his pocket and stumbled to the eastern window, letting the cooling air hit him. He took a sharp intake of nicotine before turning to Harper. "Can you send Drinker and Rook up when you see them, please?"

"Certainly." Harper stood from the stool, straightening his jumper. "You're doing the right thing." He made towards the stairwell.

"And Harper?"

"Yes?"

"Thank you," Ryan said and nodded as he exhaled.

"For what?" Harper asked.

"Perspective."

———

Ryan shuddered as he sat on the end of his and Cassy's bed, recalling Harper's story from the night before. He'd contemplated sleeping in his nightshift room to give Cassy peace from his inevitable drunken snoring, though he decided that it wouldn't have been fair to leave her alone after giving her his thoughts on delaying the wedding. As always, she was understanding and supportive, fully believing in his motives. She had witnessed everything that Rich had been through, and they both wanted him there for their big day.

Ryan knew he was lucky to have her in his life. The best partner and mother of his children that he could've wished for. The room felt empty without her after she left for her morning shift in the sanitation room.

He rolled a pair of red socks over his feet, getting a vague image of how horrifying a human-skin-flag would look. That would never be allowed to happen here. Ryan would put an immediate stop to it. He had to before, at the beginning of the war. Not everyone who found refuge at the vineyard was accommodating to different races or religions in the early days. Safe to say, they were banished—or secretly executed. The vineyard was fortified to keep out the hate that fuelled The Fast War. Harper had reminded him of that last night.

Alfie began wailing in his cot. Ryan pulled on a black T-shirt and slipped into a pair of tartan pyjama pants. He reached for the bottle of breast milk from Cassy's bedside table and leaned into the cot.

"Here you go, baby boy." He smiled, looking his son in the eyes. "Fortunately, Daddy doesn't have a hangover, so you're lucky I'm being polite."

"What's a hangover?" Maisie asked as she stepped into the parent room. Her blonde hair was a mess, and her eyes were barely open. He was surprised to see that she successfully dressed herself.

"It's an adult thing." Ryan looked at her as he pulled Alfie into his arms. "Here, hold your brother while I do your hair." He patted the bed for her to come closer.

Maisie sat and cradled Alfie with the bottle. Ryan positioned himself behind her and grabbed two hairbands from the desk.

"Why does he have different hair and eyes to me?" she asked with innocence. "Like you and Mummy both do?"

Shit. Fuck. He knew the day would come eventually when he'd have to tell Maisie about her real mum and potentially her dad, though he never met the dad. The truest link he had with Maisie was not knowing his real parents either. At least she'd get to know about Claudia, whom Ryan and Mikey lived next door to when Maisie was born. Today couldn't be that day, and it wouldn't be until way after the wedding. It was never going to be a good time.

"It's because babies' features change as they get older," Ryan mustered from some dusty corner of his brain while trying to tie her hair into two rough bunches. It wasn't an outright lie, but it would do for now.

"Where's Mummy this morning?" Maisie went into random question mode, bringing a grin to Ryan's face.

"She's doing a stock-take shift in the chemical cupboard with Aunty Steph. They need to make sure we can keep making soap."

"Why do we need soap?"

"It stops you from smelling like Daddy's feet." Ryan tied the last bunch of hair and moved his hands away.

"Why do your feet smell?" she asked, carrying on with the questions.

"Because I walk around a lot." He took Alfie from her and held him against his shoulder, patting his back. "Talking of which, can you grab me a pair of slip-on trainers please?"

"What colour do you want?" Maisie asked, disappearing into the clothes room.

"Whatever matches your favourite colour this week."

She returned with a pair of black and white striped sliders. "Here."

"Stripes?" Ryan asked, pulling the footwear on with his toes before opening the door with his free hand.

"I like Zebras," she said with a giggle. "We're learning about Africa at the moment."

"Very good. Got your bag?"

"Yep." Maisie stepped out the door and locked it, handing the key to Ryan.

"How has school been with Johanna taking over more lessons from Dominic?" Ryan asked, putting the key in his pocket.

"It's good. She's not as loud as Dominic. I think everyone in the cafeteria can hear him talk when he's doing lessons."

Ryan laughed, holding out his hand for Maisie to grab. They headed down the long corridor, then downstairs to the cafeteria. The school was inside the library next to the reception. He said goodbye to his adoptive daughter and walked to the opposite side of the reception, finding himself outside the former tourist-theatre, which now served as their rice-growing room. He knew Drinker and Rook were taking over the threshing after their nightshift. The least he could do is ask how it went and relieve them to get a decent morning/afternoon's sleep.

He'd forgotten about the wave of heat that came from this area of the winery, with the electric-patio heater in the corner blasting warmth across the old-screening room. In the centre of the theatre, a smaller area was sealed off with plastic sheeting, and floodlights hung above their indoor rice patch. Drinker pulled one of the sheets aside and stepped out, followed by Rook.

"Morning," Ryan called with a small salute. "Everything okay last night?"

"Aye," Drinker said while approaching. "We spent the morning reading your sister's notes about the corn oil."

"It's very impressive," Rook added, taking a pair of gardening gloves off. "Where did you all learn about veg oil?"

"Before the war, actually," Ryan answered. "Our old friend learned about it during the petrol crisis. He learned a lot of things that became invaluable in due time. Without Doc, and Cooper, everything here wouldn't have been as easy as it has been. We definitely wouldn't have the functioning 4x4s out front, or even this rice room." He cleared his throat, not wanting to get too emotional. "Thank you for covering last night. If you're still interested in helping to bring in the grapes, I'll wake you up during the afternoon."

Both men thanked him and left through the double doors. Ryan looked over the makeshift indoor greenhouse, peering through the gaps of plastic and remembering the first time Cooper had shown him the display. He whispered to Alfie, telling him about Cooper and Doc and everything they had bought to the community's survival. Without them, there was a high chance they may not have survived, and Alfie would never have been born.

"We've made it this far," Ryan continued whispering to his son. "We won't stop." Whatever Rich was fighting, he could pull through with Mikey helping him. There wasn't anything realistic about why Rich would be showing Termite behaviour, so it had to be something else. Maybe it was rabies. Perhaps it was delusional heatstroke. All Ryan knew was that when he got better, the wedding would go as planned, and Rich could be there for his friend's wedding.

15

North Uist, Outer Hebrides. Thirty Miles Northwest of Mainland Scotland

Burrowed deep in the hills of a remote Scottish island, well out of trace from any thermal imaging or scanning, a smart-radio notified its owner of a full battery life. She pulled the cord from the port, unplugged the charger from her extension-adapter and placed it in her pocket. As she stood from the fold-up chair, she glanced at her bed, longing for a decent sleep. Her shift was nearly over, and the calling of the sheep-skin blanket was teasing her.

She switched off the mining spotlights and left her room in the darkness of the underground, pulling closed the poorly fitted door. It wasn't a perfect fit for the makeshift doorframe, but it was the best they could muster from a broken coffee table. At least the men treated the women who served here with respect without ever trying to pry a look into their private quarters. The females captured for the breeding program were another story, and she didn't care for them one bit. They had all collaborated in one way or another with the Islamic scum.

Whether they were just friends or people they survived with, they were still sheltered with the same mud-rats that tried to bring western culture to its knees. They served no other purpose than to breed now, and anyone spineless enough to call it 'rape' was just as dispensable.

The dimly lit tunnel between her and HQ was filled with what could be perceived as a cloud of fine dust. The average person would've associated it with the aggregate they were tunnelled beneath, but that wasn't the case. It was bone. Fine fragments of human bone. Even though she'd chosen the room furthest from the slaughter cave, there was no escaping the remnants that the power-saws kicked into the poorly ventilated tunnel system. The only reprieve was knowing this current location was temporary. Soon, the time would come to take back what was meant to be.

She buttoned her lumberjack coat, pulled up the snood to cover her nose and mouth, and shouldered her MP5 sub-machine gun. As she passed the other sleeping quarters, the men's snores echoed off the tight walls—all enjoying their deep sleep before coming to take over her shift.

"Loud bastards," she muttered, exiting the far end of the passageway and stepping into the first opening of HQ.

The man-made area wasn't much bigger than a school bus interior and lit from what everyone thought was the worst display of Christmas tree lights. Two six-foot-long tables arranged into an L-shape sat at the nearest end, with nothing more than a two-way radio on top. The exit to the right led to the slaughter cave, and the door on the opposite side opened into the tunnel which would take them to the outside.

She left the charger on the empty table while looking over the rota to see who would be taking over on communication watch after her. "Gavin?" she called harshly.

"Yes, ma'am?" The nervous voice replied, and the young civilian showed his face from the door to the right. His wavy brown hair matched his unwashed skin, which hadn't seen a bath for weeks. Gavin was petrified of her, like most of the men.

Who wouldn't be scared of her? She was the daughter of Admiral, after all.

"See to it that dinner is waiting for me in my room by the time I get back." She scowled. "I don't want to have you turned into livestock if you miss another request."

"Yes, ma'am." Gavin adjusted his glasses and sat back at the HQ staffing table, pulling the chair out with shaking hands.

"Any news from Team Spike about Rat Nest?"

"Nothing new, ma'am." Gavin pulled the chair in and made sure he sat up straight. His uniform may have only consisted of the distinguished grey T-shirt and black pants of Captain Jeffries's unit, but he wanted to make sure that he looked professional. This was a cause he believed in, because if he didn't, he'd be dead by now. "All 'official' thermal scans have stopped until further notice. The European Alliance has no reason to believe we're here or have any knowledge of where Project Zodiac is currently located."

"Good." She exhaled, seeing a mist form in front of her face. "I'll be back in two hours. If dinner is where it needs to be, I may consider calling you *Private*. Don't fuck this up."

"Thank you, ma'am. And yes, ma'am."

The gale-force winds bellowed as she approached the exit, sweeping through her curly red hair. The vibrance of her mane was matched by her freckles, standing out against her skin which had seen minimal daylight in recent months. The breeze may have been harsh, but it was a welcomed refreshment compared to the stuffy living conditions.

She pulled her hood over and reached into her pocket for the smart radio, holding it up in the air. "Fucking Scottish signal." Her voice sounded muffled under the snood. "Fucking Scottish everything!"

Admiral's men made no secret of hiding that the inhabitants of the Hebrides tasted disgusting, and the only good thing about them was how easy they were to take over. Admiral had made sure to prevent her from entering his men's world of systematic cannibalism, but even she could tell be the smell of the locals boiled flesh, she'd rather eat out-of-date dog food.

The smart-radio pinged above the howling winds; a notification lightened up the screen.

. . .

Message from Catfish Program user: Rennes Patsy.

"Finally!" She punched in her lock code, bringing up the text message.

•*Kurustovia45 confirmed effective, dosage duration of seven days.*
  •*Zodiac has received shipment.*
  •*Awaiting confirmation for Team Spike to exterminate Rat Nest.*

A wave of satisfaction warmed through her veins, bringing her senses up to a heightened state. The bitter cold of the multi-coloured Atlantic sunset was powerless compared to the exhilaration that burned as she hurried back through the tunnel. She needed to contact Project Zodiac at the Milton Keynes hideout, and she couldn't hide her eagerness to report that Rat Nest was about to be exterminated.

Those people had to go. Ryan Field had to go. She would never allow him the chance to apologise or repent for what he did to Connor. *Project Zodiac will bring you face-to-face with your actions.*

The air got heavier with each step, and she couldn't tell if it was from the usual bone fragment mist or if she had temporarily lost control of her well-known, focused demeanour.

"Sort yourself out and relay the message," she scolded herself as she approached HQ. No doubt Gavin would fear for his life by not having dinner ready as she returned early, but what the hell? It would keep the boy on his toes.

16

Ryan sat for breakfast with his family in the cafeteria, holding Cassy close as she fed Alfie while Maisie tried to catch cherry tomatoes in her mouth.

"How did Drinker and Rook handle the grape harvest yesterday?" Cassy asked.

"We already know that Drinker is a grafter, and Rook matches that energy," Ryan answered, tossing a cherry tomato towards Maisie's mouth. "They both seemed interested in the whole process, including the purifying of the rainwater."

"Any thoughts on Rook?"

"He's definitely more professional than Drinker—as a soldier, that is. You can see it's what he's done since he left school."

"Do you think he's suspicious in anyway?" Cassy stood, trying to burp Alfie.

"Regarding what he's been accused of? No. It's not our issue," Ryan said dismissively.

"Regarding anything else, though?"

"It's hard to say. Harper wants him to fit in here, like, really badly. Maybe the die has already been cast regarding Rook's trial, and Harper would just rather Rook was integrated into society instead of being confined to a prison cell. He wants to be useful. I think he misses being on the front lines. He's offered to help me with sniper training later."

"Do you trust him with a gun?" she quizzed him.

"If he had ulterior motives, he's had plenty of chances to go for a gun and do something. If I'm going to better myself with a sniper rifle, I may as well have a teacher that knows what they're doing." Ryan looked up, greeted by Rook who sported the familiar all-black attire of Penbrook's excursions.

"Morning... *boss*." He made a smirk. "Dominic told me to call you that."

"What the actual fuck-suffering shit?" Ryan turned to Dominic on the table behind him. The big man had his back turned, but it was clear he was giggling as he ate his toast.

"Language!" Cassy scowled.

"Don't worry. It won't become a permanent thing," Rook said and winked.

"Better not." Ryan frowned at him. "Are you good for today?"

"Yes. Well, when I've had some food. If that's okay?"

"Of course. I have to drop this one at school, anyway." Ryan nodded to Maisie. "I'll meet you at Point A of the trench in half hour?"

"Sounds good." Rook headed to the hot counter, engaging in conversation with Sandra as he chose his morning meal.

"Come on, Smelly-Bum. Time for school." Ryan stood and kissed Cassy's cheek before holding his hand out for Maisie. He stared at Cassy. *Soon we'll be married.* "Have fun in the soap room."

"Will do," Cassy replied. "Lyndon is looking after Alfie today. It's his first day-care shift."

"He'll be fine. He's a smaller version of me."

"That's what I'm worried about."

"Very funny. Love you," Ryan responded dryly.

"Love you too," Cassy said with a cheeky smile.

Ryan said goodbye to Maisie outside the library, then headed upstairs to the gun inventory. He took Sam's hunting rifle and one of the L96's before heading all the way down through the basement and out into the trench.

"Ryan? Is that you down there?" Mikey's voice called out from above as Ryan shut the second reception door.

Ryan stepped left from underneath the footbridge and looked up. "How's Rich?" he asked.

"Stable," Mikey explained as he peered over the rails.

"Any closer to finding out what's wrong with him?"

"There are a few possibilities." Mikey rubbed his hands together, scratching the inside of his index finger. "And one of those possibilities is what we don't want it to be."

Ryan's hopes dropped. "Any idea how that would've been possible?"

"He works outside a lot and has taken on many of Cooper's former roles. He could've touched something that held the diseases spores... I dunno."

"Think Connor could've left something when he was in here and Rich came into contact with it? If the little cunt went out his way to leave us a note, there's a chance he could've rigged something while in the corn patch?"

"That doesn't sound too far-fetched." Mikey scratched his finger harder.

"You okay?"

"Fucking bug bite. I'm going back to Rich now. I'll let you know if anything changes."

"Alright bruv. Harper and the twins leave today. Ask them if we can steal anymore supplies," Ryan suggested. "They gave us an extra mouth to feed. It's only fair."

"Talking of the extra mouth." Mikey turned to the winery's entrance, acknowledging someone out of Ryan's sight. Rook peered over the railing and into the trench.

Ryan pointed for him to use the ledge on the outer-wall and join him down below. "Welcome to the trench. We used to use this for night-watch shifts outside without having to venture out into the grounds."

"Used to?" Rook asked, observing the wooden panelled walls.

"Before the area was thermal scanned," Ryan explained. "We didn't know who was out there or their intentions. Even before Father, we were confronted by a shitload of horrible people. Now, since the liberation, we only need one person on a top-floor night-watch now." He nodded up to the restaurant. "Once we install fire extinguishers where the traps used to be, we'll have a full alarm system back."

"It's more impressive every day," Rook commented.

"What is?"

"Here. What you've done. How you survive. I can see why Harper talks about it here so much."

"Hmm." Ryan noted, wondering just how many people Harper had told and what else he'd shared with his superiors. "Anyway, it's sniper school today. I bought down one of our L96's and Sam's hunting rifle."

"I've not seen that one in your inventory." Rook pointed to Sam's weapon. "And that ain't no hunting rifle."

"It's not?"

"No." Rook picked it up and ran his hands over the smooth wooden body before tapping the sturdy stock. "Karabiner 98K, or Kar98K, for short." He looked through the scope and then pulled back the bolt-action lever. "Judging from the modified attachments, it looks like a Vietnam issue."

"Vietnam?" Ryan's mouth dropped.

"Yes. Where did he get this?"

"I don't know. Sam was once a jewel thief. He spent some time on the west coast of Africa doing some sort of dodgy deals. It's where he said he got that... and why he didn't want a record of it in the inventory."

"How did he get it back into the country?" Rook asked, handing back the rifle.

"I never asked him. Knowing Sam, he probably had some form of paid help." Ryan confessed, remembering Sam casually talking about some of his dodgy dealings. "Well, you've already given me an introduction to this weapon. Care to teach me how to get better with it?"

"Sure."

Ryan guided Rook to the northeast corner of the trench before crawling into the sheltered lookout point. Point A. He was well aware that the last time he lay here, he watched Termites running around the top of Maidhill, trying to goad him into leaving the grounds and going after them.

Half an hour into the training, a thunderous downpour hindered Ryan's learning as heavy, southernly winds disturbed his attempted shots at the two mop buckets on Maidhill's southern slope.

"God dammit!" he growled as another bullet missed.

"You have to take into account that you're firing from a lower position to an elevated position, at a distance of well over seven hundred metres, and in these conditions," Rook said as he kept his eyes to the binoculars. "It's not going to come quickly."

"It's definitely easier to fire from the top floor to the road," Ryan admitted, trying to hide his frustration. "But there was a whole bunch of them."

"Whole bunch of who?" Rook asked, pulling the binoculars down.

"This doomsday cult, a couple of years ago. They stood out in the road and threatened to burn our maze down unless we handed our animals over and repented our sins to the lord."

"What happened to them?"

"Me and Sam happened." Ryan pulled his eye away from the scope. "Most of my shots hit, but those people were heavily grouped together."

"Bigger target." Rook nodded.

"Sam picked off the ones who tried to run away. He had the skill set, and Dominic learned everything he could from that showdown."

"Would you say Dominic is your best shooter now?"

"Yeah." Ryan brushed the scope of the L96 and flicked the safety on. "I don't know if I can waste much more ammo for lessons. Are there any pointers you can give me?"

"Today was going to be hard, given your position to the targets and the weather." Rook pointed to the weapon. "Your body shape is good, and you know how to handle the gun. If you can hit targets on the road from the top floor, you'll be good to hit targets at ground level anywhere up to three hundred metres. You'd be best aiming for centre mass," he pointed to his torso, "or aim for the enemy's weapon if you need to disarm them."

"Okay." Ryan nodded. "I'll have to leave Dominic to the longer shots."

"I can give him some pointers too."

"Maybe if we get some extra ammunition. I don't think we can afford to waste any more."

"Where would you get more from?" Rook scratched his head.

"We used to have a relationship with another settlement. We traded water for bullets. Their armoury might not have been touched," Ryan said as he sat up. "And no, I'm not saying where it is. I don't want the European Alliance to know we might have ammo reserves."

"Oh, don't worry," Rook laughed. "I wouldn't tell them anyway. They don't really listen to Americans. That's why Lieutenant Harper has to work so hard to get them to listen."

"Really? Why?"

"The twin towers. The reason for the war. They think we all had something to do with it."

"That's fucking stupid," Ryan scoffed. "One C.I.A agent and a team doesn't represent everyone."

"Tell that to the governing board." Rook shrugged. "They don't even consider us part of their military. We're just skilled mercenaries in their eyes."

They shared a quiet moment as the rain thundered on the clad roof of Point A. Everything since the release of the inside-job video had reshaped the world and led them to the point where no American was fully trusted in the new world.

Ryan lit a cigarette and rubbed his forehead. "Getting back on topic..." He exhaled out the small lookout window. "Which of the rifles would suit me better?"

"I'd personally use the L96." Rook took the gun from Ryan and looked through the scope.

"How so?"

"I'm just more familiar with it. Your friend, Sam, had more time with the Kar98. But this will do the job just as effectively..."

The second reception door slammed against the inner trench wall. *The winds are getting fucking strong.* Ryan peered back into the trench, seeing Harper burst out in a fluster.

"Ryan?" Harper shouted, a clear tension in his voice. "Ryan?"

Ryan quickly crawled from the dugout and waved, catching the lieutenant's eye. For the first time, he saw an urgent look on Harper's face. "What's going on?" he asked.

"The recon unit in Milton Keynes has come under attack," Harper said calmly, but shielding a panic. "The threat has not been identified yet."

"Attack? From who? How? How the fuck is that possible?" Ryan demanded.

"We don't know. We're waiting for a call back as the team evacuates."

The twins ran over the footbridge above and disappeared towards the helicopter.

"If you go, I'll come and provide support," Rook offered, also stepping from the dugout.

"Even if we were going, you're on suspension, Sergeant." Harper barked, then turned to Ryan. "All we know is they're armed, heavily. You need to start locking down."

The last part felt like a warning, like Harper knew more about this than he was letting on. This was the first report of conflict since being told the war was over.

17

The animals were bought back in at a pace that made the previous weeks' emergency procedures appear lazy. The only struggle was rounding up the cats who thought it was just a game. Once inside, there was very little protest from any of them, like they had adapted to the temporary homes.

In the top floor, Ryan, Mikey, Drinker, and Rook checked through the weaponry while Harper, Francesco and Alessandro waited for a green light to go and provide assistance. The Milton Keynes recon team had abandoned their ground vehicles and evacuated in their own unarmed Little-Bird. The attack came from a tunnel buried beneath the cricket club. Ryan's heart dropped into his stomach upon hearing the descriptions. Two different sets of attackers. Some dressed in grey T-shirts and black combat pants... Admiral's men. The other attackers were tribal-looking, crazed, and dressed in bloody, unwashed rags... Termites.

"These aren't normal tunnels," the captain of the recon team groaned over the radio's loud speaker. "Whatever made these were big. I'm talking about proper construction equipment. That's how they avoided your thermal scans!"

"How many?" Harper asked. "And where are they headed?"

"Fifty plus, between four APCs."

"APC?" Mikey asked, slumped on the barstool.

"Armoured Patrol Carrier. Like the vehicle we came in the first time," Drinker explained.

Harper gripped the radio tighter and closer to his mouth. "Where are they headed?"

"To you. Something called Project Zodiac," the captain huffed. "Evasive manoeuvres!"

"Captain?"

"They have heat-seeking capabilities. We've just deployed our decoy flares. We can't tail them any longer. Heading back to Rennes. Incoming port side..." The smart radio cut off. Everyone stared in silence at the device in Harper's hand.

"What's Rennes going to do about this?" Ryan asked. "Are we on our own?"

"I'll make the call now." Harper shuddered but added, "We do have one thing on our side. The French APCs are fitted with a tracking beacon. Rennes can tell us where they are at any point."

"We know they'll be here at some point, though," Mikey pointed out. "Project Zodiac or whatever it was called."

"Ever heard of that?" Ryan asked the four servicemen. They all shook their heads. "Wonderful," he said sarcastically. "Now I have to go and tell everyone a group of Termites is coming our way."

"Hold up," Harper called out, holding his finger in the air as he spoke over the smart radio. "Okay, thank you." He hung up and looked at Ryan. "The APCs have halted."

"Maybe they're waiting for back up," Rook suggested.

"That's a possibility," Harper agreed. "But the longer they stay there, the longer it gives Rennes to organise a search and detain team."

"Maybe," Ryan said. "But we can't put all our eggs in that basket. We need to start preparing now. When will we know if these APCs start moving our way?"

"Rennes control will call right away."

"They'd better." Ryan stormed down the stairwell, already switched into war mode.

Termites were coming.

———

The cafeteria glowed under wavering candlelight as the basement generator powered down. Mikey walked out of the stairwell, joining Drinker by the table nearest the podium.

"Just been to see what medical supplies the twins dropped off," Rook said as he entered from the medical corridor. "Just so I know what I'm working with, if I need to assist you."

"Good to know." Mikey nodded. "I hope it doesn't come to that."

The three were alone, minus Munky, who cleaned himself on the floor by the hot counter. Everyone else had eaten early and were told to get an early rest in case of an early morning alarm. Harper and the twins volunteered to take on a nightshift in the trench.

"This is the quietest I've heard it here," Drinker said out loud, a slight echo bouncing back from the dome ceiling.

"This is how it always was before we got confirmation of the war ending," Mikey said, pulling out a chair and sitting next to Rook. His palms were sweating, and his chest was tightening. "I haven't missed this level of lockdown."

"Are you okay?" Rook asked, seeing Mikey's nervousness.

"I'll be fine." Mikey pulled the hand-held radio to his mouth, clicking the receiver. "All okay up there?"

"Uh-huh," Ryan responded, who was on solitary duty in the top floor. He wouldn't leave that window until Harper received the call.

"That's why I'm anxious," Mikey carried on. "Ryan never says that unless he's on edge. I'd avoid him for now, guys. He's seeing black. This isn't just a battle for him. This isn't just the hate he feels towards them. This is us being more defenceless than we were a month ago because we were told to take our traps down by the same people who told us that no threats were nearby."

Neither of the new recruits had to say anything. Both were aware of what Ryan had done to keep his people safe, and if Rennes had put Penbrook in more danger, there was every chance Ryan would bring a war directly to them. Military-backed or not, they wouldn't be safe from the hell he'd open.

Even if any harm that came to the vineyard was pure accident, for Ryan, it would be beyond personal.

———

Months of peace and prosperity felt like they were an illusion as Ryan sat in the restaurant. *It's been a long time since I've had to do this.* The feeling that someone could be watching the vineyard from up on Maidhill returned. Ryan stared back at the darkness across the road, not hiding himself from view with his SIG716 in clear view. *How long have they been hiding? Could they be hiding nearby, too? Did Rennes know they could be underground?*

If someone was willing to attack European Alliance soldiers, then the vineyard was well on the cards too. Whether he'd forgive Harper if Penbrook came into direct harm through negligence was a question he'd ask later.

For the first time since he held a gun to Connor's head, the corners of his vision faded to black, matching the nightfall that covered the very spot he was glaring back at. *You will not harm my family.*

———

The sun started to rise behind Maidhill. Ryan answered the smart-radio within a second of its ringing. "What's going on?" he demanded.

"The APCs have started moving south. They're coming!" Harper shouted as he ran along the trench. "I'll be up shortly." The second reception door thudded open, with the twins following him inside.

They're coming. They're actually fucking coming. The confirmation shook Ryan's confidence. The first wave of vomit landed on his feet before he fell to the floor, holding himself up by his elbows. Four more waves met the carpet and splashed back into his face.

"Get a fucking grip," he whispered, spitting the last bits out and wiping his face. *Not today. Kill them all.* He reached for the hand-held radio. "Mikey, wake everyone. Termites are coming."

Harper sprinted into the restaurant, followed by the twins, Rook, Drinker and Dominic. Mikey was the last to come after pounding on all the doors and telling everyone to get to the cafeteria. "What do we do?" he huffed.

"Mikey, you'll get Rich and wheel him out to the cafeteria. He's too close to the fire exit out back. Take the third hand-held with you," Ryan ordered. "Drinker, there's two MG75's in the gun room. You'll take them down to the basement. Open the outside door to the trench and aim the guns through the second reception. It's a chokepoint, so those guns will shred anything that comes through." He looked at Harper. "It's the same defence we used in the winter."

Harper nodded. "If it works, it works."

"Dominic and Rook, you'll be up here on look out. You're our best shooters if we need to go from a distance," Ryan continued. Both men nodded. "Harper, you'll be up here and relaying all information you get from Rennes."

"Check."

"Francesco and Alessandro, you're with me and taking our arsenal downstairs. Once you've handed out weapons to everyone who is trained, join Drinker in the basement and help him set up the MG75s."

Francesco and Alessandro looked to their lieutenant for clarification that this civilian could give them an order. Harper nodded to them, which was met with a salute to Ryan.

———

Penbrook's remaining population gathered in the cafeteria. The news slapped them all with an unforgiving horror. It was real. Mikey moved Rich out of the medical corridor and to the centre of the dining area, keeping his IV drip in check. Drinker had carried one of the heavy machine guns downstairs and was setting up the tripods for them. Alessandro and Francesco handed out weapons to all the adults, keeping the remaining ones by the back of the podium.

Ryan stood with Steph and Lyndon, passing them a Glock each. "In the event that we have to evacuate," he looked back to Cassy, who sat with his children at the table behind, "get everyone to the rendezvous at Gatwick. If you have to go on foot, take the country paths and go through Surrey Golf Club. It should take no longer than two days."

"What about you?" Steph took the gun and unloaded the clip, looking up with teary eyes. "I can't lose you, too."

"You won't." Ryan reached in and hugged her. "We now have five men with us who have military training." He turned his attention to his nephew. "Remember, keep your dreadlocks tied back when you're outside. You don't want to get caught on anything."

"I know," Lyndon huffed nervously. "Want me to stay and help?"

"No," Ryan said with a shake of his head. "Your job will be to protect our family and help get everyone to Gatwick. I know you've come far and seen a lot in the last year, but that is where you are needed."

"Okay." Lyndon stood a little straighter.

"You're as dumb as your uncle." Steph had forced the joke to calm the mood. "Come on. Let's make sure the animals are secure." She looked back at Ryan, her cheeks turning red before disappearing towards the water corridor. The temporary, and potentially final, home of the deer.

Ryan watched the door close behind his sister and nephew. *We've held off more of them before.* He approached Cassy and his family, his heart aching as tears poured from his fiancée's eyes. The protective rage built up inside, searing at the sight of his love being made to feel this scared. "I won't let them hurt you." Ryan held her tightly.

"Why is this happening?" Cassy bawled into his shoulder. "I thought they were gone."

"So did I." He couldn't help but feel a lie had been staring him in the face this whole time. "You know what to do if we have to go, don't you?"

"Yes."

"Good. I love you." The hand-held radio crackled in Ryan's pocket. He looked to Mikey who was listening on his own device. "What's the situation?"

"Just go a sit-rep. They're coming anticlockwise from the M25, near a town called St Albans," Harper reported.

"That's North London," Ryan answered. "Will take them an hour or so to get here."

"Correct," Harper confirmed. "Start getting everyone in your defensive positions. We've also just got a report from the recon team."

"They made it back to Rennes?"

"Barely, but you need to see this."

"Coming now," Ryan replied before turning to the twins. "Alessandro. Francesco. Give Drinker a hand in the basement!"

They hurried down the stairwell. Ryan went to head upstairs before Mikey grabbed his arm. "None of this adds up. They've been hiding this whole time?" He scratched his head. His skin had turned pale white, with beads of sweat rolling from his hairline. "But now they come out? This has to be planned."

"It's what I'm thinking, too," Ryan agreed. "And what good is it for them to make us aware they're coming?"

"The same reason Connor left a note. To taunt us," Mikey suggested before his face dropped. "Or distract us. It's what they did before."

The answer shook Ryan and everything he'd been questioning for the past two months.

––––––

"What do you need to show me?" Ryan asked while hurrying into the restaurant.

"Project Zodiac." Harper rubbed his forehead with his handkerchief. "It's you."

"What? What do you mean?"

"The recon team reported that before the underground attack, they found a board with the phrase Project Zodiac. There was a map to the vineyard, labelled Rat Nest. Underneath that, a full description of you. Whatever Zodiac is, it runs through you."

"Sounds like an assassination plot, sir," Rook said from the window.

"Connor really is coming after me," Ryan realised out loud. "He's just getting other people to do it."

"That's not all," Harper added. "These tunnels were big enough to hide them all for months, and it seems they have something to hold off the side effects of Kurustovia45."

"Hold off?"

"The team found empty medical supplies in the tunnels." Harper handed Ryan the smart radio. On the screen, hundreds of glass vials and tubes covered the concrete floor. "There were no human carcasses. In fact, they'd been living off berries and fruit from the nearby forest and whatever flour they'd harvested before they abandoned their above-ground headquarters."

Ryan slumped to the chair. "What does this mean?"

Rook stood away from the window and took the smart radio. He studied the photo before handing it back to Harper. Ryan noticed his demeanour alter slightly. "How long before they get here?"

"About an hour," Harper answered. "At their current speed."

"And any word on Rennes sending us support?" Rook asked.

"Not yet."

"We're ready for an attack or a siege. They aren't leaving here alive," Ryan sneered firmly. "I made that mistake once."

Rook moved his eye back to the scope and clicked his fingers to get Ryan's attention, pointing to the north end of the carriageway. "How far away are your barricades?"

"Roughly a mile in both directions. Why?"

"I could park those eighteen wheelers across them. It'll slow them down."

"Good idea. I'll come with." Ryan turned for the door.

"No. I think you should stay here. Your people need you." Rook stood away from the window. "Plus I have the proper training if I come into contact."

"How fast do you think you can do it?"

"Running plus driving... I'll be back inside in fifteen minutes."

"Okay, take that." Ryan pointed to the spare hand-held radio. "Mikey has the third one. Call in if you see anything."

"Do you want me to send Alessandro and Francesco out to provide air support?" Harper suggested.

"No, sir. It'll be better if I do this by myself." Rook clipped the radio to his belt.

"Park at the north end first." Ryan pointed left out the window. "Jen has the keys to both lorries. She's in the cafeteria. Good luck."

"Check." Rook disappeared down the stairwell.

———

Dominic scanned the carriageway as Rook ran unchallenged after parking the first at the northern roundabout. The second lorry pulled away, heading south and out of sight as it moved under the train station footbridge.

"Rook's on his way to the second roundabout," Dominic called out.

"Fucking hell, he's fast on his feet," Ryan said, gripping his SIG716 tightly. "Rook, have you seen anything?" he asked into the radio.

"Negative. Everything is silent. Reaching southern roundabout now," Rook answered.

"Understood. See you back here soon."

"Any heavier weaponry I can have?" Harper asked from behind, pointing to his sidearm. "Don't think I can do much damage from a distance with this."

"Yeah." Ryan nodded to the galley door. "There's a spare M16 in my old kitchen."

"Thank you."

Having well-trained personnel helped raise Ryan's confidence, and Rook's simple but brilliant idea ensured that whoever was coming would have no alternative but to travel from the roundabouts by foot, whichever direction they took.

We're fucking ready for you. Ryan began to psyche himself up.

"The convoy is heading east," Harper returned from the galley kitchen, relaying the information being sent to him from Rennes. "They paused at the junction that leads to Maidville, then continued."

"That's bought us some time." Ryan exhaled heavily as he bought his radio up. "Mikey. Rook. The APCs missed the turning to Maidville. They're either circling round to come from the southern route or coming from over Maidhill."

"I hear you, bro," Mikey answered.

"Heard from my end. Parking the second lorry now," Rook reported.

"Understood, both of you." Ryan placed the radio on the table and turned to Harper. "What's the update on Rennes sending support?"

"They've put together a search and detain team to bring in Admiral's men. They're currently discussing rules of engagement, for here," Harper answered.

"Rules of engagement?"

"The governing board wants Admiral's men alive."

"Even if they open fire first?" Ryan laughed like he couldn't believe what he was hearing.

"That's what they're drawing up the rules of engagement for," Harper explained calmly.

"They'd better hurry up then, because if I have to shoot before listening to whether I can or not, I'm shooting. I don't particularly trust those suits in France..."

No one was prepared for the next interruption.

"Ryan, you need to come downstairs. Now!" Mikey cackled into the radio.

"What's happened?"

"Drinker and the twins have set up one of the MG75's in the basement."

"Good. I asked them to."

"Well, the twins have just found part of a fucking syringe in the basement. Right next to where Rich passed out."

"A syringe?" Ryan glared at the radio, then at Harper. Only one person had been associated syringes, and he had conveniently removed himself from Ryan's reach. "Rook... do you know anything about this?" The radio stayed silent. "Fucking answer me now."

No answer came back from Sergeant Kieran Rook.

18

The confusion in the room became muffled under the pulse beating in Ryan's ears. Everything made sense now. "Who have you bought into our home?" His voice echoed behind the dull thuds of his heartbeat before his body took over and swung the SIG at Harper. "Who have you bought into our fucking home?" he bellowed.

"What are you doing?" Harpers eyes widened.

"I said, tell me who you've bought into our home."

"I don't know how he would've snuck those syringes in or how no one would've seen him using."

"Dominic. Get away from the window. He has Sam's rifle." Ryan turned his attention back to Harper. "Rook wasn't using, was he? You fucking idiot." He pressed the silencer to Harper's forehead. "He's been supplying Kurustovia to Admiral's men."

"And Rich has been showing Termite behaviour," Dominic added, pointing his L96 directly at Harper's chest.

"He infected..." Ryan couldn't finish the sentence. He was fighting not to pull the trigger.

"I don't know what's going on, with Rook or any of this," Harper pleaded.

Ryan handed him the radio. "Call Rook and find out then. I want answers."

Harper calmly took the device. "Sergeant. You better tell me what the fuck is going on."

"I have an idea what's going on," Rook answered. "I told you before I came here, I'm being set up."

"Don't give me that shit. All this happens after you arrive here. How did you get the needles to Admiral's men in Milton Keynes?" Harper asked.

"I've never been to that location, sir."

Ryan snatched the radio and asked, "How did you infect Rich?"

"Rich...?" Rooks voice trailed off, like he was trying to process a stupid question. "He was already sick before I was brought here."

The reply hit Ryan hard in the gut. It wasn't a lie. Rich had gotten sick the week before, but there hadn't been any syringes near where he'd passed out. "How do you explain the syringe?"

"The same way I would explain the syringe remains that were found in the helicopter upon my arrest," Rook answered casually. "And why the recon team found vials in Milton Keynes. Don't you recognise the vials in the photo?"

"What does that mean?"

"They're the same as the ones the twins bought here. I told everyone that I wasn't the only one with access to the medical supplies back in Rennes."

The twins. The twins have fucking medical access. And now they were inside. Downstairs with Ryan's family. "Mikey, did you hear all of that?" No answer. "Mikey?"

Roaring gunfire ripped up the stairwell. It sounded too similar to one of the MG75's. A loud scream echoed from the crowd inside the cafeteria, up the floors and into Ryan's ears. Then, nothing at all.

He clipped the radio to his waist and began to run for the stairwell but was stopped in his tracks. A soft sobbing entered the room. A voice Ryan knew better than any others... Maisie.

"I wouldn't do that if I were you," Alessandro ordered, holding Ryan's daughter in place by the shoulder, with a syringe pressed against her neck. "It wasn't meant to happen like this... all you had to do was *kill Rook*. Now, join us downstairs, won't you? You wouldn't want anyone else getting sick."

19

With his hands above his head, Ryan stepped into the cafeteria behind Dominic and Harper. Everyone was kneeling towards the podium, where Francesco looked over the crowd with the other mounted heavy gun. All the other weaponry lay in a pile behind him as he aimed the barrel into the centre of the community. The MG75 could tear everyone apart within a matter of seconds.

"If anyone tries anything, they all die, and I inject your daughter," Alessandro hissed. "Harper, black man, kneel there." He pointed to the back of the crowd.

"What do you think you're doing?" Harper asked, kneeling on the tiled floor.

"Shut up. You're not in charge anymore," Alessandro shouted, leading Ryan up to the podium with Maisie in front. "Take a look at all these people. This'll be the last time you see them."

"They'll fucking kill you," Ryan growled. He saw Cassy crying and holding Alfie close as she knelt in the middle of the pack. Both Mikey and Drinker had busted faces, and even Lyndon had a split lip. The twins had taken control forcefully and quickly.

"Not much chance of that happening. We have all your weapons and your inventory. Everything is counted for and ready to ship out. We'll take your supplies, your women... and the meat." He glanced over the women in the crowd, with eyes widening like a child walking into the pick-and-mix section of a sweet shop.

Ryan had to hold back the instinct to swing for him. Maisie was still uninfected, and everyone was alive. He had to play this without emotions. "You know there'll be a team coming from Rennes for you? You won't get far."

"That's what the Termites are for, *idiota*. They distract the impending search team while we get back to the islands." Alessandro cackled vilely. "And now, Sergeant Rook is out there. A sole survivor of 'The Penbrook Massacre'. The drug smuggler who turned on the community who took him in. He will be a living patsy, instead of the dead one he was supposed to be, and for that, I thank you."

"Why go through all this? Why not just kill us?"

"Kill you? How could you be arrested if we killed you?"

Arrested?

"No," Alessandro continued. "Zodiac had other ideas for you, but now we have to improvise because you didn't play the game. Talking of games... Remember the one Connor played with you? He gave you a choice last time... a tasty choice from what we've heard. Now, I'm giving you one. Go outside and face the oncoming Termites, or we kill everyone."

Ryan could never forget that choice Connor forced on him and that his outburst was what got Sam and Doc killed.

"Don't take too long. What's your choice?"

Ryan looked over at Cassy, who held her mouth while hyperventilating, trying to console Alfie. *This won't be the last time I see you,* Ryan told himself, weighing up the situation. The convoy was taking the southern route to Maidville, buying him at least half an hour to devise a plan. "Take me outside then."

"Very well." Alessandro looked over the crowd, pulling his pistol out and pressing it to Ryan's back. "Don't try and change his mind. My brother won't hesitate to open fire on all of you... children included." He then coldly whispered into Ryan's ear, "Don't you dare look at or say goodbye to anyone."

Ryan knew that disobeying would have disastrous consequences, no matter how much he wanted to rip Alessandro's throat out. All he knew was that facing an approaching group of Termites didn't terrify him anywhere near as much as seeing everyone being held at gunpoint. At least on the outside he'd have a chance, no matter how small of being able to save them—instead of letting them face straight execution.

"Unlock the doors," Alessandro ordered, keeping the syringe firmly pressed against Maisie's neck while prodding his pistol between Ryan's shoulders. "Go on then."

"Go on then what?" Ryan scathed as the doors opened, letting in the morning light.

"Get outside your grounds. They're waiting for you."

"Who?"

"Are you really that stupid?" Alessandro laughed, almost in a childish, undermining tone. "Do you honestly think the APCs were going to circle all the way round? Now, face the Termites, or I'll shoot you here."

They're already here, coming from over the hill. Ryan didn't have the luxury of time to come up with a plan. He stepped out onto the footbridge; the creaking wood echoed up through his legs and into his bones. The grounds felt foreign, like he was stepping into a nightmare he'd never seen before. Nothing looked like it was supposed to look. Death was waiting in the air.

Something wet spat against Ryan's back, accompanied by a sharp whistle and thunderous crack. The familiar boom of a rifle followed. It was a sound he knew all too well. Sam's rifle.

Maisie yelped, causing Ryan to turn, expecting to see the needle plunging its contents into her neck. She stood frozen, her eyes wide and blood matting her icy-blonde hair to the side of her head.

Alessandro thudded backwards to the floor, his right arm missing a huge chunk on the bicep. The cows and horses rattled the disabled railing that they were tied to, distressed by the commotion. Ryan pulled Maisie away from the door, holding her close.

"Are you okay?" he whispered, tearing up and checking her over. She didn't speak, staring out into the open. Ryan checked her neck, then picked up the syringe. It hadn't been pumped. From inside the cafeteria, Cassy wailed loudly above everyone's distress and moans of anguish. *They think I'm dead.* He looked back to Alessandro, who began to open his mouth and howl while reaching for his sidearm.

Keep him quiet!

Ryan's vision changed colour, with the familiar blackened peripherals merging into a dark red haze. He leapt forward, pinning Alessandro's good arm down with his knee and wrapping his thumbs around his throat. Killing him couldn't just be personal. He'd have to do it quietly to keep everyone alive, no matter how much he wanted to smash the pilot's head into the tiled floor.

Alessandro fought back, throwing Ryan off to the side. "Francesco!" he attempted to call out before Ryan cut him off with a quick kick to the mouth, causing him to fling over on to his stomach. Ryan jumped on his back and locked the Italian's throat between his forearm and chest, squeezing with all his effort and tightening harder than he'd ever had to.

A hand grabbed him from behind, pulling him away by the scruff of his neck. Instinct told Ryan to swing for a punch, but the person anticipated it and caught his hand. Rook held the grip tightly before putting his finger over his mouth.

"We'll need him alive," Rook explained in the calmest tone, nodding to Alessandro before striking the wounded man in the head with the butt of Sam's rifle, knocking him unconscious. "Where is everyone?"

Ryan's thoughts shot back to everyone inside. Cassy. Alfie. Steph. Lyndon. Mikey. Jen. Everyone. Hearing them all crying on the other side of the double doors. He looked back towards Maisie, who still hadn't moved. Blood dripped off her chin and down her dungarees.

"Shut the doors," Ryan whispered with a wheeze. His voice wavered behind the hateful surge he needed to control.

"Alessandro?" Francesco shouted, sounding concerned. "Se non mi rispondi in cinque secondi, li appro."

"Five seconds?" Rook translated the only part he understood while closing the front doors. "What happens in five seconds?"

Ryan didn't need an interpreter to understand the rest, taking

Alessandro's sidearm. He didn't know what model it was, but he checked the magazine and safety.

"Cinque," Francesco began the countdown.

Ryan hastily tiptoed towards the cafeteria entrance, visioning where Francesco stood on the podium around the corner.

"Quattro."

His attack would have to be quick.

"Tre."

Ryan cracked open the left door, hidden from view behind the stairwell, and slipped inside, gripping the pistol and pulling it up to firing position.

"Due."

He swung round, eagle-eyed at Francesco's shocked expression. Two rapid bursts left the sidearm, both cannoning of the mounted gun. Francesco fired a quick burst instantly. Screams erupted from everyone, and red mist exploded into the air from the front of the crowd. Francesco ducked and jumped off the back of the podium, heading towards the fire escape and into the water corridor. Ryan fired five more bullets, all missing his target as Francesco disappeared out of sight.

"Someone get on that gun!" Ryan screamed. Harper jumped up and ran to the podium, swinging the MG75 towards the water corridor. Mikey had already made his way to the front of the crowd, helping someone who was injured and out of Ryan's sight. "Drinker, Dominic— Rook is in the reception. Tell him to start scanning the road and provide support. Keep a watch on Alessandro. Kill him if he moves," he ordered quickly, then ran over to Cassy.

"I thought you were fucking dead," she cried, gripping his arm.

"I'm not. Are you okay?" He looked her over and checked Alfie, who was screeching as hard as his infant lungs would allow. "Maisie is in the reception. Take Steph and get her to the Medical Room Two. Get Lyndon to look her over."

The deer burst into the cafeteria from the water corridor, causing Harper to nearly fire on instinct, but fortunately, they missed the crowd in the middle and darted towards the kitchen area.

"Lock the kitchen doors!" Ryan shouted. "Keep the fucking deer from getting out."

Cassy stood and hugged him tight. She'd seen him in action enough not to question when he was making sure everyone was safe, no matter how much she didn't want to let him go—because she knew once all was secure, Ryan was going after Francesco.

From the other side of the corridor wall, the thunderous slam of the emergency exit being broken open echoed into the cafeteria.

"Go get Maisie." Ryan kissed Cassy. "I have to stop him." He found himself going into manic autopilot. He didn't have time to run upstairs to get his SIG, so he resorted to picking up a Glock as he jumped over the podium and reached the water corridor. He peered round. The doors to the rice room swayed as the wind came through the emergency exit on the opposite side. Ryan ventured forward. Francesco swung from behind the fire exit door, returning fire with his own sidearm. A bullet ricocheted beside Ryan, forcing him to pin himself against the wall and out of the line of sight.

A few seconds passed before footsteps pounded on the car park's gravel, getting further away. Ryan ran through the rice room and out the fire exit, jumping over the trench and meeting the car park. Francesco had at least a fifty-metre head start by the time he reached the driveway, and the gap was growing at a pace that Ryan couldn't understand. He pulled up the Glock and aimed, firing seven shots. All missed. Even while weaving, Francesco was incredibly fast as he fired back blindly in Ryan's direction, with bullets cannoning off the winery's wall.

Not taking his eyes away, Ryan kept up the pace and followed, determined to close the gap. Francesco veered right as he reached the end of the driveway and ripped open the entrance to E1. He didn't know any of the pathways inside the maze, but Ryan did, and the quickest route to the outside was from D1. That was his chance to get to him.

It was now a cat and mouse chase inside the maze.

20

E ven with the screeching of the Hebridean winds, the smart-radio was loud enough to ping above the sharp gusts. She pulled out the device and read the notification:

Message from Catfish Program user: Spike.

Rat Nest compromised.
  Rat did not take the cheese.
  Seeking immediate evac.

A disappointed groan escaped her mouth as she replied: *What's your status?*

A few minutes passed before an eventual response.

Alessandro M.I.A.

Trapped in grounds.

She gripped the phone tightly and punched in her final message: *Get rid of your phone and get to the evac point.*

"Fucking useless Italian cunts!" she roared, ripping open the thin wooden door into the tunnels and stomping towards Gavin's desk. "Get Team Zodiac on the radio. Now."

The young private shook as he pushed down on the transmitter. "Team Zodiac, this is Hill Base. Over."

"We read you. Over."

She snatched the radio and held it close. "Team Spike has been compromised. The rat did not take the cheese. What's your status? Over."

"Waiting to release Termites. Should we try and assist Team Spike?"

"Negative," she replied. The situation was futile. The vineyard had previously taken out a much larger unit of Admiral's men and Termites at the beginning of the year. Team Zodiac may have consisted of ten of their best fighters, but they needed to be alive to finish off their project. "Team Zodiac is not to engage. Connor needs you all unharmed for stage two. Release the Termites on the vineyard—they're disposable after all. Over."

"Copy that. What do you want us to do about the Italian? Over."

"Get the Termites to kill him and destroy his phone. Out." She placed the standing microphone back on the table and looked at Gavin. "You know what they say, don't you?"

"No?" the young private asked, wary of the focused look in her blood-driven eyes.

"If you want something done properly, you have to do it yourself."

"Oh. Yes."

"Send word to Admiral," she ordered, tying her read hair back. "I'm heading to the vineyard to deal with the rat problem myself."

"Yes ma'am." Gavin started tuning the radio to Admiral's frequency before he warily turned to her again. "May I ask something?" he asked quietly. "Isn't the European Alliance sending a team to detain Team Zodiac?"

"Yes." She grinned and added, "And I'm sure they appreciate your concern. The Italians may have fucked up their part of the project, but Team Zodiac... they'll be exactly where they need to be."

———

Ryan stepped into the opening of D9, knowing his path got him to the second-to-last section quicker than Francesco would've managed. Every rushed footstep had been taken with extreme caution and as softly as possible. He heard Francesco's movements deeper inside the bushy walls trying to navigate through the winding pathways of the E-section.

With one bullet left, shooting blindly through the hedges wasn't an option, and while all that was going on, he didn't know how much ammunition Francesco had left either. *Get ahead and cut him off. Take the shot.*

Ryan pushed right, taking him to a narrow pathway that would come out by E9. From there, he could turn back and come out ahead of his target. Minimal sound came from his calculated paces, moving sharply with his pistol aimed in front. Francesco's heavy exhales were loud and clear from the other side of the walls. They were getting closer to each other.

With a controlled swing round the corner of E9, Ryan checked the ground for fresh prints before turning into the next opening, bringing his finger to the trigger as he approached. Francesco's footsteps and heaving became harder with each second.

Ryan held his breath, carefully reaching the next corner. As he veered closer, Francesco ran into his arms and caused Ryan's finger to tense and squeeze the trigger. Both fell to the ground. Ryan blinked hard and shook off the dizziness. The gun shot happened next to his right ear, which screamed as he tried to regather his senses.

He's armed. Ryan reminded himself, looking towards Francesco's right hand. The Italian raised his sidearm, pointing it directly at Ryan's face, gritted his teeth, and pulled the trigger.

Ryan didn't have time to register it.

Click.

They were both without ammo. Ryan sprung off his feet and attempted to pin him down, only to be kicked off Francesco's body with a power he'd only ever felt once. He flipped all the way over and landed hard on his back, his previous rib injury screaming like it wanted to return. As his vision adjusted to the sky above, he caught Francesco's fist coming down toward his head. He moved to the side just in time, and the pilot's wrist snapped on impact with ground.

How fucking hard can he punch? Ryan's eyes widened. He desperately raised himself to his feet and tried to get air in his lungs. Francesco pulled his hand up, glaring at the splintered bone that stuck out from his forearm before turning his crazed gaze to Ryan. His teeth exposed a manic smile. *He's infected too.* Ryan froze.

Even with one arm, Francesco would be nearly impossible to defeat.

To his shock, Francesco turned and bolted at full pace towards the outer sections, rasping maniacally. Ryan stood alone, his thoughts trying to understand why but were denied by shock. *Why didn't he fight? Why is he more concerned with escaping?* His brain raced. *What's his motive?*

Instinct won, and Ryan ran after him. Francesco had already cleared the long pathway, using that inhuman speed to his full advantage. The power that came from his pace left clear tracks in the ground to follow. Ryan tried to keep up, but knew he was well behind as he weaved left, then right, then left again. Francesco had found his way to D9 before turning right to D10. Ryan watched him disappear up the final stretch, knowing that with the traps gone, Francesco would be out of the maze and safe from Penbrook. *This can't happen.*

A crashing thump of a body meeting wood echoed over the walls, then D10's gate slammed open against the outer wall. Ryan turned right to the final pathway, seeing the opening and running with all he had left before stopping at the gate. He glimpsed through the crack and out to the distorted carriageway. Francesco cleared the mid-road barrier, holding his injured wrist as he sprinted for the treeline. Two loud cracks tore through the air, followed by the thunder-like booms which always accompanied them. The Kar98K had its personality etched into everyone's ear drums.

The first bullet slammed off the steel barricade, before the second tore through Francesco's left ankle, severing the foot completely. The vocal eruption of agony was louder than the gun that caused it, echoing round Maidville's empty skies for at least five seconds.

"Ryan. Are you there?" Rook asked into the radio.

"Yeah," Ryan wheezed after unclipping it from his waistband and keeping himself hidden behind the gate.

"Tango down. He's on the other side of the road."

"I saw. Good shot."

"Do you need assistance?" Rook asked.

"Yeah. Drinker and Dominic." Ryan scanned the treeline opposite. "Tell them to use one of the quads and bring a stretcher. Keep an eye out from your point."

"Check."

"How's the situation inside?"

"Alessandro has been put under," Rook explained. "Mikey and Lyndon are working on Johanna's leg. Fortunately, she was the only casualty."

One too many. Ryan's rage soared. Johanna didn't deserve anything like that. The thought of taking prisoners left his mind as he looked back to the whimpering Italian.

"Mikey says she'll make it," Rook added, sensing the brief silence as Ryan descended into blackout mode. "Wait for Dominic and Drinker."

"I hate these people!" Ryan roared into the radio, eyes glued to Francesco.

"I don't blame you, but the twins serve us better alive than dead. Focus on the task in hand."

"Tell Drinker to bring my SIG. I'll see you when we get back. Eye's peeled till then."

"Check."

———

"Where are you?" Dominic shouted from Ryan's left.

"Dio exit," he called back. "You?"

"Cio."

"Okay. Coming to you now." Ryan pushed the gate open and then made sure it closed before hurrying along the maze's outer wall. Cio's gate opened with Drinker and Dominic emerging. Ryan took the SIG and checked the magazine. "I'll follow you over. The prick's missing a foot. We have to get him inside before he bleeds out."

The three jumped the steel barrier and reached Francesco, who'd crawled a few metres away from where he was shot. Ryan pressed the silencer to his back. Dominic turned the pilot over with ease, lifting his shoulders onto the stretcher. Drinker grabbed his calves, knocking the stump on one of the handles.

Francesco screamed again while trying to swipe his good hand at Dominic. "Get off me, you dirty monkey!"

The insult jarred Ryan, forcing him subconsciously to raise the barrel at Francesco's forehead. "Seeing as you wanna be racist... You say anything like that again, and I'll turn your head into a fucking bowl of bolognaise. How the fuck does that sound?"

Dominic restrained both wrists with zip-ties, despite one of them being broken, and then chucked a zip tie over to Drinker to secure the good leg to the stretcher's frame. "Don't let him get to you," he looked at Ryan. "His words mean nothing to me."

"*You* people mean nothing to me," Francesco spat in Dominic's face.

Ryan's finger moved closer to the trigger before Dominic put his hand out. "It's okay. This isn't the time."

Drinker grabbed the handles at his end. "Let's get this cunt inside. You can do what you want with him later."

Despite seeing red, Ryan reluctantly let them pick up the stretcher, though he made sure to slap Francesco's bad leg and bring out another retching scream. "That's not even half the pain you're about to experience."

This scream rolled up the hillside and towards the sky before fading away, and a new sound rolled down the slope and into Ryan's ears. A sound that froze him on the spot.

A maniacal laugh. A hyena-like laugh.
A Termite laugh.

21

Ryan swung the SIG towards the hill, searching the winding dirt tracks that vanished under the thick grove of trees. Nothing moved.

"Go!" he roared to Dominic and Drinker. "Get him back inside. I'll be right behind you." Their footsteps slapped on the tarmac, getting further away as they pushed back through the maze. Francesco had turned his agony into amusement, taunting in his native language. Ryan blocked it out and pulled the radio up. "You heard that, right?"

"Copy. What the fuck was that?" Rook answered.

"A Termite. They're up the hill."

"Keeping all eyes on it. I saw Francesco throw something just before you got to him."

Ryan lowered the radio, catching an object on the ground in the corner of his right eye. It was a smart-radio, identical to the ones that he'd been introduced to last week. "It's a phone. Can they be traced?"

"They all have location settings for incoming caller ID," Rook answered.

"So, we could find out where the people they've been talking to are?"

"Affirmative."

"I'm going for it." Ryan clipped his radio to his waist, moved his hand to the weapon's trigger, then approached the new device while watching the treeline behind the sewage plant. Each step was met with a rise in heart rate, though, fortunately, his eyes didn't let him down and play tricks on him like they had in the past. He was calmer than he had any right to be. A faint whistle hummed high in the air as he knelt, rippling from above. He looked up, spotting the spear as it arched down in his direction. He snatched the phone with his left hand and dodged out of the way, letting the projectile crash to the ground.

A bullet tore over the vineyard grounds, hitting someone hidden on Maidhill's west slope.

"Tango down," Rook informed.

Ryan had seen that type of spear throw before. The last time it had been used was to bait him—a distraction from their real intentions.

They just pulled Rook's focus away, he realised, feeling his alertness surge. The next spear shot out from behind the car park, slamming clean through the steel barrier before losing momentum and thudding on the ground.

The Termites kept themselves hidden this time, leaving no target to shoot at. Ryan turned and jumped the barrier, using his hand with Francesco's smart-radio for leverage. Another loud churn of metal tearing was met with a surprise as his legs gave way, and a burning sensation tore through his trailing hand, like it had snagged on something. The spear stuck through the barrier, just missing his left leg. He pulled himself to his knees and bought his hand up.

The smart-radio wasn't there, and neither were his third and fourth fingers. Just open flesh and bone shards. The trickling blood felt like acid being poured on his hand. Every gust of wind stabbed its way into the nerve endings, lighting an invasive agony that refused to let numbness take over and made sure every movement would be met with physical torment. He knew he couldn't let the pain win now and piled all his effort into being present at his current predicament.

Looking beyond the open wound and towards the car park, he caught a Termite bursting from the treeline. He never forgot how they looked. Middle Eastern. The blood-stained rags. Eyes that were predominantly white and crazed. The teeth clamped together hard and covered with drool. Its arm was arched back with a spear in hand, pointed directly at him; only fifty metres separated the pair.

Ryan forced his right arm up, pointing the SIG with one hand just as the Termite released its launching arm. He tried to squeeze the trigger, but the involuntary shaking made it impossible to aim or fire.

The Termite flung backward, with body-based debris shooting out of its exit wound from behind. Ryan didn't hear the rifle shot. He couldn't hear anything but knew he was alive. *Get up.*

He sprinted as fast as his legs could muster before colliding into the maze wall. A spear cut him off to the right, shattering through the timber. Instinctively, he turned in the opposite direction, running towards D10 and where he'd exited a few minutes ago.

They're leading me away from Drinker and Dominic. They wanted them separate.

A chilling numbness shot into his hand. Then the pain kicked back in. A raw, bone-curdling fire rushed all the way to his shoulder. While trying to ignore it, he pushed along the wall to D10, hastily opened the gate, and slammed it shut behind him. The latch didn't lock in place, and it opened slightly, followed by a spear that ripped through the outer wall and somewhere into E10.

"Ryan. There's too many of them," a faint voice called through the radio. He knew it was Rook, but all the collating sounds merged. The warnings from the radio. The Termite laughter. The gunfire from the top floor. He couldn't make sense of anything. He felt like he was drunk. "They're trying to cross the road. Get inside now."

Above the warning, he managed to pick up on the sound of bare feet pounding towards him. He shook off the haziness, pulled everything back into focus and raised his gun, resting the barrel on the back of his wounded hand while bearing through the pain.

As he pushed further inwards, more of the outer wall and pathways tore apart as spears crashed through. He was getting dizzier with the force he exerted on himself. A sharp turn right. Then two lefts. Another right. Ryan's shins met a spear sticking out from the hedgerow, sending him flying forward and landing on his left hand. His teeth nearly broke as he desperately repressed a scream, to which his throat took the worst of it as it became a silenced roar. Somewhere to his left, a gate clattered against the outer wall, followed by a sea of footsteps pounding into the maze.

The gates should be on my right. He looked around, trying to recognise the area he'd fallen into. He couldn't tell. It looked like the path into E8, which also looked like C7, and D9.

"Don't contact me," Ryan whispered weakly into the radio. "I need silence." After he turned it off, he shut his eyes and concentrated on every kind of noise that now surrounded him.

Ryan was lost in the maze. Trapped with Termites. The cat was now the mouse.

———

Mikey tripped up the last step and stormed into the restaurant, reaching Rook by the window. "What the fuck is going on? Why has Ryan turned his radio off?"

"He's not alone in there." Rook kept his eye on the scope. "I took down as many as I could, but they barraged across the road. I've never seen people move that fast. It was like a fucking wave."

"He's in the maze? With them?" Mikey's voice quivered as he looked out the window, taking in the vastness of the perimeter. "This can't be happening." His fear turned to anger. "I'm going out there. I'll give my radio to Drinker. If our grounds are breached internally, warn him and take out as many as you can."

"Check."

Mikey rushed downstairs. The anxiety of losing his best friend melded with something he didn't normally entertain... rage. Nearly everyone was armed in the cafeteria, minus Lyndon who was tending to Johanna's wounds while Teddy tried to comfort her. He rushed to Cassy, who held Alfie close. Her face was blush red, with tears dripping off her chin. "I'm going out to get him. I'll bring him back," he promised.

"Is he okay?"

"He's turned his radio off. He's trapped in there with them."

That did nothing but add to her suffering. Cassy dropped her head and cried harder. Mikey waved his hand for Jen to join him. "Look after Cassy. I'm going to get Ryan."

"On your own?" Jen protested.

"Don't do this. Not fucking now," he said pulling his hand away, jaw clenched tightly like he was on some kind of amphetamine. Jen had never seen him in that state. "I need to save him. I need to kill them."

"Okay," Jen accepted in shock, holding Cassy as she sat but not looking away from him. Mikey never spoke to her or anyone like that.

He stormed through the cafeteria and into the reception, tossing his radio towards Drinker who caught it just in time. Without warning, he picked Harper up with both hands around the neck and pinned him against the wall.

"I'm going out to get my friend," Mikey hissed, saliva hanging from his chin. Harper couldn't free himself, and Drinker looked on in dumbfounded terror. "When we get back, you've got some fucking explaining to do." He dropped Harper and opened the doors. "Lock these behind me. Rook will call down if we get breached. If that's the case, I expect you to do everything you can to hold them off."

Neither responded as Mikey pulled the G36C up, sprinted over the footbridge and towards the driveway, disappearing out of sight and at a pace he'd never been capable of before.

———

Ryan held the gun as tightly as his hand would allow, trying to follow where the footsteps were heading. A loud brush came from the other side of the wall to his right, followed by multiple footsteps that led to the opening in front. He was surrounded.

A Termite burst from the corner in front, unaware they were facing away from Ryan. He squeezed the trigger twice, both suppressed bursts hit the target in the back, dropping them to the ground. The recoil pulled on his left hand. He'd never struggled to control his breathing so hard before, and now the pain was becoming overwhelming. Behind it all, he knew silence was his only friend. *I will not be defeated.*

Another flurry of footsteps came from his left, a few sections deeper. Between focusing and ignoring his hand, he pushed on to the next section in his path, quickly glancing behind to cover himself. He stepped over the Termite's body and swept the open area in front, which resembled C8, but he couldn't be sure. Most of the sections were designed to look similar to confuse intruders. Blood trickled heavily down his forearm and into his sleeve, gathering in the elbow crease of his hoodie. He didn't know how much blood he'd lost, and that was starting to weigh on his mind.

Panting came from behind. Ryan swung and aimed quickly. The rampaging Termite only caught a quick glance before Ryan fired two shots into their chest. On their way down, they managed to let out an ear-piercing screech.

Ryan stood fully silent, listening hard. All the footsteps around him halted, then started heading inwards towards his direction. He turned back and pushed down the opposite pathway, a hundred and fifty metre stretch with no turnoffs. Two Termites stopped at the far end, locked onto him like a predator hunting its prey, and charged at full speed. Ryan went to aim but heard something next to him. A Termite burst from the left and grabbed him by the waist, throwing him to the floor. He instinctively got himself on top of the Termite, pushed their face into the ground with his knee, brought the gun up and pushed the barrel into the back of their head. A quick trigger squeeze rendered them lifeless, but he wasn't aware of the next oncoming Termite.

The blade came down hard, piercing all the way through Ryan's right forearm. The force knocked him back, pulling the Termite down with him. His arm felt like it was melting from the inside, both flesh and bone were on fire, making the first wound feel almost unnoticeable.

The two other rampaging Termites had nearly made the distance down the long stretch, bearing down as the third got up and pulled the knife out from Ryan's arm, holding it high and ready to plunge it straight into his abdomen.

A loud explosion came from above. The Termite's head exploded to the side. Two more explosions. Ryan squinted, trying to make sense of what happened. The Termite who had stabbed him, and the other two, lay lifelessly beside him.

"Ryan," Mikey yelped, skidding to a halt beside him, checking him over. "Can you walk?"

"Uh-uh." Ryan forced as he spat on the ground, trying to regain composure behind the insane tearing sensation in both arms. The fingers in his right hand were useless, leaving him unable to grip anything. Without thinking straight, he managed to pick the gun up with his remaining fingers on his left hand and held it close to his chest. Mikey grabbed him under the armpits and pulled him to his feet. The sudden jolt of movement ripped through his body, causing him to cry out like he hadn't before. More footsteps thundered around them.

"This way." Mikey nudged him towards where he'd come from, pulling his G36C up and leading the line. Ryan did his best to keep up, but his vision was fading.

They weaved right into another open area. Mikey knew where he was going and navigated the remaining pathways until pulling up to the gate at D1. He reached out to open it as Ryan collapsed, barely breathing.

Mikey took Ryan's radio and turned it on. "Ryan's hurt. Get the fuck here now with a quad and a stretcher," he ordered.

A Termite burst out from D2 and headed straight for Mikey, slamming him into the gate. Ryan tried to stand, but his legs gave out and his face hit the dirt. Struggling to keep his eyes open, the world around him faded. The last thing he saw before falling unconscious was Mikey taking the Termite by the back of its neck, picking it up off the ground and crushing its head into the timber.

22

The laptop pinged. He lifted the screen and read the message, dreading each word that may appear before him. It was a direct message from Admiral Caven.

Care to explain why Team Spike have failed Project Zodiac at the first stage?
Can I trust you to see out Stage 2 with full effect?
What do you plan on telling Connor about the rat not taking the cheese?

The shame that came with today's events was unfathomable. Of all his missions and teams, this was a smear on the pristine record he prided himself on having. He didn't feel safe here on most normal days, and now he had to worry about Admiral bringing the world down on him.

The twins should've killed Ryan after he didn't take the bait, not toy with him.

Now, he could lose everything, and his family would be forced to live in the refugee camps.

He'd die before letting that happen.

———

The metal-shark boat pulled away from the sandy shore of North Uist, humming across the gentle waves and kissing the Atlantic Ocean before turning south and beginning the journey along the Scottish west coast.

"It'll be roughly ten hours until we get to Blackpool beach," the captain called out from behind the deck. Captain Worrell was a podgy young man with receding, golden hair and dull grey eyes. He looked older than he was, jaded by his late teens spent fighting in The Fast War. "There is a fully fuelled ATV and a travel bag waiting for you at our destination. From there, it'll take you a good eight hours to get to Milton Keynes for your stopover and refuel, then another three and half hours to Maidville," he informed.

"ATV?" she asked dryly, looking over the starboard side while smoking one of her dad's cigars. All-Terrain-Vehicles were her least favourite form of transport. The heavy-duty quad bikes may be extremely nimble but provided no protection from incoming gunfire. It certainly wasn't the worst news, though, and she wouldn't let it dampen her spirits as the boat bounced off the waves. She welcomed the salty air as it brushed her skin. This was the most time she'd spent outside in months.

"Is Admiral okay with you going alone?" Captain Worrell asked above the roaring engine.

"He doesn't have a choice." She turned and winked, "He was reluctant with the idea of me joining the fight to begin with, so now I have to show him that I can do more than our supposed allies in Rennes could."

"You know you don't have to prove anything to him, or us."

"Oh, I know. How much do you know about this group?"

"The vineyard? Only what I heard from Connor," Worrell answered. "I was lucky enough to speak to him before he left."

"Go on." She tossed the cigar stub into the sea.

"Their grounds are extremely well defended, and they have a serious amount of weaponry. From what our source in Rennes told us,

Connor took out two of the big players there before his arrest. Left Ryan alive, just to toy with him."

"Toy with him? I expected better from Connor..." She scoffed, shaking her head. "What can you tell me about Ryan?"

"A few details... Average height and build, nothing imposing." Worrell scratched his forehead. "Blond dreadlocks... a small family."

"That's enough to identify him."

Everyone had underestimated this guy so far. She wouldn't do the same. She needed to know exactly who her target was. One day, Admiral would tell the story of how his daughter, Hannah Caven, killed Ryan-fucking-Field.

23

B lood was everywhere, splashed across the walls like a music sheet that matched the harmony of the Termites laughter. Spears rained down, thudding into puddles around Ryan and drenching him in waves of blood that dripped off his skin, just like it had done with Maisie.

Maisie.

Maisie!

Ryan awoke slowly, greeted by the sun which seemed to burn through the bedroom window and into his eyes. He pulled his hand up to shield it, seeing the tightly wrapped bandage around his forearm. The pain returned with immediate effect, squeezing the muscles and drilling deep into the bone. He swung his legs off to the right, sitting over the edge of the bed. He looked at what remained of his left hand, which looked like it was being held in place by surgical dressing. Only his thumb, index and middle finger protruded from the gauze, which like his right forearm, replied with a wave of unimaginable discomfort. His feet hit the floor, and Cassy jumped in front of him from Maisie's room.

"Oh baby. You're awake." She knelt beside the bed, hugging him as gently as she could.

"How long I was out for?" Ryan's voice was dry, making him reach for the grapewater on the bedside table.

"Don't try and grab it." Cassy shot her hand out and took the bottle, bringing it to his mouth. "Mikey says the knife went between your radius and ulna, chipping them along the way. You need to rest it to avoid any permanent nerve damage."

"Nerve damage?" he murmured after he swallowed.

"The use of your fingers and thumb." She lowered the grapewater.

"How long was I out?" he asked again.

"All of yesterday and this morning. You didn't lose as much blood as feared. It was the shock that caused you to pass out."

"Has Mikey banished me to rest and recover?"

Cassy shook her head. Tears built up under her wide eyes. "You know he normally would, and I really want you to, but now isn't the time."

"Where's Maisie?" Ryan stood slowly with Cassy's aid. He went to move to her room, but Cassy stopped him in his tracks.

"She's asleep now, and I've only just got her to sleep. She's traumatised. She hasn't said a word, and she's not eating."

"No. No." he sobbed, carefully pulling Cassy closer to him. "I'll make sure she's okay. I'll help her get past this. We'll get her past this."

"I know we will." She cried into his chest. "I was so scared. I thought it had happened. I thought you were gone."

"I'm sorry. I can't believe I let this happen to us."

"You didn't do this." Cassy pulled away, looking him in the eyes. "You thought you were doing the right thing. Don't even put this on yourself. Not now, because it's not over."

"What do you mean? It's not over?"

"Mikey needs you. He's in the basement. I'll help you get dressed."

Ryan took each step gingerly, avoiding knocking his arms on the handrail. The darkening entrance to the basement caught him off guard, like a monster was waiting in the depths of a blackened dungeon.

"He's waiting for you in there," Cassy whispered over his shoulder.

"Are you not coming?"

"I can't. I need to be with Maisie... and I don't want to know what you decide."

Ryan's heart dropped. *Decide? What am I walking into?* He limped inside and looked right. Two hospital beds sat between the four central pillars, illuminated by some of the spotlights from the medical rooms. The occupants became clearer as he cautiously approached. Alessandro and Francesco, both unconscious. Rook stood on guard with Mikey's G36C in his arms, turning after hearing Ryan's footsteps.

"How are you feeling?" Rook asked as he walked over.

"Doesn't matter how I feel." Ryan glared at the hospital beds and asked, "What's going on?"

"I'll let Mikey explain. I'll be over here in case you need me. You're not going to do anything to them are you?"

Ryan carefully raised both his bandaged arms. "I couldn't pull a trigger if I wanted to."

"True." Rook nodded at Ryan before walking to the stairwell entrance.

"Oh, Rook?"

"Yes?"

"Thank you. I don't know what would've happened if you weren't here."

"No need to thank me." Rook glanced over to the twins. "I should thank you for not killing me, like they wanted."

"Yeah." Ryan agreed, feeling ashamed that he let himself get played. *Dirty fucks.* "Have they said what or why I was supposed to?"

"They've been under for the past twenty-four hours." Rook shook his head and added, "As much as Harper protested, you should be the one to find out why. If they held my family hostage like that, best believe I'd want the first answers of why."

"Thank you."

Ryan slowly approached the beds, seeing blooded bandages and emergency medical equipment on a table between both beds. He held back the urge to go for the scalpel and slice both of their throats.

"I had to put them under." Mikey's voice came from nowhere, making Ryan jump to the side. His friend stood against the barred cell doors from the other side, gripping them tightly and breathing heavily. "Glad to see you up and about."

"What the fuck are you doing in there?"

"I don't trust myself. It's taking control of me."

"What is?" Ryan asked, looking into Mikey's crazed yet calm expression. Then it hit him. "You're infected, aren't you?"

Mikey nodded. A tear fell from his right eye, dripped down his cheek and hung from his chin. "It looks like it." He dropped his head. "Probably happened the night I was on second reception duty. They fucking chloroformed us before they did it."

The fucking tissues. "I'm sorry." Ryan's guilt soared. *I should've spotted it.*

"We all decided to let them in." Mikey dismissed. The words didn't help Ryan, and a lead ball formed in his gut, making him want to vomit. "Rich has been under while it's been eating into his frontal lobe," He huffed, "I think he's slipped into a coma, and he doesn't have the self-awareness to wake up."

"How can we repress it?" Ryan asked, "Without having to feed you human meat?"

"Those two are infected." Mikey nodded to the twins. "They must have something they take to keep it under control. Like the vials Harpers friends in Milton Keynes found."

"What if they won't give it to us? Or what if they don't have it here?"

"That's why I need you here. To make a decision."

Ryan turned back to his friend. "What decision?"

"To put us down." Mikey sighed in defeat.

Ryan stared back, not believing what he had just heard. Mikey held eye contact, with whites wider than he'd ever had. His fingers shook on the iron bars, rattling the rivets at the frame.

"I'm going to pretend I didn't hear that." Ryan said shaking his head.

"You don't have much of a choice. Do you know what I did yesterday? I managed to force a live-human skull through the gaps of an eighteen-inch thick-timber gate, and then I pulled their trachea out with nothing but the strength in my arms. Strength that I didn't have before."

Nothing in that description sounded at all like his best friend. Mikey was truly sick, and it would be with him forever, but he was still Ryan's best friend. Nothing would change that.

"What you did yesterday... is save me." He approached the cage door. "That's what you did. Don't ever ask me to put you down again..."

"If the twins don't have anything to suppress this, you're going to have to." Mikey pressed against the bars, slowly bending forward the one in his right hand.

Ryan turned the conversation to the twins, realising that trying to talk Mikey down wouldn't work. "How do I wake them up?"

"Well, hopefully they don't slip into a coma either. We don't know enough about this disease and everything it does to the brain. If they don't wake up, you're going to have to..."

"I'm not fucking discussing that Mikey." Ryan said sharply while dropping his head, "I'll wait for them to fucking wake up."

Alessandro stirred first, groaning weakly before the pain set in and jolted him awake.

"I'm glad it was you who woke first." Ryan stood away from the cell, approaching slowly while trying to keep his arms as still as possible. "Normally I would have killed you by now, but we seem to be at a bit of an impasse, and I need something from you."

"You want to keep your friends alive?" Alessandro chuckled menacingly. "Hand yourself over to the Termites, and I'll give your friend the serum."

"Yeah, I had a funny feeling you'd say that. See, the issue for you is, one, all those Termites are dead, and two... you held a syringe of that shit to my daughters neck."

"I'd happily do that again."

"Well, you won't get the chance. So where is your stash?" Ryan asked, cutting to the point and to avoid getting angry.

"Turn yourself over to the convoy that bought the Termites here, and I'll give it to your friends. You have my word." Alessandro relented.

"I've got a better idea. Tell me where it is, or I'll solve this issue the other way."

"What other way?"

"The syringes aren't the only thing that can hold off the effects, are they?" Ryan's mouth twitched. He was actually going to enjoy what he was about to say, and that horrified him. "Yesterday, you said you wanted to play a game with me, like Connor did. Now you get to play that very same game, and it has similar outcome." Alessandro picked up where Ryan was going, and the vile sneer faded. "You give me those syringes, and you tell me how much is needed per dose... or I cut your brother up in front of you and feed him to my best friend."

"You... you wouldn't."

"I've done worse," Ryan said nonchalantly. No change in his expression, just the cold seriousness of the cards he was about to put on the table. "Bad news is, neither of my hands are working properly at this moment, so I'm not sure how efficient and quick it'll be when I carve Francesco up." He stood next to the bed. "You have given me reasons to do things that'll make your peoples actions look like child's play in comparison. Should I run out of your brothers meat before you give up this... serum... I'll be serving you after."

"You'd be arrested!" Alessandro laughed uncontrollably, then silenced himself before another burst. "Go ahead, do it!" The foreboding fear was replaced by a curious satisfaction, then instant regret. Ryan picked up on it.

He cocked his head. "Why's that a good thing?" He knew one of the side effects of Kurustovia45 was vocal outbursts.

"They wanted you to get arrested before." Rook interrupted as he walked over, "By killing me."

"Project Zodiac!" Alessandro cackled. His hyena laugh echoed off the basement walls.

Ryan watched as Alessandro fell into a hysterical fit. *What the fuck is Project Zodiac, and why do they need me arrested?*

24

S ilence hung in the cafeteria as Ryan sat on the edge of the podium, holding a scalpel in his right hand.

"Project Zodiac," Ryan said loud and clear, "Is a plot that was designed to frame Rook for infecting Rich and Mikey. We all know I would've killed him, and truth be told, I would've if he had been in the building at the time. Fortunately, the twins weren't aware he was out when they planted the syringes downstairs." He looked over everyone. Torment and anger painted their faces. "I would've been arrested, leaving you without me, and only Mikey in charge as the disease ate away at his mind. In the fallout of all this, the convoy and Termites would have attacked you while I was gone. You would've become cattle for them, wherever they're hiding now."

"Do you think Mikey will actually eat human meat?" Sandra asked.

Everyone had already figured out Mikey's condition, but no one knew he had asked to be taken out of the equation. Ryan told them of his plan to feed the twins to Mikey, and it didn't come as shock. Even Jen wanted him to do it. Ryan knew he couldn't though. When it came to deciding what to do with the twins, the vineyard's hands were tied.

"No." Ryan shook his head dismissively. "Unless he was losing his mind, which he isn't for now as fortunately Alessandro accidentally gave up the serum during one of his outbursts. Even if Mikey needed to eat them or not, I'd carve them up just for the fucking fun of it, but I can't do that, can I?" He turned his head to Harper, who stood beside the stairwell door.

All eyes locked hard onto the lieutenant.

"You'd be sentenced for war crimes," Harper said loud enough for everyone to hear. "And for interfering with an investigation."

"They're not your fucking prisoners!" Jen screamed, storming towards him. Ryan carefully jumped from the podium and got himself in between the two. "Have you seen what they've fucking done?" she said.

"I have," Harper replied calmly.

"They infected Mikey. They infected Rich. They shot Johanna. They threatened to infect Maisie, while holding all of us at gun point..." She turned her gaze to Ryan. "... they tried to kill you." Tears rolled down her cheeks. "Why are you not killing them right now?"

"You have no idea how much I want to," Ryan said regrettably. "If I do, I won't be here for Maisie, and I won't be able to get Mikey the treatment he needs."

"The twins have just tried to kill us. All of us. You're going to just let them go free?" She glared at Ryan.

"They won't be free," Harper interjected. "We'll be taking them into..."

"You stay the fuck out of this," Jen snapped. "You were the one who bought them here." She turned back to Ryan. "You already let Connor go. Are you really going to do the same here?"

"That's not fucking fair!" Steph stormed forward and stood in front of Jen. "If anyone has anything to say about that, it would be me. You still have Mikey. I don't have Doc. All I know is that my brother has had to make decisions that all of us here couldn't begin to comprehend. So, if you want to be angry at someone, be angry at Harper, but don't even bring Ryan into this. It's out of his fucking hands."

Everyone watched as the two women stared each other down.

"Well maybe I should just go down there and kill them my-fucking-self." Jen sneered.

"I won't let you do that." Ryan said stepping forward, even though he knew that one punch to his arms would probably be enough to immobilise him.

"You're going to stop me?"

"If I have to. You think I'm going to let you give birth in a fucking prison cell?"

Jen stared back, taking in what Ryan said.

"I didn't think so. It's about the bigger picture here." he said as calmly as he could, though clearly irritated by her earlier retort.

"Fuck you." Jen stepped past him and stood in front of Harper. He didn't see the slap coming, or have time to react before she stormed up the stairwell.

"That slap didn't happen," Ryan icily demanded as he approached Harper. "I just hope you're fucking happy with what's happened here, and what your governing board has put us through."

"Jen didn't have to do any of that," Steph said over his shoulder.

"The father of her unborn child has been handed a brain-rot, death sentence that is only avoidable from consuming proteins found in human meat. I'd say she's pretty justified in doing whatever she wants, including killing the twins." He squinted at Harper. "You'd better stay on guard down there with Rook until your back up arrives."

———

Hannah checked the petrol gauge as she reached the outskirts of Nottingham city centre. Her tank was half full, more than enough to get to Milton Keynes.

She pulled her flask up and took a mouthful of distilled water, refreshing her throat after the speedy journey from Blackpool. At the beginning of her route south, she passed the city of Manchester, the location of the second largest bomb detonated on April 24th, 2024. Six years later, the hundred-mile radius around Manchester looked like a scene from all the apocalyptic movies. The M6 motorway was void of the expected abandoned vehicles, as most had been flung over the western shoulder into gardens and fields, like an EF5 tornado had torn through the area. None of the trees or plant life had regrown to what they once were, and everything from the road to the bridges were coated in a rust-coloured dust. Even the air tasted different, tainted by the array of pollutive chemicals that stuck to everything in the area. Only Greater London looked worse than the northern city.

Nottingham was one of the few English cities lucky enough to avoid being a target for the nuclear weaponry. What it did leave was a larger population for the inland invasion to wipe out, and they had tried with every ounce of their contempt for the west. The battle of Nottingham lasted the longest of all the intercity skirmishes to break out. Six months of resistant fighters holding the city, with the petrol campaign starting in the suburbs, pushing all survivors into the centre. The arrival of Captain Morgan Jeffries and SAS Task Force 205 had caught the Russian/Islamic Coalition off guard and forced a retreat, ending the siege of Nottingham. It was the first big victory in the fightback of The Fast War. The survivors of the battle had been transported to the refugee camps in Milton Keynes, where they were looked after and nursed back to health. Until the mutiny, and everyone was forced to choose a side.

Hannah sat at the top of Maid Marian Way, looking down the long stretch that forked into the city centre. She could navigate the city with her eyes closed. She was born here, and went to university here. After hearing about the horrors that had happened to the city, she begged her father to let her join the fightback. He refused at first- until he and Task Force 205 had been captured by the R.I.C two years into the war. After what happened to him and his men at the hands of their captures, Admiral decided it was better that his daughter knew how to defend herself. He never spoke of what happened, but it changed him. This is what bought on the mutiny, leading Task Force 205 to start rebuilding the country as they saw it should be.

Her phone pinged. She attached the flask to her belt and pulled the phone out, reading the notification from Admiral.

Team Zodiac is initiating stage 2 as of tomorrow.

Do not engage Rat's nest for at least a week.

There is a stopover being prepared for you at Milton Keynes ground-base 4, southern outskirts.

Connor has been denied the chance to kill the rat. Make him proud.

"I will make him proud," she whispered, tucking the phone back into her pocket, "I'll tell you all about it when I see you, Connor."

She twisted the ATV key and roared the engine, saying goodbye to her beloved home city after her quick detour. After many years away, she hoped to see Nottingham rebuilt one day. Maybe she would see the city sooner than she wanted. In the event of an emergency, Hannah's predesignated extraction point was her old university campus, two miles from the city centre.

Now that she had a week before executing her mission, the journey to Milton Keynes would be taken at a much calmer pace, but she revelled in the knowledge that her prolonged stay over at 'ground-base 4' would give her more time to rehearse the shot, and the escape.

She wouldn't need a rescue team.

———

For the first three hours of the evening, Ryan sat cross-legged against Maisie's bedroom door, listening to her from the other side. Her breaths changed from heavy to rapid, followed by the occasional sobbing before extended periods of unnerving silence. He didn't know how to help her through this kind of trauma, but he was going to make sure he was there when she needed him. The blistering throbbing deep inside his arms made it impossible for him to drift off, so he sat and bore it.

"Are you coming to bed soon?" Cassy asked as she peeked her head around their bedroom door, switching the light on to the small hallway of their family room. "You've been here for hours."

"No." He looked up. A sea of red surrounded his green eyes. "You should sleep. I'll stay here in case she wakes up."

"I've slept enough, for what I can." She sat beside him and kissed his shoulder. "And you've done enough."

"I wish I had."

"What do you mean?"

"I could've put a bullet in the twins instead of taking them prisoner." He sighed heavily. "It would've saved us a lot of bother."

"Would it though?" Cassy used her finger on his chin to turn his head. "In that scenario, Mikey wouldn't have the serum, and we wouldn't be able to get any information from them."

"I doubt the fucking European Alliance would've shared any of that information with us."

"Even if they didn't, they could still find out who the twins were working with. Like you said, it's about the bigger picture."

Ryan rested his head on her shoulder, torn between what was right or wrong. The whole situation felt like a balancing act, and whatever decisions he was faced with would cause long lasting damage. He wasn't a superhero. He knew that. The world needed to stop testing him like he was one.

His eyes started to close, and the pain in his body subsided. He felt safe while tightly holding his future wife. Finally, exhaustion took over and he drifted into a heavy sleep.

———

Henry's standard morning call woke Ryan in a microsecond. Cassy had put a pillow under his head and covered him in a wool blanket. He winced as he pulled himself up and sat back against the door, still not fully accustomed to the missing appendages. He carefully rubbed his eyes with the side of his thumbs, adjusting to the dark autumn morning.

While standing, he peeked his head back into the main bedroom. Cassy lay asleep, with Alfie in the cot next to her side of the bed. He stretched his arms out, and a loud crack came from the middle of his back, right next to his old rib injury.

"Fuck," he whispered harshly, but silently as he could.

"Daddy?" a small voice called from behind.

Instinctively, he switched the light on and turned. Maisie stood at the door. Her skin was pale white against her dark-red pyjamas, and her arms were outstretched, ready to be picked up. Ryan didn't wait and leaned down, ignoring his discomfort and pulled her up with his left forearm, resting her head on his right shoulder.

"Have you eaten?" he asked quietly. She shook her head. "Are you hungry?" She shook her head again. "Want to get away from the bedroom for a bit?" She nodded that time.

Ryan crept to Cassy's side of the bed and tapped her on the shoulder with his elbow, waking her slightly.

"We're going for a little walk. Be back up soon. Love you." He leaned down and kissed her on the cheek. Cassy's eyes opened and she saw Maisie in his arms.

"Hey." She smiled, reaching her arms out before Ryan pulled away.

"She isn't talkative right now," he mouthed subtly.

"Okay." She sat up and kissed Maisie on the back of the head. "Love you both. See you soon."

Ryan leaned into Maisie's bedroom, turned her light off then pulled the door open into the main hallway, closing it behind him softly to not wake Alfie. His wounds screamed from the minor activities. "Wanna get a drink? I think the first lot of orange juice is ready." He distracted himself and put all his attention on her.

She nodded into his shoulder again.

As he stepped into the cafeteria, he quickly glanced at the clock above the doorway to the reception. Ten past six. There was hardly any light outside, and the last traces of the heatwave had said goodbye as autumn kicked in. The kitchen lights started flickering. *Sandra is down early.*

As he made his way to the hot counter, Sandra jumped back in surprise.

"My God!" she exclaimed. "It's been a while since you've given me a fright."

"Sorry." Ryan feigned a grin as he kicked the double door open into the kitchen. "Didn't actually intend to this time." He pointed to Maisie.

"How is she?" Sandra approached, stroking his daughter's back.

"Thirsty. Think she wants to try the orange juice, don't you, smelly bum?"

Maisie nodded again.

"I'll get some right away, dear," Sandra said with a smile, heading to the walk-in fridge.

Ryan sat Maisie on top of the work bench. "Just going to give you a quick look over." Her hair felt more brittle than normal, and some blotchy patches had formed on her skin in the past few minutes. Her eyes stayed staring forward, apart from the few times they glanced at his wounded arms. He wasn't going to tell her about how they were acquired just yet, but didn't doubt she was smart enough to know by now.

"Here you go." Sandra returned with a full pint of fresh orange juice.

"Thank you." Ryan reached for it, taking a sip before handing it to his daughter. She took the glass and pulled it slowly to her mouth. "That's a taste I've missed." he said, watching Maisie experience it for the first time. There was no reaction from her, which given the circumstances was a good thing. If she didn't like it, she'd have probably dropped the glass.

"It's good to get those vitamins in before a day like today," Sandra chirped, which confused Ryan.

"What's so special about today?" he asked.

"You don't know?" she gasped. "Drinker said he was going up to your room to tell you."

"I passed out last night. Maybe Cassy thought it was best to leave me till the morning." Ryan thought aloud. "What's going on?"

"The search team from Rennes found Admiral's men."

"This is a good thing, but what's so special about today?"

"These men, they're being taken back to Rennes," Sandra explained, folding her tea towel and placing it on the oven top, "but the transports are stopping here on their route."

"To pick up the twins, I assume?"

"Not just that. It's Harper's boss. He wants to meet you personally."

25

The sudden cold turn had become ever-present during each new morning, with increasingly bitter gusts sporadically blowing through the particularly clear sky. After the failed winter of last year, maybe the upcoming season would bring the familiar frost and chills before depositing a pathetic snowfall that normally came to England.

To counter the chill, Ryan wore his black, long sleeve T-shirt with camouflage-patterned arms, matching his combat pants as he stood next to the graves at the back of their land. He lit a cigarette and sat on the hard ground, crossing his legs and taking a puff.

"I'm lost." he admitted out loud. "I don't know what's going on. I feel fucking neutered." Inhaling some more and looking at the blue sky, "A year ago, I could've killed the twins, no questions asked. Look what they did to Johanna, Rich, Mikey... Threatening Maisie. Shit, I would've actually enjoyed killing them."

Munky, the ginger cat, strolled up beside him, purring loudly as he rubbed his back against Ryan's knee. The felines company helped take the edge off the loneliness of the moment, so Ryan stroked the cat's chin before turning back to the graves.

"There's a rule book to play by now, and it's not our rules written in it," he continued. "I've been playing by it and look where it's got us." His voice tightened. "Letting Connor go was enough, and that still resurfaces in my thoughts every fucking day. But now, Rich is in an indefinite coma, and Mikey has that fucking disease which can only be held off by a shot of something that only the twins know, or he becomes an easy-to-manipulate cannibal."

"You can't control everything." The voice replying was Doc's. As much as Ryan welcomed the logic of his deceased friend, he knew it was only in his head. For a fraction of a second, he didn't care that he could be losing his mind again.

"I'd love to believe that this is really you talking." Ryan looked back up to the sky. "But I need to try and keep myself together through all of this." He stood and looked at the graves. "Guess I just needed to get it off my chest."

He headed back to the winery with Munky following. Mikey stepped through the fire exit and walked over the footbridge. He'd showered and put on his favourite blue hoodie and white jogging bottoms.

"I thought I'd find you out here," Mikey said and sparked a cigarette. "How you holding up with all this?"

"Bollocks to how I'm feeling." Ryan dismissed and hugged his best friend. "How are you feeling? Does the serum work?"

"I'm fine." Mikey chuckled, hugging back before letting go. "It definitely works, almost instantly. If what they say about the intervals are true, I'll have to shoot three milligrams every seven days."

"No side effects?"

"Not from the serum itself, but this disease could have some drawbacks whether I take it or not."

"What do you mean?" Ryan asked, his brief happiness faded.

"Well, remember Doc theorised that we may have outsmarted Father because this illness rots the brain anyway. The cure only delays it. Even though it's a massive extension of time, it'll still affect my decision-making," Mikey explained.

"Fuck sake."

"I wouldn't worry about it. If Alessandro and Francesco can still function a helicopter, then the serum is good for the long run. It could affect my medical judgements, though, which is why I think Lyndon should primarily focus on his medical studies and training, instead of taking on the extra roles he's volunteered for."

"I'll let you talk to him about that then," Ryan declared, stepping onto the footbridge.

"You're his uncle," Mikey pointed out. "Prick."

"And you're his teacher. Twat!" Ryan retorted, happy they could still share the same old back and forth. "Fuck, it's just good to see you out of that cage."

"It's good to be out. I feel more like myself again." Mikey nodded, before rubbing his chin. "Had to apologise to Harper, for what both me and Jen said to him."

"Hmm." Ryan looked away, not wanting to be interested.

"He isn't responsible for this. Even you know that," Mikey said firmly. "It's easier to pin it on him as we don't have anyone else to blame."

"You think we'll find out who's behind all this then? The twins weren't working on their own."

"I don't think we'll personally find out, but I don't doubt that Harper will. Francesco and Alessandro have tried ripping up all his plans for a return to civilisation. He won't stop until he's smoked out who's pulling the strings back in Rennes."

"Hmm," Ryan grunted again, flicking his cigarette into the trench. "Anyway. I'm glad you're here for when Harper's boss arrives," he said, changing the subject. "This should be fun." Even the least intelligent person would sense the sarcasm in his tone.

The roar of multiple helicopters bore down on the vineyard, coming from over the northern horizon. Drinker had tried to convince Ryan not to have defences set up, but was quickly reminded that right now, he didn't know who to trust.

Dominic had been told to stay on the top floor and keep his rifle ready until given the order to stand down. Ryan and Mikey armed themselves with their preferred assault rifles, standing outside the front doors in full display. Inside the cafeteria, everyone else had been armed too, should there have been any ill intentions with the new visitors.

In the basement, Rook administered the serum to the twins to calm them down. Harper handcuffed the pair after releasing the bed restraints, with Drinker leading Alessandro at gun point, and Rook doing the same with Francesco, though he forced him to hop all the way there. They exited the basement through the second reception and into the trench. A ladder had been placed for them to climb out. It took longer than they wanted for the twins to climb with their injuries, but no one was going to help, and Ryan wasn't going to let them go through the cafeteria and out the front doors. There was a very real chance that someone would take a shot.

I wouldn't even blame them.

"Don't look at them," Mikey whispered, keeping his eyes north to the approaching helicopters.

Ryan didn't say anything. He was summoning what strength he had to stay focused on the meeting and not execute the twins in front of the now visible air convoy. Two smaller helicopters, similar to the Little-Birds, flew on the outside of the formation. Two larger choppers filled the middle space. They were much longer with two horizontal rota's, and not the typical back tail rota of the other helicopters. Ryan knew they were people carriers, even if he didn't know the correct term for them.

"Stand there and shut the fuck up, ya ham doughnut," Drinker ordered as he pushed Alessandro in the back, a few metres to Ryan's left. Francesco hopped over and was given a crutch to lean on as he stood next to his brother.

The convoy hovered above. Harper signalled for them to land just outside the car park on the northern side. The largest of the two people carriers landed in front of the team, the other to the left, and the Little-Birds landed last on either side. The dust storm kicked up from the arriving party turned the air nigh-on unbreathable and made the twins chopper look like a fart in a jacuzzi by comparison. After a few minutes, the engines all gradually powered down and the haze cleared. The tail ramp lowered from the largest in front. Two squads of armed soldiers filed out from both sides and formed a perimeter around the chopper, with two holding their aim on Ryan and Mikey.

Neither Ryan or Mikey flinched, holding their weapons tightly and ready to raise them, even if Ryan couldn't pull a trigger just yet, he wasn't going to stand down. Their gazes turned back to the exit ramp. A tall, broad-shouldered man marched down, hands behind his back. He wore the same combat sweater as Harper, and his grey trousers were perfectly uncreased. His dark blue eyes were clear and focused, analysing Mikey and Ryan. He turned his gaze towards the twins, brushing his perfect, side-swiped brown hair. Clear disappointment appeared across his face, and he lowered his head whilst shaking it.

Everyone stood in silence.

"So, do you have anything to say for yourselves?" he called to Alessandro and Francesco. No answer. General Woodburn waved his right arm in the air. The exit ramp lowered for the second people carrier. Four armed men ran out, taking the twins under their arms and leading them back to the helicopter. Ryan saw some more prisoners inside, all wearing black cargo pants and grey T-shirts. Admirals men. One glanced back at Ryan, a slow, wicked smile formed on their face before the ramp closed. It was like they wanted to be there.

"Don't," Mikey said, quickly putting his hand across Ryan, whose right arm flinched.

Woodburn spotted Ryan's movement, and slowly strode over to the pair. "Thank you for returning the prisoners, though they were instructed to be unharmed."

You fucking what? Ryan's blood boiled, and he instantly went to step forward to square up to him.

"It was me," Rook announced, stopping Ryan in his tracks as he interjected into the conversation. "All of their injuries came from my shooting. These two had nothing to do with it."

Woodburn's eyes bounced back between Rook and Ryan. "Hmm. Well, there will be an investigation when we eventually get you back to Rennes, Sergeant Rook."

"Understood, sir."

Woodburn looked back to Ryan, his eyes lightening. "You must be Ryan. Boy, have we heard a lot about you."

"Probably more than I've heard about you," Ryan snapped back. "Everything I get told is either an order or classified."

"Well that's why Lieutenant Harper is one of my most reliable men." Woodburn glanced to Harper. "And a trusted friend. Despite all that has happened, I hope you can continue to work with him."

"You'll understand if I'm having a hard time doing that. He brought the twins here."

"That's where you're wrong." Woodburn sighed, "It was me who signed off on Francesco and Alessandro working directly with him."

"What?" Ryan's voice dropped.

"They requested a transfer to his team when air transport was assigned. I confirmed it. Harper was just following orders. My orders. The twins were here because of me."

26

H arper watched from the side as Ryan fixated on General Woodburn, praying the joint-leader of Penbrook didn't act on his now well-known impulses. The relationship he'd been trying to build with these survivors was hanging on by the finest thread after what those fucking twins had pulled off. Even the very foundations back in Rennes required a shake-up with the revelation that Admiral had moles within. Everything he worked on needed repairing, and a major flush out would need to be put in effect.

"It wasn't just you who was tricked, Ryan," Harper said out loud, wanting to get a foothold in the conversation. He stepped over, holding back from putting his hand on Ryan's shoulder. "This is what they wanted. They played under all our noses, and if they had their way, you'd have killed Rook, and then been sent to one of the same twelve cells that the twins are now going to rot in."

"He's right," Mikey admitted, stepping in front of Ryan and clicking his fingers in his friends face. "Look at me. We all got played. And I'm sure the *general* has some news for us about how they plan to fix and prevent future attacks." He emphasised Woodburn's ranking to put him on the spot to defuse the situation.

"And you must be Mikey," Woodburn assumed.

"That's right."

"Lieutenant Harper's reports about here have been spot on."

"I bet they have," Ryan said coldly.

"You've been following the orders that come straight from France, out of good faith while also putting yourself at risk..." Woodburn looked around the front side of the vineyard. "May we talk inside? I have a lot to tell you about what's going to happen, because from what I understand and as you said yourself, the phrase *classified* is starting to piss you off."

The corner of Ryan's mouth twitched, and he stepped back, relaxing his posture slightly but making sure he kept his guard up. "Not inside. I want to keep eyes on that helicopter filled with Admiral's men." He slowly raised his left hand in the air and stuck his thumb up, before pointing with his remaining fingers to the fore-mentioned chopper.

Woodburn looked to the top floor, seeing a dark figure move away from the opening of the front facing window, and presumably covering the prisoner transport. "You folks really are impressive." he commented before turning to his own protective unit. "Stand down," He ordered.

His men lowered their weapons and assumed a more casual stance, as unlike Woodburn, they were unaware that they were being watched from the top floor. "Your man on the top floor isn't jumpy, is he?" he questioned.

"He's ordered not to fire first. So, if all is secure here, everything will be okay," Ryan replied.

"Good," Woodburn nodded. "I'm sorry our first encounter has to be under these circumstances."

"Me too, but it's how it is these days," Ryan said bluntly. "What have you got to talk to us about?" He got straight to the point.

"Very well. First of all, the European Alliance recognises you as a part of its official population due to your cooperation. This means that you are under not just our regulations, but also our protection. Seeing as how our direct actions put you under duress, it is our obligation to reimburse you for damages, and to help you move forward."

"Like a compensation package?" Mikey doubtfully asked.

"That's what those lawyer adverts on TV once called it," Woodburn said with a smirk. "But yes. We know we've asked a lot of you, and this is the very least we should do for one of our potential prospects for development. This compensation package will be arranged after an inventory meeting with Lieutenant Harper, who will compile a list of things you need to further your community's survival."

Ryan was taken aback. This was the first time someone from the outside had offered to assist with supplying them without it being a trade deal.

"Rennes is in awe of what they've heard about you, and consider you a vital part of the future, and relocation program."

"What's going to happen to the twins, and the men you captured yesterday?" Ryan pressed on. Though he was stunned by the offer, he had more urgent answers that needed clarification.

"This should be classified," Woodburn admitted, tapping his finger on his chin. "Interrogation will be as standard. We need Admiral's location to prevent any more of these situations, and to find out who has been helping them from within. After that, they will stand trial."

"Trial? Why? Everyone knows what they did." Ryan pointed out sharply.

"We know, but who will we become if we don't offer everyone a fair trial? No better than the very people who tried to obliterate us, that's who. This is what needs to happen to ensure democracy can return, and our children can have a better future."

Mikey chimed in, "Will there be a jury?"

"Yes."

"Witnesses?" Ryan added.

"Yes. Everyone who wants to testify. Unless they plead guilty to all of it, then it's not necessary."

"What would the sentencing be?"

"That's not for me to say. That's up to the judge," Woodburn answered, straightening his back. "That's a while away anyway, so it's best to leave it from your mind until you're called upon to testify and make a statement. There are bigger and better plans for your community between now and then."

"What do you mean?"

"It's going to grow. Regarding the relocation program, Maidville has been selected as the focal point for British citizens. It makes sense for remaining survivors dotted around the country to move here. You already have better amenities than all the others combined."

"Everyone moves here? They'll just leave what they have behind?" Mikey asked. "How can we just suddenly integrate people we don't know?"

"They don't have much to leave behind, and a stronger populace is always good for both rebuilding and defences." Woodburn pointed to the front of their grounds. "You have a sign out there, and many dotted around the local area, saying you want to help people and that everything can prevail. This is who you are, and no one has done it better than you."

"Do you still plan on bringing refugees over from France?" Ryan added. "What's the plans with them?"

"Locations have been identified for each nationality."

"They're going to be segregated?"

"Separated is the best term. It'll help them preserve their country's cultural identity as time moves forward."

"Isn't this just potentially going to create nationality issues?"

"It hasn't in France so far. They all have their own ideals and beliefs, but I don't think any have the will to start an inter-sectional conflict- as long as they respect each other, and you. This is where Maidville's importance comes in, in the eyes of the European Alliance."

"Have they made a decision?" an eager Harper asked.

"They have." Woodburn nodded before turning back to Ryan and Mikey.

"Decision about what?" Mikey shifted his gaze between the pair.

"With London being out of commission for the foreseeable future, and considering how the population has reduced radically," Woodburn began, "the European Alliance sees Maidville as the future capital of a new England."

———

A community meeting was held within minutes of General Woodburn's departure, as Ryan and Mikey had to get the news off their chests. They, nor anyone else could could fathom the ideas that awaited their future. Only two days had passed since they were nearly taken off the map, and now they were the golden egg of the country.

Woodburn had also offered to take Rich back to Rennes, so he could receive full medical care while he was in his coma. Mikey agreed with the offer, deciding that it was for the best and increased Rich's chances of recovery along with twenty-four hour supervision. Ryan was unsure of letting someone go, so they agreed they would have an answer the following morning when a returning crew came to pick up Harper, Rook, and the twin's Little-Bird.

Among the grand plans laid open for them, there was one strong legislation that Ryan hated more than having to take the traps down and had to be prevented from going into a full verbal tirade with the general. Once Mikey ran out of the serum, he would be taken to Rennes under protective custody, where he'd be held until another serum could be replicated to aid his condition. The European Alliance wasn't comfortable with someone running round with a disease that required cannibalism to ease the symptoms.

Mikey understood the scenario, and the reasoning for it. Ryan, on the other hand, couldn't bear to lose more people, never mind his best friend. Jen, as everyone found out, wasn't happy either until Mikey told her that she would be allowed to join him, and might even give birth in a more secure environment. Rook suggested he be deployed to Penbrook for the duration of Mikey's stay at Rennes. A trade for a qualified medic was only fair, not just to help further Lyndon's education, but also to be considered as a part of their compensation as it was their fuck up that had caused Mikey to get infected. Harper agreed with Rook's suggestion and managed to convince Woodburn to talk to the governing board.

During the meeting, the other news regarding Maidville and Penbrook's future had been met with a lower than enthusiastic reception. As Ryan looked out at everyone, he saw they were just as burnt out from the past years' worth of strangers on their doorstep. He didn't like that they had lost all hope and optimism for helping people in need. They had been stung too many times since Father's arrival.

Sandra never lost her faith and declared this to be the big final break they had been waiting for after what felt like a lifetime of hell. She promised everyone the best feast they'd had for years to try and get everyone back into a positive mindset. Everyone appreciated the effort and indulged her as they sat in the cafeteria for longer than normal. Even wine was brought out as she tried to get everyone talking about what could become of this change. Shops. Summer events. All the things that made a community work before the war.

Ryan noticed Harper had stayed in the medical rooms with Rich the whole time. Ryan wasn't sure whether it was because he didn't feel welcome in the cafeteria or because he felt responsible. Rook relieved Harper to get some sleep, and he took over caring for Rich.

Everyone left after the meal and headed to their family rooms. Drinker said he'd do the night lookout for Dominic, so he could help Sandra clean-up, which was met with a sarcastic thanks from the big man.

"None of this is going to be easy," Cassy said trying to reassure Ryan as she sat next to him on the empty podium.

"Everything is changing." Ryan looked over the cafeteria, where Dominic helped wipe down the tables with Sandra. He stood and picked up his nearly empty plate, with a few spoonful's of beetroot risotto remaining. "I'll take care of the washing up." he smiled, walking past the married couple.

"You're a gem," Sandra said.

"Least I could do." Ryan entered the cafeteria, holding the door open for Cassy and walked to the sink at the back wall. "And the food was amazing tonight." he shouted back through the closing door.

"I'll help you dry up." Cassy reached for the plate rack and pulled down the dish towel.

"Thanks. You know I prefer the actual washing part." Though he hadn't tried washing up since losing two of his fingers.

"I haven't forgotten since that night."

"Oh yeah." Ryan perked up a bit as he turned the hot tap on, remembering their first kiss. "You blatantly followed me that night to do that. I had actually planned to kiss you another time."

"Oh really? How?" Cassy asked, placing a plate on the drying rack.

"Well, it was going to be a sunny day, and preferably no fighting happening anywhere near us. The sun would glow on your dirty skin, and I'd look into your eyes and just... smooch!" Ryan took a handful of soap suds and attacked Cassy playfully.

She teasingly protested, hitting Ryan with the cloth. They laughed until they ran out of breath, slowing down to heavy giggles.

"Do you know what's funny about how you planned it?" Cassy wheezed.

"What's funny about it?"

"It didn't happen how you imagined, but it still happened."

"What's the funny part?" Ryan asked, looking for the punchline.

"That's been our whole life since we've been together." She stood against the sink. "Every path has been different, but we still got there."

"Why does this feel like one of your 'look on the bright side' comments?" he groaned.

"Because it is." She kissed him. "Remember, you nearly didn't let Jen into our community when you first met her?"

"She kind of gave us all the reasons not to," Ryan said, remembering that hard conversation with Mikey and Doc.

"And yet you still understood her situation. Letting her in was one of the best decisions you made, even though you thought she could turn rogue on us."

"It was a leap of faith, and you're right." He sighed in defeat. "It was for the best, and against my judgement. What are you getting at?"

"You had Doc and Mikey help you with that decision. I know Doc's gone, and we'll lose Mikey for a bit, but you're not on your own to make those kinds of choices anymore." She pushed off the sink and stood in front of him. "Mikey has told you not to put this on Harper, and so have I."

"I know. I know."

"We wanted to help people, and he's the right person to help us... help people."

"Did you need *help* with that sentence?" he teased, wanting to change the subject with immaturity.

"Fuck off." Cassy laughed then added. "I'm just saying that Jen's relationship here didn't start great, because of what the world had forced her to do. Don't blame Harper for what was out of his control."

"Jen didn't bring someone here who threatened to poison our daughter."

"No, she didn't," She rubbed her hands on the cloth and tossed it on the sink. "But as you said, 'our daughter'. I'm raising her too. If I can see that Harper isn't responsible for putting her in danger, then I'm asking you to try and see it too."

27

I t was well after midnight as Hannah passed Milton Keynes, turning off the M1 motorway and steadily drifting to the southern outskirts of the town. She turned right as she reached the border of the woods, looking for a specific red pick-up truck.

There it is.

She pulled up to the wreckage and turned her engine off. Thick darkness engulfed the wooded road. She reached into her travel bag and grabbed the U.V torch, shining it at the trees nearest to her. One of the trees had a glowing arrow pointing her deeper into the woods. A mixture of saliva, lemon juice and blood had been painted on the trees, glowing brightly to lead her to the opening of tunnel A. The member of Team Zodiac who set up her stay-over had left the directions before taking off and returning to the team in Blackpool.

It was an ingenious and resourceful way to ensure that no one would find the entrances to the underground-bases. This particular tunnel and the main chambers existence would remain unknown to idiots of the European Alliance, despite them luckily finding Ground-Base 1 a couple of days ago.

Hannah reached the first tree and shone her U.V light further into the wooded area, exposing the next tree to guide her. Twigs cracked under each step, reminding her that even though she thought she was alone, Admiral would scold her for being so heavy footed. Her breath clouded over the luminous marking. She paused for a second and shook her head.

If there were people here, they'd have seen your ATV lights anyway.

She repeated the process with the trees until she reached what would be the last one, with the clear arrow pointing down. She pulled a few branches away from the ground and found a wooden hatch door. Switching to her normal flashlight, she pulled the door up exposing an opening into a dark, vacuous void. Moving the beam of light around, the switch for the cable lights dangled in front of her. With a quick click, the tunnel illuminated, exposing the steps carved into the ground for five metres before breaking into an open cavern.

This wasn't like the tunnels back in the Scottish Isles, which were hastily made after they had been forced to flee Milton Keynes in the spring. No, these tunnels were constructed to hide the true numbers they had in their cattle, and just how big their forces were.

Ground-Base 4 was well over seven feet high, twice as wide, and lined with reinforced concrete. Two rail tracks ran down the middle of the passage, which was used for the body-transport-carts. Admiral had seen the World War 2 mountain bunkers in Poland, bringing back that vision with him. The Nazi's may have been batshit mental, but they were damn efficient engineers.

This is where Admirals men kept their food, and the people that were to be slaughtered. All the rounded-up prisoners were held in the local football stadium before being bought here. Most of the main activity had happened above ground, but this area was kept out of sight. It had a higher death toll than any of the worst European Camps of the twentieth century. That was beyond a pretty big reason to keep the location out of sight of the European Alliances eyes.

No doubt they'd use it to stain Admiral and Father's vision. Hell, they'd probably even be called Nazis by all those fucking idiots out there, of which she knew Ryan had once, like the short-sighted fuck that he was. Admiral's people weren't fuelled by hate or discrimination.

They'd harvest anyone that served them no use, background disregarded. It wasn't personal.

Hannah closed the hatch behind her and stepped down into the tunnel, peering through the open doors on both sides. Some butchery equipment remained, and the bloodstains on the wall were so old that they'd turned to a muddy brown, and it was no surprise the floors were exactly the same colour. The next section opened up into a large waiting area with a singular table in the middle. A note was waiting for her.

Miss Cavern.

There are forty hours left in the solar-power generators. Your extra equipment and weaponry are waiting for you in room CHD18. It's made up for you to get some sleep. By the time you return, the solar should be charged for another two days for you to stay hidden.

There is a map to guide you through Maidhill to your vantage point.

Kill him.

"Typical," she muttered, disgusted that the room they left for her was not only a slaughter room, but it was also a children's slaughter room. Although it wasn't the room's child death toll that bothered her. It was the smell, which seemed to hang in the air longer than any adult death, like the fear stuck to the concrete walls, and the wailing tears overpowered any scent of flesh or disembowelment. "I wouldn't even have to do this if the fucking Italians just did their job."

She marched through the tunnel, counting the door numbers until she reached CHD18. As she opened the door, she was hit by warmth and greeted into a dimly light room with a double bed, surrounded by thick candles that had been burning for hours, covering the room in a lavender scent. The cleaning down hose had been refitted to the side and sported a shower head with a plastic curtain hanging next to it, and a towel folded on the bed next to a clean, grey T-shirt, black combat pants and clean socks. Another note sat on top.

. . .

We know the Italians fucked up.
  We pulled together some extra supplies before I left Zodiac.
  Enjoy this moment of comfort before you have to clean up their dirty work.
  See you soon.

To the right of the bed, she spotted the HK714 rifle and two lots of twenty-round magazines. On the floor lay an MG42 heavy machine gun, which she knew was vital to repressing the vineyard's top floor lockout. The mass of weaponry would no doubt be heavy to haul across Maidhill to her vantage point. Once she fired that first and hopefully only shot from the HK714, the whole vineyard would be looking for her, and she'd have to give them a reason to keep their heads down. The MG42 would give them that reason.

––––––

Ryan was due to meet Mikey for breakfast to decide Rich's future but chose to take a small diversion before they met up. He found himself outside Harper's room and heard the lieutenant from the other side of the door, already performing his usual early morning workout routine. Ryan knocked twice gently and stood back, giving some space.

A couple of seconds passed before Harper pulled the door open, sporting a green T-shirt and grey briefs. He looked surprised to see him at this hour.

"Free to talk?" Ryan asked.

"Sure." Harper left the door open as he pulled on his combat pants and tied his boots up. He closed the door behind him and followed Ryan downstairs. They stepped into the reception and pushed the entrance doors open.

Ryan offered Harper a smoke, which he respectfully declined.

"Must be nice seeing your family today?" Ryan asked as he lit his cigarette.

"I am. First time for a while," Harper answered. "I've been doing a lot of shifts, even when back at Rennes."

"Do you worry for them when you're away?"

"I never stop. Not in this world. Now that I know people back home have an agenda against all of us."

"I can relate." Ryan exhaled. "How would you react if it's one of your friends back home that's a threat to them."

"I would want the same as you. I want this threat resolved," Harper insisted.

"That's not what I asked. How would you react if someone you're friends with put them in danger?"

"I don't know. I'm lucky enough not to have faced that situation."

"Well, I have." Ryan turned. "This is where I stood when Alessandro was holding a syringe of that shit to my daughter's neck as he pretty much wanted me to 'walk the plank'. This is where I stood when Rook fired a shot that saved our lives. Another person you bought here."

"I..."

"Let me finish, please, Lieutenant. I'm not a big believer in fate, destiny, or any of that shit. I prefer to try and see a situation for what it is. Which admittedly, I've struggled with the past couple of days, as I've wanted to spill blood for what happened. I'm not pleased about what's happened, and I don't think that'll leave me until Maisie says she's okay, but... I'm sorry."

"What? What for?" Harper was caught off guard.

"I'm sorry I pinned it on you. I'm sorry that I thought you were involved. You may have bought the twins here, but you also bought Rook, who saved our lives." Ryan extended his hand. "But I can't have this happen again, and I need you to understand that."

Harper reached and accepted the apology, making sure he didn't squeeze Ryan's hand at all. A visible veil of relief crossed his face, but perhaps it was mostly happiness with the peace offering. "I hope I can keep working with you, and I'll make sure this never happens again. I can promise that something will be done to check service volunteers more efficiently."

"That's a good start, friend."

Harper's lips curled slowly into a smile. "I'm glad we can move forward, friend."

"You can thank my future wife for that." Ryan joked, flicking the cigarette butt into the trench. "I'll let you get back to your routine. Mikey and I have an important decision to make."

28

The vineyard car park was packed as the helicopters took off and left for Rennes. Everyone waved and cried as they said their goodbyes to Rich, not knowing when or if they would see him again. It was the hardest decision they ever had to make, but easily the better of two evils. Mikey had compared Rich's survival on the limited supplies they had, versus the full medical facilities at Rennes. It was for the best that they let him go into their care.

The group's animosity towards Harper had eased, as most wished him a safe journey home, and Rook got a hug and handshake from pretty much everyone, thanking him for being in the right place at the right time. Ryan gave the pair an extra bottle of wine of each, knowing that with their upcoming time off, a cheeky glass could help keep their nerves intact.

Harper promised to return in seven days with the supplies that everyone had listed, and with an advisor's selection of what animals could be integrated into their current livestock, even the potential of a bull for breeding. The twins' Little-Bird was piloted by the extra crew, and the two chopper party departed over Maidhill and disappeared into the cloudy morning sky.

Ryan was the last to go in, saying goodbye to Cassy as she headed into her morning shift of detergent mixing and stock taking of the basement chemicals. Footsteps crunched on the gravel as he stood alone.

"I'm sorry," Jen's voice croaked from behind.

"For what?" Ryan turned, seeing her tear up.

"For what I said to you, and about you. It wasn't fair, and I was just hurting." she admitted, looking at her feet.

"I know you were. That's why I never took it to heart." He hugged her. "Can I tell Mikey I saw you cry?" He knew that would wind her up and lighten the mood.

"I know I'm being soft right now, but don't take the piss."

"Okay." Ryan chuckled. "But I know you're not crying because you have to apologise. What's up?"

"I'm afraid of what Mikey's taking." She said and shivered.

"The serum? What about it? It seems to be doing what it needs to do."

"What if it's just a front? What if it has long-term, hidden effects? What if they planned for us to trust in it? They planned to blame Rook for everything. They planned well ahead for all of this."

"Yeah..." Ryan tapped on the door as his brain went into over-drive, picking up on something. "They did. What are you suggesting?"

"I don't know. I'm confused. Scared. Fucking hormones. I don't know." She stamped her foot in frustration, wiping a tear away with her sleeve.

"Is Rennes looking like a better option now?"

"Possibly. I know it wouldn't be permanent, and should this serum be a bad thing, at least it won't be on Penbrook's doorstep. Mikey was the one who bought it up." Jen's eyes fixated on him. "I think he needs to talk this out with you."

"Okay. I'll talk to him later." Ryan scratched his head, "He didn't say anything to me earlier."

"We spoke after your meeting about Rich. I may have spooked him into thinking about Rennes."

"Well, thanks for that," Ryan said sarcastically. "I was just starting to feel better."

"Don't guilt trip a pregnant woman, muppet." She slapped him on the shoulder.

"Ow. Those hormones are seriously playing with you." he joked, though his arms screamed as he flinched. "Okay, I'll talk to him at lunchtime."

That was becoming a regular thing. All the positive news was followed by a possible negative. On the other hand, this one had been spotted early, and maybe they could get ahead of whatever could go wrong with the serum.

Whoever was behind all this, had thought out every step to play on the vineyard's weariness and paranoia.

―――――

"Jen spoke to me after Rich left." Ryan said as he sat in the patient chair in the therapy room. Though it wasn't an official session, everyone knew not to disturb them when they were in medical room three.

"I thought she might," Mikey said, sitting in the chair opposite. "Did she apologise?"

"She has nothing to apologise for."

"Jen was out of line."

"She was hurting." Ryan winced as he carefully leant on his left elbow. "But you know that's not why I'm here, or what you need to talk to me about."

"It was hard enough to make the decision for Rich," Mikey sighed, leaning back, "but this could be the best outcome regarding my situation. We know it's only temporary, until they've successfully created a safe and fully working serum."

"You know the serum is fine. The Italians wouldn't have taken it if it wasn't. So, what's your real reasoning for wanting to go to Rennes?" Ryan stared at him, knowing full well that Mikey had something up his sleeve.

"You can read me like a book." Mikey grinned wickedly at his friend.

"It works both ways with us. So, get the point."

"Okay." Mikey straightened himself. "Regarding what this General Woodburn guy said, we're giving ourselves and livelihoods over to Rennes. So, I want to see who these people are."

"You want to do some form of reconnaissance?" Ryan raised his eyebrows. "Where has this come from?"

"Maybe I'm learning from you. Harper I have no doubt we can trust, but this whole governing body trying to make up to us for their fuck up? It doesn't feel like compensation. It feels like *bribery* for our *trust*."

"You lied to Jen about your real intentions?"

"I didn't lie. I just didn't tell her." Mikey shrugged as he looked out the window, knowing full well, it was a lie. "I don't trust this divine plan they have, even if it comes from good place. I mean, Look at Harper. He was following Woodburn's orders, who was probably following someone else, and so on. We need to find the head of the snake."

"Okay. What happens while you're gone?" Ryan huffed.

"Lyndon can take over my duties. He's strong enough to take care of most injuries and wounds. If someone has something life-threatening, then Rook can aid him. When Rook isn't helping Lyndon, he can be your right-hand man, and you can learn from his military experience." Mikey leaned forward, cupping his hands together. "Rennes claim they to want to help. Let's take full advantage of them."

"And I thought I was the only crazy fucker here."

"Believe me. I wouldn't do it if it weren't for that." Mikey pointed to the syringe on his desk. "You know what they say, *When needs must*."

"Yeah." Ryan pinched the bridge of his nose. "They do say that."

"This is also good for Lyndon, as I said."

"You actually think he's ready?" Ryan felt a small moment of pride, thinking about how far his nephew had come. "He does praise your teachings."

"And I praise yours."

"What do you mean?"

"Well, since we lost... Doc..." Mikey cleared his throat, "We lost that pragmatic, logical edge, and I've had to take that on board to help keep you level. It's somewhat nullified my emotional outlook, and I see things more like you and he did," he explained. "A year ago, I would've said *fuck off* if you told me to go to Rennes. This year, I'm saying let's get our money out of these suit-wearing, law-making pricks."

"From a *logical* point of view?" Ryan smirked, remembering Doc's favourite phrase.

"Logical." Mikey nodded.

"When do you plan to go?"

"When Harper comes back next week with the compensation package, I'll request to be placed close to Rich."

"Think they'll give the green light for that?" Ryan asked doubtfully.

"One of Penbrook's civilians giving themselves up and throwing trust at them? They'll eat it up. I never thought I'd be the one to do something like this, but yes. Let's get a foot ahead in this war. I'm sick to death of these people trying to ruin our life here. They have to be brought into the light, so I'll be the one to shine it."

––––––––––

Misty rain pattered against the bedroom window as Harper tucked his son, his youngest child into bed. Little Troy Harper had used up all his energy after spending the first day in two weeks with his dad. The newly turned seven-year-old probably ran over five kilometres during the whole afternoon in the family gardens.

Harper kissed his son on the forehead. "Today was the best day I've had for a while, and you best believe I needed it."

He left the room, making sure to leave the door open a bit before checking in on his daughter, who was nose-deep in another science fiction book.

"What are you reading this week?" He sat on the end of Katie's bed. Like her brother, she had the same dotted freckles as her dad, but jet-black hair like her mother.

"An alien invasion book. It's not the best." Katie looked up from the book. "I've read two since we last spent the day together." She already sounded more like a fully grown woman, instead of the twelve-year-old she was.

"I'm sorry. You know it's my job to try and help these people."

"You've been spending so much time with them."

"That's because these people are needed to help make a safe place to live, and they don't have the security we do," Harper explained.

"What's so special about them?" Katie lay the book face down and sat up straight.

"How they've survived, and their strength. One day we will be able to finally move away from this military base. I know it's safe here, but this isn't a place for you and your brother to grow up."

"And you think where they live is the future? Why can't we go back home?" Katie huffed.

"You know why we can't go back home. It's not there anymore." The words stung as they left his mouth. The very thought that the land of the free was now uninhabitable was heart-breaking.

"I hate this world. We were happy there." She folded her arms, looking at the family photo on her bedside table. She had just turned six before their evacuation, and Troy was barely half a year old.

"We can be happy again," Harper reassured her, though surprised she still remembered their home. "I won't lie, it won't be the same, but it'll be better than this."

"When?"

"I don't know, but the quicker and harder I work, the more chance of it being sooner."

"Okay." Katie finally smiled, hugging her dad. "I'm sorry. I just missed you so much."

"I missed you too, but I'm here all week. Plenty of catching up to do," he said as he stood. "Don't forget to turn your lamp off when you're done reading."

"I promise I will." She groaned. "I only left it on once."

"I know." He snorted, amused by the fact she was nearly a teenager and already sounding like one. "Night Pumpkin."

"Night dad."

Harper left the room, walking along the dark hallway. Canned laughter came from the living room, where his wife, Carol, was watching her favourite sitcom on DVD.

"Troy was asleep before he hit the pillow," Harper announced with a yawn. "He ran himself out of energy."

"He really missed you, Adam," Carol commented, turning her electric wheelchair to her husband. "We all did."

"I missed you too." He kissed his wife and smiled weakly.

"I can see this last trip has hurt you. Talk to me." She nodded to the armchair beside her.

Harper reached down to the table, picked up the remote control and paused the DVD. "Did you hear about what happened?" he asked.

"I heard your pilots weren't who they said they were."

"It's true." Harper sat in the armchair, pouring himself a glass of wine from the bottle Ryan had given him. "It nearly made a huge dent in the relationship we've been trying to build with the vineyard."

"You couldn't have known what would've happened," Carol said, noticing her husband drinking quicker than he normally would have. "What actually happened?"

"Well," Harper rubbed his eyes and sat forward. "Two of them have been infected with Kurustovia, and one of them is Mikey." He saw Carol's eyes widen. She was aware of who Mikey was to these people. Harper poured himself another glass. "A woman was shot in the leg. Ryan's daughter was held hostage with a needle to her neck, and he... he lost two of his fingers fighting back against a Termite invasion."

"The Termites came back?"

"That's a conversation for another time."

"Okay." She knew she wouldn't get that conversation. Adam always tried to shield her from what horrors were out there.

"And it was me who bought all of this to their doorstep," He said and sighed.

"They were orders. They weren't your decision."

"I failed again."

"You've never failed." She pushed her control stick forward and wheeled over to her husband to hold his hand. "You didn't fail me. You didn't fail us. You didn't fail the vineyard. So, stop blaming yourself for the bad people in the world."

Harper looked at the stumps where her legs should've been. It was a constant, haunting reminder of the violence that broke out after the release of the world trade footage. Harper never forgave the domestic terrorist who fired the improvised RPG at their family car as they pulled into JFK airport. They were lucky to have been evacuated on a jet with medical facilities. It was the only reason she was still alive.

"I haven't met these people yet, but from everything you've been able to tell me about them, I can't wait to," Carol spoke softly. "If they truly are the people you say, they will know it's not your fault too."

"That doesn't change the fact I bought a threat to them." He began to cry, gripping her hand tight, "She's just a little girl."

"Who?"

"Maisie. Alessandro and Francesco were going to make her live the rest of her life with that... illness."

"Adam. The twins are monsters. You're not," she reassured him. "The world is mad enough with everything that's going on, and people are doing things that are making history books look tame. What did your therapist say to you when helping you move forward after what happened to me?"

Harper looked up, tears streaming. "She said, uh..." He paused, trying to remember then said, "It's not what happened that matters..."

"It's how you deal with it," Carol finished the sentence.

Harpers smart-radio buzzed in his pocket. It was Ryan.

"Sorry, I have to take this. Thank you, honey." He kissed her while standing and held her face for a moment. She always knew how to take the weight off his shoulders. Harper wiped his eyes and walked to the kitchen, closing the door behind him. "Ryan?"

"Is this a bad time? You sound ill."

"Just a small case of the sniffles, nothing to worry about," he lied. "How can I help?"

"I'm going to pass the phone to Mikey. He has something to talk about."

29

He'd been dreading going to the laptop, but whatever message was waiting for him was going to be there whether he liked it or not. Not long after powering up and connecting to the net-server, the first message from Admiral pinged.

Update?

He composed himself by finishing his scotch and started typing.

Zodiac is in position.
 Additional: The medic, Ryan's right-hand man, wants to turn himself in.

He poured himself another glass, eagerly waiting for the response.

Let him. Separate them.

Hannah will move into position after.
This will break them from the inside.

————

Harper awoke abruptly as his smart-radio vibrated hard against the bedside table, causing him to knock the charging cable out as he reached over. The minor disturbance hadn't pulled Carol from her deep sleep, which was aided by the multiple painkillers she took daily.

He picked up the phone and staggered out of the room, trying to adjust his eyes to the screen, noticing it was three thirty a.m. There was a text from Rook.

Sorry for the timing.
Can you meet me in comms?
You'll want to see this.

His brain struggled to think what Rook could've possibly discovered at this hour of the morning, but nevertheless, he confirmed and changed into his dark grey track suit and running trainers. It was only an hour and a half earlier than his normal wake up time, so he thought he might as well start his exercises by jogging to the communication room of the aeroport. More to the point, he wondered what was waiting for him.

Once outside, the sharp autumn winds had no trouble waking him as he jogged across the open town, past the opera hall and all the way down the French highway, slowing as he reached the aeroport entrance. Rook waited outside, his scraggly hair covered under a black beanie, the same colour as his zipped-up windbreaker.

"Sorry sir, but this is important, and I've kept it among as few people as possible," Rook said, opening the glass door into the check-in area. He showed the lieutenant upstairs and led him to the control room, where a solitary worker was stationed. "This is Senior Officer Eliza Fultz." he said, introducing the young woman. Her green overalls were creased, and her brown hair was tied back in a messy bun. Dull eyes were hidden behind thick glasses. "This is Lieutenant Harper."

"Lovely to meet you, Miss Fultz." Harper tried to smile but had to repress a yawn. "So, what's so urgent that you've summoned me at this hour of the morning?"

Rook and Eliza shared a concerned glance before she sat in her chair and pulled up a map of England on the screen, where she pointed to the southeast region of the country. A small red blip appeared on the screen. "This is your communication from three hours ago," she said bluntly in her thick Bavarian accent. "Where you spoke to two gentlemen called Ryan and Mikey, before calling the governing board."

"You can trace calls?" Harpers eyes widened. "And listen in?"

"We can now." Rook stood over the monitor. "The twins were in communication with someone, and the Termites were damn sure not to let Ryan get that phone."

"Didn't the prisoners hand their phones over?"

"They did. Which makes this more concerning." Eliza zoomed the map outwards. Two larger blips appeared. One was in central England, and the other was on Africa's west coast.

"What the hell are those?" Harper wondered out loud.

"It's a text communication, from unregistered models." Rook said, as he looked back at Harper. "Someone out there is talking across continents."

"Can we see what's being said?"

"No." Eliza turned in her seat. "Direct calls can be monitored due to the open Nat type which our network requires. Messages are protected by multiple encryptions to prevent them from being intercepted by hostiles programs, which is why we can't pinpoint their exact locations or read what is being said."

"Who have you told about this?" Harper looked at the two.

"Just you, sir." Rook admitted, scratching where his ear should've been. "If we have a mole inside, we don't want them to know we have a way of finding out where their contacts are."

"Hmm." Harper peered at the screen. "Can you find out who these two devices belong to?"

"Negative," Eliza said dryly. "For all we know, this could be a one-way conversation, with one phone sending and the other receiving."

"Okay." Harper rubbed his chin and thought for a while. "Keep this between us. Miss Fultz, alert one of us if you pick up anything."

"Affirmative, sir."

30

I t was a long and anxiety-induced week for Ryan, knowing that his best friend was leaving, even if it was temporarily. The grand promises for the future had a dark cloud hanging above them. Foreboding greyness in the uncertainty of what lay ahead.

Mikey suggested they have one final therapy session before he left, to help get all the detrimental thoughts out of his system.

"Today's the day," Mikey said to start the session. "How are you feeling?"

"Fuck you. You know how I'm feeling."

"Kind of predicted that response."

"Then you can predict that not having you to calm me down is a disaster waiting to happen," Ryan stated.

"We can still talk. They've given us unlimited communication time," Mikey said in a soothing tone. "You can call me whenever you need."

"It's not the same."

"Yes, it is. If you need to talk. Unless you're worried about something else?"

Ryan didn't respond.

"What are you actually worried about?" Mikey pried. "Rook will help continue Lyndon's training."

"I'm not worried about that. Lyndon has stepped up. I've seen how he's been helping Johanna recover. You've taught him well." Ryan deflected, looking away while grinding his teeth before blurting out. "I know I should've killed Connor. I let him get away with what he did to us, just like I did with the fucking twins."

Mikey studied his friends face, trying to decipher whether it was anger or hurt that had bought this on. "That might be how you feel, but deep down you know you made the right choices, in both situations."

"Maybe, but that doesn't stop it from killing me. I feel like it's done some damage."

"Go on."

"My trust. Every time I've had my guard up, it was too harsh to people. When I let it down, people get hurt," Ryan ashamedly said as he lowered his head. "I can't spot danger like I used to. I should've done more."

"You lost your fucking wedding finger and took a blade through the other arm to fix something that we did not invite on us," Mikey assured firmly. "Killing Connor is not the answer. You don't have to go on a bloodbath anymore. You already made the hardest decision at the beginning of the year... and out of all the things that have happened, that's the only thing should be eating you, but you know you did what you had to do because you were left with no choice. If you can forgive yourself for that, you can forgive yourself for handing over a prisoner when you were being held at gunpoint."

Ryan cringed, remembering the hundreds of lives burning away in front of his eyes. The melting cries of unimaginable pain and anguish that had kept him awake for months on end. "So then..." He was about to ask the question out loud that he only asked himself, or the ghosts of his deceased friends. "What do I do?"

"What do you do?" Mikey repeated. "Do what you've always done. We're all alive because of you, whether you want to believe that or not."

"Well, that's not true, for the last... incident, is it? We're alive because of Rook." Ryan sat back and zoned at the ceiling.

"Maybe so. After everything we've seen, maybe we're owed that bit of fortune of having Rook do what he did." Mikey took a sip of his grapewater. "But we owe you that too, it was you who went after Francesco, and we could've all been shot to pieces if you didn't come back inside."

"Is this supposed to help?"

"Is it helping?"

"Yes." Ryan jumped forward and hugged Mikey unexpectedly, nearly knocking him out of the chair. His arms screamed in distress, but he didn't care. "I'm going to fucking miss you."

"I know. I'm going to miss you too. But this is for the best..." Mikey paused then added, "Logically."

"Stop trying to sound as smart as Doc. You're not," Ryan replied stubbornly.

"Was worth a try." Mikey stopped the egg timer so they could have a final chat before he Harper arrived to picked him and Jen up.

The large, unescorted helicopter landed in the usual space of the northwest corner of the vineyard's grounds. Goodbyes were said all round to Mikey and Jen with tears flowing from everyone.

Harper opened the cargo ramp and multiple armed men surrounded the chopper before carrying supply crates from the back and placing them in front of the crowd. Once the exchange was done, they returned to the helicopter and provided security cover. Rook gave the departing couple a hug as he stepped off the ramp, enjoying a few minutes of conversation with the pair.

Harper approached, handing over a clipboard with a list. "I've detailed the invoice for the compensation package. It's all there."

"Thank you," Ryan answered, taking it and reading down the list. "They'll be safe, right?" he asked, looking at Mikey and Jen as they walked up the ramp.

"They will," Harper confirmed. "They're in the wing opposite my family's quarters. It's where Rich is being looked after. They have access to the whole town, apart from the committee hall and the aeroport. You'll have twenty-four hour communication access to them."

"Okay. Good. Thank you," Ryan said with slight relief.

"Goodbyes are harder if you drag them out. Trust me."

"I know."

"I'll let you know when they've settled in." Harper offered his hand. "Take care, friend."

"Thank you." Ryan shook the lieutenant's hand. "You too."

————

Hannah trundled over the rubble of the burnt down mansion and observed what was once a large garden. Some of the foundations remained where the five Termite cabins had been built, but other than that, there was no evidence that Father and his unit had been stationed there ten months prior.

She kept herself hidden as a helicopter thundered overhead, heading towards the south coast. Her ATV was parked out of sight on the eastern slope, covered by three panels of garden fencing.

Hannah timed her journey as she made her way across the garden to a wall of dying nettles, identifying one of the paths that were cut into it. She needed to memorise it all from her vantage point to the ATV. Soon, all hell would be following her, and she didn't plan on getting caught.

31

R yan found himself spending more time with Maisie as school was officially cancelled for the foreseeable future. The only two teachers were Dominic, who had taken on full security duties from the top floor, and Johanna who was still recovering from her wound. Ryan couldn't deny that he also needed the time off from his regulated schedule.

He sat with his daughter in the reception, looking out the front doors despite the autumn breeze getting colder every minute. The rain had finally eased off after a two-day storm.

"Cold," Maisie muttered as she clung to his arms.

It definitely wasn't the highest level of articulation she was known for, but at least she was starting to talk more. Ryan stood and went to close the door before Lyndon rounded the corner, nearly colliding with his uncle.

"Fuck. Sorry." Lyndon stood straight, before glancing at Maisie. "You didn't hear me say that." He winked at her.

Maisie giggled into Ryan's shoulder, which made him shake his head at his nephew. "Why did you look so startled?"

"Was getting some air. Just nervous about checking on Johanna's wound."

"You can ask Mikey if you want." Ryan dug the smart-radio from his hoodie pocket with his good hand. "Not much battery left, so be quick."

"I'm scared he'll tell me that I did something wrong," Lyndon admitted.

"Of all the things in this world..." Ryan laughed. "That's what you're scared of? You've been smashing it, and you have Rook on standby if needed. Now, buck up and make the call."

Lyndon smiled and dropped his head, taking the phone. "Yeah, you're right." He headed outside and dialled the number.

"I'll be out in a second. I need to ask Mikey something when you're done."

"Are you joining us for lunch?" Cassy asked from behind, walking over with Steph. They both wore protective goggles and full body overalls. Both ladies removed their disposable gloves and tossed them in the bin by the door.

"Yeah, I'll wait for Lyndon to finish using the phone." Ryan passed Maisie over.

"Who's he calling?" Steph asked while looking out the door.

"Mikey. Just checking to see he did something right." Ryan pointed out the door. "He's determined not to fuck up."

"Sounds like he's the same perfectionist I heard you once were?" Cassy whispered, peeking out the front door and looking over her nephew-in-law. Steph had joined Lyndon, giving him a hug.

"He is. Fucking proud of him." Ryan smiled, lifting Maisie's head by the chin. "Your cousin is doing really well, isn't he, smelly bum?"

———

Harper burst into the communication room. His red hair was distressed, and his eyes were a combination of awake and sleep deprived. "What have you got?"

"The anomaly that was only messaging," Eliza answered. "It's back, and it's an open communication."

"A phone call?"

"Affirmative."

"Location?" Harper's eyes glued to the map's live feed.

"There." She pointed to the bottom of the screen.

"Maidville?"

"Affirmative. Northeast of the town centre."

"That's up the fucking hill." Harper panicked, grabbing his smart-radio and dialling Ryan's code. *User busy.* "Fuck. Fuck."

"I've decoded the connection's firewall," Eliza said, moving the cursor to the red blip. "Patching in now."

"Okay." Harper turned, redialling Ryan. No answer.

A voice came over the speaker. One that sent chills down Harper's spine. He knew it.

Admiral Cavern.

"... confirmed?" Admiral asked the person on the other end of the conversation.

"Target is confirmed. He's even hugging his... wife?" a female voice answered.

"Two birds?" Admiral Caven asked, though it was clearly leading to an answer.

"One stone." she answered.

Harper nearly vomited his heart out. His hands tensed up in a hyper-panicked state, barely dialling the number correctly again.

User busy. "Ryan!" He screamed.

"Take the shot," Admiral ordered.

Seconds passed. A muffled gunshot passed through the speakers.

"Target down," the female voice whispered, coldly and proudly. "Switching to the MG42."

―――――

The first bullet barely made a sound as it tore over the carriageway and trespassed into the safety of the vineyard's grounds. Hannah watched his blond dreadlocks separate as the bullet split through the back of the neck and out the front of his throat, catching his wife in the side of the head on its way. Blood sprayed like a beautiful mist as Ryan's body flopped forward onto his partner's, with both dropping to the ground in a heap.

"Target down," Hannah whispered into her headset, grinning while she did. "Switching to the MG42."

Even at half a kilometre away, the first screams from the grounds reached her position. The top floor lookout would be searching for the location of the shot. She shifted her body from the mounted sniper rifle to the heavy MG42.

"Time to light it up."

———

The restaurant's windows exploded. The volley of bullets was deafening as the rounds smashed into the walls of the top floor, reverberating through the brickwork down into the reception. Glass rained down onto the car park.

"Get in!" Drinker pulled Maisie away from the open doors by the shoulders, catching a glimpse of where the muzzle flash came from. "Shit. How many people are outside?"

"About ten working in the allotments. Where's Alfie?" Ryan panicked as he slid beside them, pulling Cassy with him.

"With Sandra in the cafeteria. He's safe."

"Thank you," Ryan huffed before turning to check on Cassy and Maisie. They were unharmed, but the crippling fear had returned to Maisie's eyes. He tapped Drinker on the shoulder. "The gunfire is focused on the top floor. Get Rook and go help Dominic." He turned to Cassy and said, "Take Maisie into the cafeteria and stay with Sandra and Alfie. I've gotta help get people inside."

"Aye, got it." Drinker took off.

"Stay with mummy." Ryan kissed his daughter on the forehead. "I'll be back soon."

He withdrew his Glock and pushed towards the side of the door. The barrage halted. He held tight and pulled the pistol up to firing position. Rifle gunfire returned from the top floor, hopefully pinning down whoever had opened up on them.

As he swung out the opening, his intention was to check on everyone outside, but his eyes were pulled to a few metres in front of him.

His heart stopped. Blood dried up in his veins. His skin froze behind a horror that paralysed him. His arms dropped, legs taking over as he stumbled to the sight that killed him inside.

In the middle of the car park, Lyndon's body lay slumped over Steph, in a widening pool of crimson.

32

Ryan shook uncontrollably as he slumped on the podium in total darkness. Vomit hung from his chin, dripping over his trainers and forming a huge patch on the front of his T-shirt. He felt dead. The voice coming from the smart-radio beside him tried to pierce through the crippling hell he was burning in.

"I tried to call you." Harper said over the loudspeaker, echoing through the empty cafeteria. "The line was busy. I'm sorry."

"He was trying to call Mikey. He wanted advice. All he wanted was some fucking advice." Ryan wheezed softly, spitting bile on the tiled floor. "I need to get back to my sister." He hung up sharply, stumbling into to medical corridor and reaching the first room. The top of Steph's head was covered in gauze, with Rook fitting the final piece in place.

"The impact isn't fatal, but she will need immediate surgery to remove skull shards." Rook looked up. "I'll recommend this to Rennes. Arrange an emergency pick up."

"She's going to make it?"

"If we can get her there, yes."

Ryan slid down the door into a sitting position, bursting into tears.

"Thank you." Holding the smart-radio out. "Can you make that call for me, please?"

"Sure." Rook said, taking the device and punching in Harpers code.

Ryan crawled into the corridor and leant against the wall, hyperventilating heavily as his arms cramped. His body caved into crushing emptiness, like when he was forced to watch Doc and Sam die.

His legs gradually carried him to the next room, the door was open and waiting for him to fall in, like it was forcing him to confront it. He reached his left hand out to the top of the bed and pulled the cover down, revealing Lyndon's pale face. Blood soaked his dreadlocks.

He does look like me, Ryan screamed to himself. A flurry of guilt and anger split his heart right down the middle. *It was supposed to be me.*

"I don't know why this had to happen." He fell onto the side chair, holding his nephews cold hand. "I don't know why. I don't know what I could've done. I don't know why it had to be you. I don't know why I'm still alive. I want this to stop. I wanted you to be happy. I wanted everyone to be happy. I want you back." Ryan sobbed, dropping his head.

"You know why you're alive." Lyndon's voice answered. Ryan looked up. His nephews lifeless face hadn't moved. *"You know why. Be the monster you're supposed to be."*

Ryan shook his head, wanting the voice to stop. It was all in his head, but the blackness returned. The numbness instantly replaced with a burning rage.

"On my life, I would give my own to have you back."

"You know you can't do that."

"No. I can't." Ryan placed Lyndon's hand back under the sheet and covered his face one last time. "I'm truly sorry. I hope you have the peace that I couldn't give you. I don't think you know how much I love you."

Ryan forced himself to turn away and shut the door behind him. There weren't enough bullets in the world to stop him from making this right.

———

He opened his laptop in a panic and began typing his message to Admiral, praying the connection could keep up with him.

Hannah did not kill Ryan. She killed his nephew.
  She needs to get back to the Isles now.

Minutes passed.

Who was the female that was hit?

He downed a whole tumbler of his scotch while typing his reply.

His sister. Non-fatal.
  She's being brought here for emergency surgery.

It felt like an age passed before the reply.

I'll contact Hannah.
  Take the sister out on arrival.

———

Harper watched with apprehension as the emergency chopper came onto the radar screen.

"Sir, the medivac is making its approach," Eliza announced out loud.

"E.T.A?"

"Ten minutes."

"Good." Harper pulled the smart-radio out and dialled Ryan's number. "Ryan. Your sister is making her final descent. I'll contact you again once she's in surgery."

"Thank you." Ryan answered weakly.

"Before you hang up." Harper said quickly, "we've just intercepted a communication from the shooter. We have their location, and we are sending a search and detain squad to bring them in."

"Where are they?" Ryan's voice intensified.

"You know I can't tell you that, but we couldn't wait to run this past high command. It'll take hours to get the green light for this. I won't let them get away."

"Are you... fuck," Ryan huffed, losing control of his breath. "They killed Lyndon. They fucking killed him!"

"I know, and I know what you want to do. I will make sure she doesn't get away with it. I swear on God, on my family's life. I promise you."

There was a period of nothing but Ryan's heavy breaths and occasional voice cracks. "Okay." Then he hung up.

Harper closed his eyes and tapped the smart-radio on his forehead. He knew what he was doing was right, and there was nothing he could do to make Ryan feel better, but it felt like he was robbing the man of justice. He wasn't sure how long Ryan would be able to keep it together before all hell broke loose.

"Clear Task Force 2819 for lift off," Harper said, stepping over to Eliza's terminal.

"Task Force 2819, you are a go." she announced into the headset.

"Roger that, ground control. E.T.A on the target, two hours-thirteen minutes," The pilot responded over the speaker.

Harper looked at the window and pulled his headset on. The chopper powered up, with, a four-man team piling in the side doors.

"We want the target alive. Bring her back to us in one piece," Harper said into his mic.

"Roger."

Harper watched the Little-Bird lift away and head north, with its taillight dimming into the morning darkness.

The screen next to Eliza's lit up, flashing red. "Sir?" She stammered.

"What is it?" Harper walked over to her station.

"S.A.M turret one has just armed."

"What? How?"

"I don't know, I... I'm locked out of the system." Eliza frantically tapped the keyboard.

"What's its target?"

"I can't confirm."

A piercing, high-pitched screech ripped through the open window. Harper looked through the blinds. Four missiles left the S.A.M turret and swerved toward their target. The chopper dispersed its decoy flares, successfully detonating the first three missiles, but the fourth hit the helicopter's underbelly, exploding into a ball of flames and lighting up the morning sky.

Harper watched in horror as he tried to figure out which of the two choppers was shot down. Was it the approaching medivac with Steph and Rook, or the Little-Bird with Task Force 2819?

Sirens rang out over Rennes city centre, and the barking's of security dogs wailed through the streets. Different parts of equipment landed in the surrounding fields, some still on fire.

"Sir." Eliza turned. "Task Force 2819 is down."

———

He removed the target screen from the laptop, saying a silent prayer for the men's lives he'd just taken, though mentally referred to them as nothing more than collateral. If there was one way he would get back on Admiral's good side, it would be by preventing Hannah from being dragged into this.

That was the first time he used the Catfish Program to directly influence the Rennes defence systems, and now there would be a target on the back of everyone with access to the local web connection. Every laptop would be confiscated for inspection.

He had the blessing of knowing that once the Catfish Program was deleted, it would leave no trace and fabricate a recent history based on the users prior activities. The downfall was that once the program was deleted, it couldn't be reinstalled onto a previously used device.

He began his final message to Admiral.

· · ·

Had to activate the SAM turrets.

They were sending a search and detain team for Hannah.

All air traffic will be grounded until user has been found.

Investigations will begin immediately. Will have to cut communications shortly.

Preparing Zodiac stage 2.

Waiting for final orders.

His finger hovered over the cursor, waiting for what would be his final message from Admiral Caven. He didn't have to wait long.

Keep your phone for emergencies.

Carry out stage 2.

Delete Catfish once prepared.

Upon the final orders, he moved the cursor to the aeroport security rota for the next two days. He ensured the southeast wing would be vacant from 15:00 to 19:00. A fully fuelled cargo plane was to be prepared for a faux mission and stationed on the runway. All S.A.M turrets would deactivate across the European Alliances stronghold until Project Zodiac was fulfilled.

He checked, rechecked, and triple-checked the final plan. Everything was there. It would all come to fruition. The bug was now in the Rennes network, and everything would still play out even after the deletion of the hacking software.

He moved the cursor over to the Catfish menu, finding the icon at the bottom of the list.

Delete.

———

Mikey and Jen had been moved to a secure interrogation room moments after the Little Bird was shot down. Both were understandably scared, tired, and confused. They had been awoken by the explosion, shocked as the flames lit up the sky and the blast thundered the windows around them.

Lieutenant Harper entered the room with two cups of coffee. "Sorry for the sudden transfer, but this was something I could only inform you of once we had confirmation."

"What was that explosion?" Mikey asked, taking one of the cups. "And why was Ryan trying to call me earlier? Why hasn't he answered our calls back?"

"There was another attempt on Ryan's life yesterday." Harper held his hands together. "In the eyes of the shooter, it was successful. We had to wait for confirmation."

"What do you mean?" Mikey stood from the table, alarmed. Jen covered her mouth.

"Ryan is alive. But..." Harper paused then said, "It was a case of mistaken identity." He sighed heavily. "Lyndon..."

"No." Jen burst into tears.

"Is he...?" Mikey slumped back into the chair, hope fading from his face. "Who did this? I need to go back."

"That's the problem. You can't."

"Bullshit! We have to go back. Now!"

"The explosion this morning was one of our surface-to-air missiles that locked onto our search and detain team. They were on course to bring the shooter in." Harper leaned forward. "We thought the original target was the incoming medivac, which was transporting Ryan's sister here."

"Steph's here?" Mikey stood again. "Why?"

"She was severely injured during the attack. Rook did the best he could to patch her up and came over with her, but she needs surgery to remove fragments. She's in the surgical theatre now, and is under heavy guard."

"We'll go back when she recovers then." Jen wiped her nose, holding Mikey's hand.

"That won't be for a while," Harper said regrettably. "Not while someone has control of our surface-to-air missiles. All air transport is grounded until this has been sorted."

"What... what can we do?" Mikey sat down, putting his arm around Jen. "Ryan needs us now."

"When Steph awakes, she's going to need a friendly face. You know that." Harper rubbed his temples. "But you can help Ryan from here. I need you to relay some information, to him."

"What information?"

"The mole here is using an advanced encryption software, so we can't identify who it is that's been infiltrating our network. We can however, locate people who are using unregistered communication devices, and this includes the shooter."

"You have their location? Have you given it to Ryan?" Mikey asked. "Please fucking tell me you've given it to him."

"You know I couldn't originally, but now I'm left with no alternative as we can't send anyone to bring the shooter in." Harper dropped his head, hating what he was about to ask. "And I need you to try to convince Ryan to capture her... alive."

"Are you fucking joking?" Mikey slapped the table and pulled his hair. The suggestion hit Jen so dryly that she started laughing at the stupidity of it. "So, you're asking me, to ask my friend, to not kill the person... who just killed his nephew?" he scoffed, wiping a tear. "At the beginning of the year, he melted hundreds of men, women and children to save our people... What do you think he's going to burn to kill this cunt?"

"I need you to try."

"You won't give him the location unless he promises, will you?" Mikey's eyes narrowed, almost hateful.

"I will give him the location, regardless of whether he agrees or not. I just want him to do what's best for the long run." Harper twiddled his pen lid. "If he can bring her in, we can get Admiral to turn himself in. This fight is closer to ending when we have her in custody."

33

Ryan found himself in his private, night-shift room. He couldn't fall asleep for longer than ten minutes without a night terror pulling him back into this hellish reality. He wanted his family to get some rest time without his screaming haunting them, so he found himself alone in the small room, sitting on the end of the mattress. The smart-radio buzzed softly. It was Mikey's number on a video call. Ryan swiped the unlock icon, and his best friend appeared on the screen.

"I've just heard," Mikey blubbered. "I'm so sorry."

Ryan nodded and looked away, wiping the dryness in the corner of his right eye. His body was incapable of producing more tears.

"I have something to tell you. The search and detain team was shot down as they tried to leave. The mole on the inside has access to their air defences. They can't bring her in." Mikey said, though it looked like he was hiding something insidious. "They want to give you the location of the shooter."

"What?" Ryan stood, eyes wide. "Where are they?"

"Just south of Milton Keynes, there's a wooded area referred to as Ground-Base 4. There's a tunnel system underneath."

"I'm leaving now."

"Wait," Mikey yelled, preventing Ryan from hanging up. "This person is a so called high-value target. It's Admiral's daughter."

"I don't fucking care who it is. I don't fucking care."

"Rennes is asking you not to kill her," Mikey forced himself to say out loud, and Ryan knew it wasn't his words, but more of a script. "They say it'll be the end of these people if you capture her. They can get Admiral to turn himself in." He shook his head, like he was disappointed with himself. "You know what I want you to do. I was just asked to pass that information on."

Ryan sat on those words, thinking them through before looking back on the screen. "Look after yourself, bro. Send my love onto Jen." He looked at his black excursion gear hanging on the back of the door. "Tell Harper to keep me updated if the location changes." He ended the call and beelined for the weapons room.

The top floor restaurant was a wreck with glass and wood splinters, and chunks of plaster and brickwork littering the floor. Window frames hung on by tatters, waving in the faint breeze that filled the whole room. It felt empty without having anybody on watch from the top floor. Until just a second ago, no one had been given confirmation that the threat was gone.

Ryan turned left into the galley kitchen, pulling down the SIG716. It was preloaded with the suppressor still attached. He reached into the bench fridge and pulled out four magazines of 7.62x51mm ammunition, which he stuffed into his shoulder bag with one of the hand-held radios. He then pulled out another Glock.17 from the drawer and placed it on the counter, putting his own personal pistol next to it. On the back wall of the kitchen, he found the shelf with assorted attachments, pulling out two suppressors for the pistols. Once tightly screwing them on, he took down with of the L96 sniper rifles and checked the magazine.

The door pushed open to the kitchen. Cassy stood with puffy eyes, signs of crying and a lack of sleep.

"Mikey called me," he said, slinging both rifles and the bag over his shoulder.

"I know," Cassy sniffed. "You woke Teddy. He came to tell me he heard you leave quickly. What's going on?"

"They know who did this. It's Admiral's daughter." He tucked one pistol down the back of his waistband. "They have her location. She's stopped near the old Milton Keynes base. I can be there in three hours."

"Can't Rennes take care of this?"

"Apparently not. All flights have been grounded. Even if they could, I'm still going."

"What about us? We need you." She folded her arms. Her skin was reddening under her dark hair. "I need you. Maisie needs you. Alfie needs you."

"Lyndon needed me. Steph needed me." He teared up.

"This wasn't your fault." Cassy held Ryan tightly by the arms.

"Maybe not. But while Rennes can't assist, she gets away. The person who killed Lyndon gets away with it."

Cassy looked at Ryan. His green eyes and blond dreadlocks gave her a flashback of Lyndon, the future nephew she had also just lost. She realised she'd never talk to him again, and just how great the teenager was with Maisie and Alfie. This was how she felt after six years of knowing Lyndon, whereas Ryan had helped Steph raise him. He nearly gave his life on the first day of the war to save him. Now, there was someone out there who had robbed Ryan of the only family he truly had before Cassy came into his life. "She'll get away with it killing Lyndon." She realised just who this person was.

"She gets away with it," Ryan repeated.

"Okay. Okay." Cassy nodded, holding back her tears. "Just, please do the thing you always do."

"What's that?"

"Come back," she sobbed.

The couple hugged tightly.

"I always come back." he whispered. "Tell the children I'll be back soon. I have to go now."

Ryan headed downstairs into the laboratory, filling up two petrol cans with corn oil, hoping that would be enough for the journey both ways. Then, keeping his head down, he opened the reception doors and walked over the footbridge onto the car park.

"Ryan?" Dominic's voice called from the trench. His big, black frame climbed out and approached him, keeping his gun up to Maidhill.

"They're not up there anymore. They've retreated north." Ryan said.

"How do you know?"

"Harper has their location."

"What do you think you're doing?" Dominic asked, looking at all the weaponry.

"You know what I'm doing. Keep everyone here safe while I'm gone." Ryan said, making it clear this wasn't a discussion. "You have Drinker to help you now, but you're in charge till I get back... *boss*." That time he had to force the sarcastic smirk.

Dominic stepped forward, pulling him into a tight hug. "I'll keep everyone safe. You have my word."

"I know." Ryan stepped away and tried to hide that he wanted to cry. "I have one of the hand-held radios in case the smart one dies. I'll radio on the way back when I'm within range."

He then turned and disappeared into the morning darkness. Fifteen minutes later, after navigating the unarmed trails of the maze, the headlights of the 4x4 shone over the hedged perimeter and the engine roared, before heading north towards the M25 motorway junction.

It was just over an hour into his journey, and he'd already thrown up multiple times, though he did his best to make sure it went out the window. The motorway signs were barely visible to make out through the fire damage and multiple layers of foliage that had grown over them. From what he could tell, he'd made it as far as junction fifteen of the M25, which would put him west of London. He weaved between the abandoned cars on the motorway and pulled up to the side, feeling the need to let out all his hate before it caused him to crash.

"Fuck!" He slammed the steering wheel with both hands, sending waves of distress into his injuries before they fired back in protest. He gritted his teeth and pushed his head back against the headrest while letting out a flurry of wild swings, "Why him? Why Lyndon? Just leave us alone!" He punched the centre of the wheel, setting the horn off.

In the trees to his left, a startled flock of birds flew into the sky in a blind panic, causing Ryan's heart to nearly stop. They cawed and screeched as they hurried away in terror, unaware of what the car horn was. He calmed his breathing and held his chest, watching the birds regroup before disappearing behind the motor side railings. For a moment, he forgot where he was and what he was doing, taken back to a time when seeing any bird was a daily occurrence. The noises and calls they made in the stupidest of hours of the morning. How they would causally stand in groups on live-wire telegraph poles, or how you would have to avoid being shit on by one as you walked under a railway bridge. A time when everything was normal. When everyone was *alive*.

"Fuck sake." He wiped his head, taking a mouthful of grapewater and spitting it out the window. He was so absorbed in his hate fuelled mission that the sensation of taste didn't register with him, and the lingering vomit stayed between his teeth.

Bushes on the opposite side of the motorway started moving, like something was forcing its way through them. Ryan stayed as still as possible, slyly reaching left for the pistol on the passenger side. Two small bear cubs emerged, biting each other playfully, followed by a large adult who looked adoringly over her young. The direction where this small family had come from was Heathrow airport, which Ryan could just make out through the trees. To Ryan's left was the Wraysbury water reserve. He could be stopped in between them and their watering hole for all he knew.

He turned the ignition back on and left the family of bears, "Just a mother protecting her family." He looked at them in the rear-view mirror "I hope you do a better job than I did."

The vehicle remains near Heathrow Airport were significantly more damaged compared to the patch of motorway nearer home, signs that a serious and large-scale attack took place around there. Ryan hadn't travelled this far north in years, and the fear of London's fallout and radioactivity had kept them from travelling no further than seven miles north of Penbrook.

Thirty minutes passed before he reached the junction to join the northbound M1 motorway, which would take him to the Milton Keynes outskirts.

A call came in- an unknown number.

"Who is it?" Ryan asked while putting the smart-radio on loud-speaker.

"It's Rook. We intercepted another call. Your target is on the move."

"Where to?"

"She's on the same motorway that you're on, heading north. It looks like you're twenty minutes behind. There is a team who's picking her up in a town called Blackpool. That's all we know."

"Thank you." Ryan hung up and pressed hard on the accelerator. "You're not getting to Blackpool, bitch."

———

The holding cell cameras powered down without triggering any failsafe systems, and the feed had been replaced with a repeating cycle from the day before, streaming straight into the guards screen. He stood outside the guard room, waiting for the preprogrammed timer to turn the card scanner green, effectively opening the door without him having to use a card. He had a box of syringes under his right arm, and his beloved pistol in his left.

"Bonjour, sir," The first guard smiled as the door opened. "Did you enjoy breakfast?"

"I love the marmalade the refugee camps are producing." the second guard cheerfully added as he looked up from his comic.

He didn't reply. Instead, he raised the pistol and fired two shots into the chest of each man. Neither had time to react, slumping heavily into their chairs, with the second falling to the ground on top of his blood-soaked reading material.

The cell corridor opened. Grunts and moans of the Kurustovia45 deprived troops seeped through the thick metal doors. He slid open the eye hatches for each, making sure Connor's door was last.

"Listen up!" he ordered, and the rambling stopped. "In thirty minutes, your cells will unlock. You will then leave your cells and apply one of these syringes." He pointed to the box that he had placed in the centre of the corridor. "You will then give Sergeant Lovell his dose and free him from his chains." He tossed the key next to the box. "In thirty-five minutes, the doors to this corridor and the holding room will unlock. You will make your way through the southeast wing, exiting the fire escape on to the north end of the runway. You will enter the cargo plane, ZX45. It is fully fuelled, and its destination coordinates are set. Flight Lieutenant Payne, from what I understand, you know how to operate one of these?"

"Yes, sir." came a voice from the cell at the back left of the corridor.

"Good. All turret systems are down. The black box has been manipulated. Current winds give you a six hour flight to Liberia."

"Liberia?" Connor whispered from his cell. The chains clanged along the floor as his raspy breathing got closer to the window. His good eye peeked through first, followed by the one that was sealed shut. "It's you!" He laughed. "It's been a long time, sir."

"Another time, Sergeant. I'm sorry Ryan wasn't here to see this." He turned back to the other cells and said, "For Admiral."

"For Admiral." they replied in unison.

He exited the prisoner corridor and stepped out of the holding room, completely ignoring the guard's bodies. Thanks to the fact he had altered the security rotas, he didn't have to worry about anyone coming this way. Everyone who occupied this wing were scheduled to be on duty in another part of town for the next four hours.

———

Harper met Woodburn and Rook in the control room, placing his laptop in the collection tray.

"Afternoon General, Sergeant." He said and smiled.

"Adam, please, until we're back on duty, let's keep it informal."

Woodburn returned the smile. It was unusual to see him in anything that wasn't uniform, but the trio had been suspended until the mole had been caught. The European Alliance was now short a helicopter and six servicemen, and they didn't have trust in anyone previously involved with Admiral.

"I don't think I'll ever get used to doing that, sir." Harper headed to the back table and poured himself a coffee.

"Well, I can't order you on your day off." Woodburn shrugged and looked around the control room. "Why did you want to meet here this morning?"

"We've got something to show you. Something we found nearly two days ago, but we don't know who we can tell, including the governing board." Harper approached Eliza's terminal. "So far, it's just us four."

"We've found Admiral." Rook said, standing against the wall with his arms crossed.

"You've what?" Woodburn's mouth dropped for a second.

"Thanks to the help of officer Fultz here, we've managed to inter-cept the communications of all the unregistered smart-radio users. We have identified this signal as Hannah Caven." Harper pointed to the screen. "But this one... zoom out please." Eliza zoomed out the map to a global scale, "It took a while longer to pinpoint as we don't have many orbitals around the equator. This one is Admiral Caven. He's in Liberia."

"Why the hell didn't you tell me sooner?" Woodburn growled.

"We had to confirm it was him, and you were busy telling the six men's families that their husbands had just lost their lives. With there being a mole among us, we had to keep it quiet."

"How long have you had this information?"

"Coming up to forty hours now, sir." Harper said apprehensively. "We had to be sure."

"Who else has been in here?" Woodburn looked at the other empty terminals.

"A few lower technicians," Eliza said, turning in her chair, "A couple of supervisors and communications officers." she started explaining, then held her head set to make sure she heard what was being said.

"Say again, ground control." She listened intently before her face dropped. "Sirs, the cargo plane at runway northern point is moving."

"What?" Woodburn exclaimed.

"The cargo plane." She pointed out the window. "It's taxying to the end."

"Cargo ZX45, what is your clearance?" Woodburn asked into the spare headset. No answer. "Cargo ZX45, this is General Woodburn. What is your clearance?"

They watched through the window as the plane built up speed and hurtled south, taking off gradually and gaining altitude.

"For Admiral." Connor's voice whispered over the speakers.

34

The smart-radio vibrated on the dashboard as Ryan hurtled up the hard shoulder of the M1. He kept his eyes on the road and fumbled until hitting the loudspeaker button.

"Rook?" he shouted above the ragged engine.

"Yeah. Ryan, there's been a situation." The sergeant sounded deflated. "Here in Rennes."

"What's happened? Is Steph okay? Mikey, Jen, Rich?" Ryan panicked.

"They're fine." Rook tried to reassure him, but his voice was clearly shook. "It's something you need to know."

Ryan slowed the vehicle, "What?"

"There's been a breakout. In the prisoner corridor."

Ryan skidded to a halt. He knew who the only occupants of the prison cells were. "How many?"

"All of them..." Rook paused. "Including Connor. Harper and Woodburn have gone down to investigate."

Ryan said nothing. He sat in silence, with cold sweats and shivers taking over as another nightmare smothered him.

Hannah's phone rang in her headphones. She took her left hand off the handlebars and reached into her jacket to press the answer button on the cord.

"Connor is out," Admiral said immediately. "He'll be joining me soon."

"Good." She smirked in triumph, though felt a stab of disappointment, *Ryan was supposed to be there to witness it all.*

"We've just received word that you're being tracked... they've sent Ryan to bring you in." Admiral pulled her from her thoughts. "We're sending the Blackpool team down to you now. Get to the evac point and set up defence." he ordered.

"Understood," she confirmed. "How long before they arrive?"

"Six hours."

She hung up and started to slow down. She knew Ryan wouldn't let her survive the six hours if he caught up to her. He wouldn't stop till this was over. She'd fucked up by identifying the wrong target before, but now she had the heads up on him. She would catch him off guard.

It ends now, Ryan.

———

"Ryan?" Rook asked for the seventh time over the loudspeaker, though that time more urgently.

"What?" Ryan answered coarsely, torn between despair and rage. *Connor is out.* He kept thinking on repeat, not knowing whether to push forward or get back to protect his family.

"We've just intercepted a call between Hannah and Admiral. We know Connor is heading to Liberia. Penbrook is safe from him," Rook said in the calmest of tones.

"Liberia?"

"Another time, Ryan. Something else has happened. She knows she's being tracked. Admiral is sending the team from Blackpool to pick her up from an extraction point. He estimates that it'll be six hours before they get to her."

"How does she know she's being tracked?"

"I don't know, but it's just our communications officer and me who has heard this conversation." Rook explained calmly. "Her signal halted at the next junction of the motorway. Nottingham, by the looks of it."

An engine caught Ryan's ear, coming towards him from straight ahead.

"She's coming." Ryan hung up and stepped out of the Land Rover, taking the L96 sniper rifle and stalked to the middle of the road while keeping his head down. He couldn't figure out how far away she was and didn't want to risk letting her know he had a heads up on her. His heart raced. He felt his surviving fingers cramping up; even the ones that were missing seemed to itch within the layers of bandages. Doing his best to calm himself, he pulled the L96 up to his shoulder and climbed the central railing of the motorway onto the opposite side. He hid behind a burnout pickup truck and slowly raised his head, trying to spot the vehicle as he zoomed in through the scope.

The rumbling engine got softer, almost dying out completely. Ryan focused on the area where the noise was, he figured it to be about three hundred metres, then spotted some kind of armoured quad bike slow down before softly hitting another burnout car. A body was slumped over the handlebars, but it wasn't human. It was a rotting deer carcass.

She was nowhere to be seen.

35

Harper and Woodburn surveyed the scene in the prisoner corridor. All the cell doors were open, and ten syringes were scattered across the floor.

At the end of the corridor, leant against the wall, Alessandro and Francesco sat lifelessly, though their eyes looked like they were still screaming. Even to the inexperienced eye, it was clear that their throats were bitten out. On the wall behind them, a symbol of the Zodiac chart had been painted in their blood.

"The whole fucking system was disarmed." Woodburn rubbed his forehead, looking at the array of needles spread across the floor. "We couldn't have shot them down if we wanted to."

"How is any of this possible?" Harper raged. "Everyone has handed in their laptops. All are accounted for."

"Not all of them." Woodburn looked over the list. His eyes nearly bulged out of their sockets. "You're not going to fucking believe this. Tech Supervisor Monreal."

"He's been M.I.A for a month."

"What better way to do all this, than to make people think you're missing?"

"Which quarters is he stationed in?" Harper asked.

"Non-family residence. Room B17 of Aeroport...." Woodburn realised. "That's this fucking wing."

Harper withdrew his pistol, followed by Woodburn, pacing cautiously down the corridor and towards the closed door.

"Monreal?" Woodburn knocked. "Are you in there?"

No answer.

Woodburn nodded to Harper, who busted the door wide open with one kick. The single-bed quarters had been stripped clean of all belongings. A couple of candles burned on the desk next to a broken lamp, and a laptop charger hung off the side of the table.

"How the fuck could he have stayed hidden?" Harper asked himself, scratching his head and picking up the lamp. "How could he have done this?"

"If he could control the cameras and rotas, he could've manipulated anything to ensure he was undisturbed. He could lock people in rooms, and elevators. Raid anywhere for food or drink." Woodburn replied, blowing the candles out. "He could listen in if his quarters were to be searched again. He was right under our nose the whole time."

"Son of a bitch!" Harper launched the lamp against the wall. He marched up the adjacent corridor and out into the airport terminal, turning left at the baggage check-in and into the security depot. After climbing the stairs, he pushed the door open to the communications room. "Do we know where this fucking plane is headed?"

"Liberia," Rook answered, dropping his head in defeat. "Liberia,"

"How could you know this?"

"Admiral just confirmed Connor will be with him soon, in what might be the last communication with his daughter."

"Last?" Harper rubbed his face, trying to make sense of it all.

"Someone has alerted them that they're being tracked," Rook said, shaking his head. "What happened in the prisoner wing?"

"Tech supervisor Monreal is the one who's been doing this. He's the mole."

"Motherfucker."

Woodburn entered. "I've spoken to the governing board. As you can imagine, they're not happy that we've been withholding information, and that we've been entering restricted spaces while under suspension. We're probably going to have the book thrown at us."

"Fucking let them," Rook snorted. "They've already done it to me."

"You don't think we can argue a case? Now they know it was Monreal, and he was one of their own!" Harper protested. "One of their own was working with Admiral, not one of us. Surely they should be investigated."

"Easy, gentlemen." Woodburn raised his hand, sitting in the chair beside Eliza. "They know they can't afford to lose us."

————

Ryan held his breath, hoping heavy footsteps would give themselves away on the crumbling asphalt. A heavy thud came from up ahead, back on his original side of the motorway. He looked through a blown-out car window, searching for anything moving out of place.

A thunderous rampage of bullets tore into his empty Land Rover, shattering the glass and metal like a sheet of ice being pelted with stones. Ryan carefully trod round the car to find the muzzle flash, locating it roughly two hundred metres ahead, resting on the bonnet of another 4x4.

Ryan pulled the rifle tight, gripping the barrel with his remaining fingers on his left hand. He let out a long heavy breath, blocking out the roar of the machine gun. His heart rate slowed and his vision focused through the scope. A slight breeze from left to right told him to aim just wide of the target.

He remembered what Rook had taught him. *Just hit the gun.*

With a gentle squeeze of the trigger, a controlled kick back, and the bullet shot across the motorway before Ryan could blink. A spatter of blood hit the rusty van behind the heavy weapon, followed by a surprised yelp.

Ryan swung the rifle over his shoulder and pulled out one of the silenced Glocks, bringing it up to firing position. The wind blew empty shell casings along the road, and footsteps dragged from up ahead. He stepped back over the central barricade and pushed tightly along the middle of the road, staying well out of the machine gun's sights. A few distinct female wheezes and moans of pain came from the outer lane of the motorway, and Ryan was now level with the rusting van from which she'd hidden next to.

His heart thumped, sending a pulse all the way through to his fingertips. He forced a couple of quick and clean checks behind vehicles but all he found were left over bullet casings, and the MG42 mounted on the car bonnet with hundreds of rounds still ready to be fired from the ammunition belt. No body. No footprints. No hand marks.

The ATV roared back to life on the other side of the road, heading north on its original journey. Ryan sprinted into the middle of the road, aiming as best as he could. Hannah sped off, with Ryan's bullets thudding off the shells of cars that she dodged between.

"Dammit!" he screamed, bolting back to the Land Rover. He swept the glass off the seat and jumped in. Now more than ever, he was grateful that having a veg-oil motor meant that it was held in the back and survived the onslaught of bullets. He twisted the ignition and skidded to a hasty start, keeping his eyes on her as she exited the ramp and headed towards Nottingham. The ATV seemed to struggle as it ascended the turnoff, giving Ryan time to catch up. He swerved in and out of the dead traffic, pulling up the ramp and turning hard, following with ungodly determination and hatred.

He was catching up fast.

This is going to happen. You are going to die.

————

Hannah winced uncontrollably every time she tried to pull back on the throttle. A bullet had passed through the flesh of her right bicep. From what she knew, there wasn't any artery damage, but she'd lost all power to accelerate hard and gain distance.

She looked over her shoulder. The Land Rover was still functioning, and was following her like a monster that smelt blood. She had the distance to get through the suburban villages of Thrumpton, Ratcliffe on Soar- but she wouldn't be able to stop at the evac point of the university campus without her pursuer seeing it. She'd have to lose Ryan in the concrete jungle of which she had home advantage.

Nottingham city centre.

36

Ryan was gaining distance on her at an impressive rate, though her smaller vehicle wove between the stationery cars easier than his 4x4 could. Many times, he tried to lean out the window with his pistol and take the shot, but in reality, it was significantly harder to mimic the scenes from action movies than he was led to believe.

The closer they got to the city centre, the more decayed skeletons appeared in the wreckages and on the sidewalks. It was like Nottingham had taken a genocide level death-toll during The Fast War, without any kind of clean-up effort put in after. Maybe the R.I.C successfully held that part of the country before the armed forces took it back. Maybe even Father and Admiral took it back. He didn't care either way.

Both vehicles sped past Nottingham train station, and Hannah smashed straight through the broken glass doors of the multi-storey shopping centre, disappearing into the dark entryway. Ryan skidded and dragged the car to the left, keeping his driver side window on the opening. Pistol raised, he reached for the SIG on the side seat, powered the engine off and tossed the L96 and spare pistol in the back. He tucked his Glock into the back of his waistband and shouldered the SIG, making sure it was on full-auto. Hiding next to the outside wall, he peered into the darkness, trying to make out the interior. The ceiling was two storey's high, with walkways on either side of the first floor, presumably for another shopping tier. Light shone through another row of exits at the far end, with multiple double doors that were once glass.

A small burst of rapid fire came from the right, thudding into the wall he stood behind. He stayed covered and waited for the flurry to stop. As soon as it did, the engine roared, heading towards the other exits.

Ryan swung inside and aimed at the moving silhouette, avoiding something she threw in his direction. He opened fire with a calm few squeezes, bursting a tire and causing the vehicle to jolt wildly, throwing her into the exit's doorframe. Ryan pushed to get the kill before a hard bang came from behind and nearly blew his ears out. The remains of a bench shot forward and caught him across the back of his shoulders, slamming his face and body into a marble pillar. His lungs emptied on impact, and his ribs screamed like they were broken again. He forced himself to stay focused, though the screeching in his ears was so intense that it blurred his vision. Looking ahead, he saw the vague outline of someone rising from behind the upturned vehicle, and pointing their weapon back inside.

———

Hannah managed to toss the grenade just as she accelerated. Bullets pinged off the pillars, causing sparks to fly in her face. She tried to cover her eyes with her hand as a bullet ricocheted into the front tire. The handlebars swung, turning the ATV directly onto its side and throwing her off. In her panic, she attempted rolling to the right, though landing on the back of her wounded arm and crashing her hip against the remains of a bench.

The grenade exploded inside the building and the gunfire stopped. She listened above the sputtering engine for some wounded cries, or worse, unharmed footsteps coming closer to her. She reached out and grabbed her MP5, changing the magazine with her good hand. She peeked over the wreckage of her vehicle and aimed her weapon into the darkness, not willing to take any chances with assuming he was dead. She fired into the void, using the puff of smoke lit by the other entrance as a reference point to where it had detonated.

She ducked as pistol-fire came back, horrified that the grenade had no effect on him. She looked up the street, knowing the area well. If she were to outrun him, this long stretch would leave her as a sitting duck. Left with no alternative, she'd have to take the first side street and find a good spot where she could look back and catch him out in the open.

She reached for the HK714, not needing to check the ammunition as she'd only fired one bullet. A bullet that was the reason she was in this situation now.

I'll eliminate the whole family with this fucking gun, even if I have to go back to finish the sister. She forced herself to believe. She didn't feel like dying today.

She blindly fired the MP5 over the top of her head into the shopping centre and pulled herself up, running as hard as she could and putting as much distance between her and Ryan as her body would allow.

———

Ryan spotted the limping figure as they hurried away. Carefully pulling himself to his feet, he rubbed his eyes and started using what little light he had to search for the SIG. He hid his nose in the collar of his hoodie. The stale air finely had a chance to introduce itself to his lungs. He kicked a few objects on the ground, all cluttering like broken pottery. Finally, he felt something long and cylindrical. He picked it up, but it didn't feel metallic. It was a bone. He tossed it to the ground and kept feeling around, eventually touching the scope of the rifle. After placing the Glock in his waistband, he shouldered the rifle and stretched his back, letting his ribs click again.

"God-fucking-dammit." he wheezed. The ribs weren't broken, but they still hurt like hell. Putting his eye behind the scope, he pushed towards the opening, stumbling on more bones.

As he stepped out into the street, he got his first view of the city. The street in front had shops on either side that once were multiple stories, but had been reduced to mere structural skeletons. Every kind of weed or shrub had taken over, completely covering what remained. Decayed bodies littered the street, with limbs scattered metres apart from the person they were once attached to.

He blocked the apocalyptic view from his mind and pushed up the slight hill, checking the street to his right.

A bullet whistled past him, followed by the muffled sound of a suppressor as it smashed into the crumbled wall on the left side of the street. There was a loud, frustrated cry from where the bullet had come from.

He peeked round the corner to see where she was. Another bullet returned, though further off target, and the anguish was much louder.

Silenced shot. Her firing arm is injured. It must have a kickback. She's using the rifle.

He burst onto the side street and jumped behind the wreckage of a garbage truck. No sniper shot that time. He spotted a dumpster about twenty metres ahead on the other side. He breathed in and rushed across, only to be met with a burst of automatic gun fire. She switched to her primary weapon, with bullets whistling just over his back as he dived behind the bin and more rounds cannoned off the other side.

The automatic stopped. She was either reloading or baiting him. He saw a smaller side street about twenty metres to the left.

I have to make that.

Ryan prepared to run again when a metallic clunk cannoned off the middle of the road. Ryan glanced under the dumpster, seeing a tin-shaped grenade rolling across the ground. A dull puff hid behind an expanding plume, filling the street with a cloud of thick grey smoke and spreading out to either side.

Weak footsteps hurried into the distance, trying to escape the side street.

"You're not getting away, you cunt!" Ryan roared, pushing through the thick smog. His foot caught the top of her discarded MP5, buckling his ankle and sending him crashing to the ground. His elbows scrapped on the road, which only raised his anger and made him push harder as he limped out of the smoke. He reached the end of the street, meeting a wide main road and an electric tram toppled over in the middle. He checked both sides and pushed forward to the tram. Another crack from the sniper rifle came from in front- another side street. The bullet did very little to the tram as he hid behind it, but this time he didn't hear any obvious sounds of distress.

She's found a way to fire without aggravating her injury, Ryan rationalised. That's when he knew that she had likely found a spot where she could rest the barrel. She wasn't on the street anymore. She was in a building.

Ryan found himself on the other side of the situation for once. He had her under siege.

37

Rook walked across the open plaza of Rennes with Sam's Kar98k. A couple of the on-duty guards gave the disgraced sergeant a dirty look as he passed them.

He stared straight back and raised his middle finger. "Fuck off, it's not loaded."

They didn't reply, but they didn't have to say anything to show they didn't like him. Apparently, corrupting a communications officer to do under-the-nose surveillance while being suspended was a sin to them. He was glad that they thought that. It meant Eliza was still in the governing board's good books and allowed her to carry on without them knowing. Fortunately, General Woodburn had been let off lightly too, as it was Harper and Rook who originally had kept the information secret and took the hardest hit from the governing board.

Rook found Mikey sitting on the front steps of his dormitory building. A cigarette was in his mouth that had burned to the tip, and his skin was whiter than paper.

"Hey." Rook approached, waving his hand in front of Mikey's face, which seemed to snap him out of it and spit the burning butt on the ground. "Are you okay?"

"No, not really," Mikey stuttered. "I just had to have a video call with Cassy... and teach her how to embalm Lyndon." He wiped his nose.

"Jesus. I'm sorry." Rook sat next to him.

"Yeah. Just when I think we've gone through enough shit, there's more to wipe off our shoes."

"If it helps, Steph is out of surgery. They expect her to make a full recovery."

"That's good." Mikey leaned forward and picked up his cigarette packet to spark another one.

"She'll be brought over here, and placed in the room on the other side of Rich." Rook explained. "She's going to need you."

"I know. Any word from Ryan?"

"Not for four and a half hours, but we haven't intercepted anything between Admiral and his daughter either. We have to take that as a good thing."

"I wish I could. I want to phone him," Mikey sputtered as he inhaled hard, and Rook went to talk before he cut him off. "Yes, I know calling him while he's out there is dangerous for him."

"Well, in the meantime, I have something you can give back to him next time you see him." Rook handed Mikey the Kar98k.

"You saved his life with that. He'd probably say it's better for you to keep hold of it."

"I would love to, but I'm not really supposed to have any sort of firearm in my possession while suspended," Rook said as he looked back to the guards. "Even if it's not fucking loaded!"

"Okay. I'll take it back to him." Mikey begrudgingly agreed, "Thank you."

Rook's smart-radio buzzed. "Eliza?"

"Sir." she said abruptly. "I've intercepted another distress call from the daughter. She's panicking."

"Can you patch my device through?"

"Doing now," Eliza confirmed.

Rook and Mikey listened to the conversation between Admiral and Hannah on loudspeaker, and the finest slither of hope revealed itself.

"I guess we can call Ryan." Mikey said and laughed in joyous relief, feeling a weight lift off his heart.

38

During the long hours and thirty-something crack-shots at him, Ryan identified the building from where she was shooting. On the right side of the opposite side street stood a large church with tables and chairs outside. She was firing from an elevated position out of one of the windows.

The surrounding pavements looked no different from the streets of Maidville. Even a city as large as Nottingham had come to the natural decay and floral invasion. Ryan tried to figure out if there was another route he could take to flank her, but the toppled tram was in the middle of the wide road, with the nearest car being at least thirty metres from him, but closer to the church.

He pulled out all his bravery and sprinted towards it, closing the gap, though now he was in more of a remote position and with a weaker car to protect him.

He blind fired the SIG, slamming bullets into the thick brickwork. He had one more clip left. He'd have to play this wisely.

His smart-radio vibrated. "Not a good time." he shouted angrily after he pressed the button.

"Ryan. We have her location," Rook answered.

"I know. I'm there."

"In that case, you should know she's out of ammo."

Ryan's face dropped. He hung up and pushed towards the church while keeping his head low and weapon raised. The church doors were like no other he'd seen. Where the usual thick wooden doors with brass clangers should be, were the remains of a sleek glass and brightly tiled entrance. He trod over the rubble and shards, pushing into the grand opening.

No rows of pews. No alter.

An island bar stood in the middle, with a few bottles of spirits that had survived over the years. Thick cobwebs and dust tainted the air as Ryan stepped further inside. Surrounding the bar was the remains of bar tables and booths.

A church that became a bar? Even after The Fast War, Ryan felt like he'd truly seen everything. He found a stairwell at the back that took him up to a balcony with more tables. Fresh blood smeared against the walls.

She's up there. Ryan swapped the SIG for the pistol, giving him more control as he pushed up the stairs and stepped onto the balcony. On the table furthest away, Hannah held something up as she tried to control her breathing. It looked like a screen. Her smart-radio.

A bomb?

"What the fuck is that?" he growled.

"My dad." she answered weakly.

Ryan saw the ringing icon.

Admiral wants to talk?

Just kill her and go...

He might have a bargain...

Or you can kill his daughter in front of him.

The three options bounced around all corners of his head, while he kept his eyes peeled on her. He rushed to her and pressed the suppressor to her forehead. She tried to appear unfazed, but he could see the very real fear in her eyes. *This is why she contacted Daddy.*

Ryan felt he had to hurt her. To kill her. Now.

Remember the last time you acted on emotion.

The voices wouldn't stop.

"Shut up!" he bellowed loud enough that it scared something away in the ground floors rubble. Hannah's expression turned perplexed as Ryan's eyes conveyed the battle it was fighting deep inside.

With a quick reach back, he caught her on the side of the head with the butt of the gun, catching the smart-radio as it fell from her unconscious hands. He stood the device on the stool against the wall. He was in full view on the camera's right side, with Hannah's body on the left as her legs dangled off the table.

The screen flashed open. A dark figure appeared that Ryan couldn't make out, keeping their face hidden.

"Well." A thick midlands accent introduced themselves. "You must be Ryan."

"And you must be the dad of the woman who's about to die." he sneered back, not even in control of what he was thinking or saying. The monster inside was out, and it wanted to play.

"We both know you're not going to do that. It's not like you to kill someone who's unarmed."

"No, but it is like me to kill a whore who took away someone close to me," he screamed, raising the pistol at her.

"Don't!" Admiral's voice quivered as he shrieked. "Please. I can offer you something."

"My nephew's life back?" Ryan cried. "Can you do that?"

"No. But I'll give you the life of everyone who you still have."

Ryan squinted. Confused.

"There will be no further attacks on your people. We will leave you alone and let you live in peace," Admiral bargained.

"Peace? We've only known war since you people came into our lives. We're already at war."

"I can make it stop."

"Like how you got Connor out?" Ryan retorted. "You think he'll stop?"

"Ask him," Admiral said coldly.

"What?"

The camera shifted to Admiral's left. The face of nightmares lit up as it leaned in. Ryan's blood froze as the one good eye looked back at him. The clean shaved head and warped left ear was a face Ryan never wanted to see again.

"You have Admiral's word. Let Hannah live, and I won't come after you like I promised." Connor's voice would never sound reassuring.

"Maybe I want you to," Ryan spat. "Maybe I want you to come here."

"We both know you don't want that. You have Cassy and your children to think about," Connor said, reminding Ryan of the promise.

Ryan moved his finger to the trigger.

"Don't!" Connor yelped. The familiar sinisterism of his voice swapped with a panic. "Don't do it. Please. If you want anyone, take me, but not her."

Ryan was caught off guard at Connor's first display of fear. He was willing to give his life for this woman.

This woman.

This woman who killed Lyndon.

"None of what happened was personal. She was there to kill you," Connor begged.

"She shot my sister too." Ryan snapped back. "She would've killed anyone to get me."

"Just let her get back to Admiral. Take me."

"My sister will never hold her son again," Ryan sobbed.

She's unarmed. This isn't you.

"Don't you want this to end?" Connor pushed.

"Fuck!" Ryan screamed, taunted by the conflict in his head, keeping the gun aimed at her. "Fuck. Fuck. Cunt. Shit. Fuck." Nothing made sense. The darkened church walls closed in on him. Judging him.

This is me. I've executed before.

"Don't do it. Save her. End our battle," Connor pressed. The camera switched back to Admiral.

The battle will never end.

"Ryan. You can stop this," Admiral said again. "Leave her there and go."

Parts of Connor's letter played through his head like a tape on repeat: '*We will never stop. I'll be coming for you someday.*'

Time stopped. The doubt and confusion lifted. He knew what he was about to do.

I'm not a monster.

The suppressor hit the ground, followed by the thumping of metal clanging on marble.

"Thank you." Admiral exhaled heavily. Even with his face hidden, his relief radiated through the screen.

"I didn't drop my weapon," Ryan said bluntly. "I just took the suppressor off." He reraised the pistol in Hannah's direction. "I want you to hear this."

The shot cannoned through the empty church, deafening and reverberating as it bounced from wall to wall.

The screams, cries, and threats coming from the smart-radio were inaudible. Ryan hadn't gone deaf. His just soul didn't care to take anything in. He reached for the phone and switched it off, tossing it out the window.

Ryan looked down at what he'd done, wondering if he had made the right decision. Nothing was right anymore. There was no good and evil. Just people doing what they needed to do to even the score.

I'm not a monster.

39

T he drive home was unbearably long and lonely, leaving Ryan
with nothing but the inner torment and ambiguity to under-
mine his already damaged mental status. He'd had a long
time to think after dragging Hannah's body through the city centre,
tying her hands and feet up and tossing her next to the engine of
the 4x4.

He cleared the shattered glass from the window shield and took off,
doing his best in the mental haze to remember the route.

His smart-radio vibrated again. "What?" He answered on loudspeaker as he found his way back to the M1, coming up to where he
had his first conflict with Hannah.

"It's Harper. I'm calling to let you know there is a vehicle coming
after you."

"Vehicle?"

"Hannah's extraction team."

"Oh." Ryan's eyes widened as he remembered, turning onto the
motorway. "How far behind?"

"They left Nottingham one minute ago."

About ten minutes behind.

"Understood." Ryan tossed the phone and slowed, looking to the other side of the road. He recognised the rusty van and blood stains. "You can always learn from your enemy."

Two 4x4's entered the M1 from the Nottingham junction, hurtling south before spotting Ryan's stationary Land Rover. Everyone but the drivers got out. Black pants and grey T-shirts as normal, fixated on what they saw.

Ryan had tied Hannah to the outside of the rear door in a crucifix position, with organs hanging from near her lower abdomen. The men were horrified by the sight, as some clearly knew her. Two of the party swept both sides of the motorway as the one in front approached, reaching his hand out to her and reading a message that Ryan had left for them on her T-shirt.

"Holy shit!" The baling, blond man exclaimed loudly, causing everyone to look in that direction.

Watching all this from under the rusty van's chassis, Ryan lifted the heavy machine gun onto the bonnet and opened fire, taking down four with the first, chaotic burst. The MG42 blew holes into people that made Sam's rifle look like a water gun, and there wasn't a single fibre in Ryan that felt remorse or guilt for the bodies he was tearing to pieces. This was for Cooper, Fergie, Hamsa, Hamsa's family, Doc, Sam, Rich, Lyndon, Steph. His jaw was clenched so tight he bit through his lip. The muzzle flashed into his eyes so wide that it could've made him appear like a Termite. He turned the barrel to the vehicles, shredding the drivers into nothing recognisable as body tissue and blood sprayed over what remained of the battered windows and interiors.

Once the bullets ran out, he stood from behind the bonnet and walked over to the mid-road carnage. One of the men sputtered, and Ryan shot him in the head with his Glock, than proceeded to spit blood over the man's body. He gathered their weapons and threw them onto the front seat of his Land Rover.

He looked at Hannah, pulling the rotted guts away and placing them next to the decomposing deer he'd cut them from by the side of the road. His eyes caught the message he'd written in blood on her clothes: 'You're the birds. I'm the stone.'

Ryan was grateful Harper had explained the whole communication between Hannah and Admiral before she took Lyndon's life, because now he was going to use *the two birds, one stone* phrase back against them all, in any possible way he saw fit.

Once Ryan cut Hannah down from the position, he lay her in the back seat again and double-tied her hands and feet to the luggage rack.

———

Dominic sat by the window, looking over Maidhill. Drinker pulled up a seat next to him.

"He always comes back," Dominic said.

"Aye, that's what I've heard."

"Any contact since he was warned about the extraction team?"

"Not yet." Drinker sighed softly, staring at his own smart-radio.

"He put himself in front of half a thousand of them last year," Dominic said, looking at the very spot Ryan had fired the shots that saved Penbrook. "Connor couldn't kill him. Hannah couldn't kill him. He's not dead."

They watched the hill intently for hours. The multi-coloured clouds deepened as the night drew closer.

The hand-held radio crackled. "You there, *boss?*" Ryan asked.

"Don't call me that," Dominic laughed, relieved.

"Fucking annoying, isn't it? I'm an hour away. Get everyone in the cafeteria." Ryan paused then added. "I've got something I need to show everyone."

———

"I know what I've done, and the target I've put on all of us," Ryan explained as he stood on the podium. Everyone was beyond relieved to see that he'd gotten back safe, and just as scared about what was to come. "But there was no peace deal to be made, even if Admiral and Connor claimed so. I wasn't letting Hannah go, because they're still going to come after us eventually."

"What makes you so sure of that?" Cassy asked, sitting in the middle of the crowd.

"This." Ryan sighed, reaching into his hoodie pocket. Before the meeting started, Ryan had run up to their family room and unlocked the drawer, taking the three items out. He pulled Sam's pocketknife out first, then Doc's glasses. "A month ago, when I went into town with Mikey and Drinker. We found these on the way back. Recognise them?"

It wasn't until he offered the question that everyone recognised the items, with gasps echoing around the room.

"We found these at the petrol station, attached to the pumps. The knife was used to hold the glasses in place... and there was a note too," Ryan said, pulling the paper out and unfolding it. He cleared his throat and began to read it out loud,

"Dear Hippy Cunt. Whatever happens to me today... whether I live, die, or get to fuck your little girlfriend in front of the decaying bodies of your people, know this: We will never stop. I'll be seeing you again.

I mean, If the taste beneath your skin is as good as your friends, how could I say no?

Your good friend, Connor."

Ryan turned the note over and laid it flat on the stand, giving his family and friends and a moment to digest what they had been threatened with.

"Why didn't you show us this before?" Sandra asked.

"I wanted to, and I was going to. There just didn't seem to be a good time with Rich getting ill, securing the perimeter, the fucking twins, and.. Lyndon." Ryan wiped his nose, "I wasn't trying keep it a secret. I just didn't know when the best time was."

"You did the right thing." Cassy said out loud. The normal innocence she displayed had been coated with a cold hatred. A part of the note was aimed directly at her, and she knew it wasn't a joke. "They tried to get you arrested, and they failed. After that, they tried to assassinate you, and that failed." She looked over her shoulders, stood, and addressed everyone. "We don't need to second guess that they would've come here even if Ryan had let that bitch go. We all know what these people are, and what they're willing to do." She turned back and looked at her fiancé. "We were at war with them anyway. We might as well face it head on."

Ryan held eye contact with her. A tear trickled down his left cheek as the regret of his actions lifted. Whether it was the safest decision, or not, he knew that he did the right thing.

40

Harper stirred his coffee and rubbed his temples as he sat at the spare terminal of the communications room. Rook and Harper had both been restored to duty since the revelation that Tech Supervisor Monreal was indeed the mole, and had got on the flight with the escapees. His laptop was never found.

Woodburn and Rook walked in with a look of apprehension on their faces.

"What did you need to see us so urgently for?" Rook asked, pulling out a chair at the terminal next to the coffee station.

"Ryan just sent me a photo." Harper opened the messages on his smart-radio, then held the screen up to the pair.

"Who is that?" Rook squinted at the image.

"What in God's name?" Woodburn leaned in, recognising the person in the photo.

"Yeah," Harper nodded, then looked at Rook. "That is Hannah Caven. Admiral's daughter. Ryan didn't kill her."

Rook looked away and scratched his forehead, taking a moment to understand what was happening. Woodburn rubbed his chin, a thoughtful look on his face.

"I don't know what Ryan's game-plan is," Harper carried on. "What do you think we should do?"

"Should we even try bringing her in?" Rook asked doubtfully. "We know this is the one prisoner that he isn't letting go."

"He might not have a choice." Harper added, the regret evident. "It might not be up to him."

"You take her away from him, you'll destroy everything you've worked towards. That trust, respect, and friendship goes out the window."

"If *we* take her away," Harper shot back, "it'll take the target off Ryan, and Admiral won't pursue the vineyard, and will turn himself in."

"Ryan had a chance to take the target off the vineyard by letting her go, he didn't take it." Rook pointed out. "There must be a good reason he's keeping her alive and in their custody."

"Maybe so." Harper agreed, then his face darkened. "But letting civilians keep prisoners isn't the future we're fighting for."

"No. Making sure the vineyard remains our ally is what we're fighting for." Rook returned the hostility.

"Enough!" Woodburn bellowed, leaving Harper and Rook glaring at each other. "We tell no one of this."

"Sir?" Harper couldn't believe what he'd just heard.

"Ryan has the upper hand, and we need to keep it that way." Woodburn relayed out loud. "He has a very big card up his sleeve by making Admiral think he killed her. If we tell anyone else, the information could get to another one of his moles, and then back to him."

"If Admiral still thinks Ryan killed her though... he'll send hell their way." Rook said, pulling the chair out and sitting. He folded his hands together and pressed them to his forehead, "Are you sure you want the vineyard to still have this target on their back."

"The relocation program starts in four weeks. The vineyard will have armed personnel for the duration of the integration. Ryan knows this." Woodburn tapped the back of his chair lightly. "Admiral and his people won't stand a chance against an even heavier armed vineyard. As long as he doesn't know Hannah is alive, Ryan has a get-out-of-jail card should they come hunting for him. I suggest..." he looked at

Harper, "...for the sake of the relationship you've built with Ryan, and for the future of Maidville, all three of us keep this a secret."

"Sir, this could backfire on all of us." Harper protested, "It's against protocol."

"I've told you before, my friend." Woodburn smiled, but remained adamant, "We're not officially on duty yet. Message Ryan to say we're on his side, then delete that photo immediately."

41

R yan couldn't get used to the fact that General Woodburn had not only agreed to let Ryan keep Hannah hostage, but also that this was all going to go on under the noses of the European Alliance. He'd been reassured that extra defences would be in place should Admiral attempt to launch and offensive on them all. In that moment however, he didn't feel like celebrating these minor victories.

In the two weeks since bringing Hannah in, Steph had pulled through her injuries and woken from her coma. Ryan had to tell her about Lyndon via video call. He couldn't be there. He could only watch through a screen as she broke down violently. His sister, robbed of her only child, and he couldn't even be there to console her.

Only a couple of days after she found out, the first suicide attempt happened through the means of hanging. Luckily, Mikey had heard her tying the bed sheet to the window handle, and broke into her room to pull her back in just before she jumped. The second attempt involved a piece of broken glass and her wrists, and again, thanks to Mikey being alert, she wasn't allowed to succeed.

Ryan had never felt so helpless to her, and it broke him to know how much she was dying inside. His regular three hours' worth of sleep every night had now been reduced to barely an hour, with him sitting on the end of the bed and softly sobbing for her.

Mikey was in constant contact regarding her condition, and his last communication caused Ryan to have such a violent meltdown that Drinker and Dominic had to pin him down and stop him from going to the basement and stabbing Hannah to death. Mikey had told Ryan that Steph was now under heavy medication. She'd been dumbed down. All to avoid the grief that Hannah had caused her.

In time, Ryan calmed himself enough not to kill her, ignoring all the urges, but they never left. In what was nothing more than good timing, Harper had called to confirm that teams were being sent to England by sea to start rounding up all the other survivor groups and bring them to the vineyard- with heavily armed units to help during the process. The distraction was needed, but after being told that Steph wasn't allowed to return while being officially committed to the psych ward of Rennes hospital, the hate poured back into his veins.

Harper needed to soften the blow, and Ryan was ready to play a card that would serve his hidden agenda well. The smart-radio buzzed.

"Harper?" Ryan answered swiftly, "Are you ready to tell me yet?"

"Fine." Harper relented.

"Go on then. Why was Connor so quick to offer himself in place of Hannah?"

"Connor is her Godfather." Harper explained, "He also saved her from a gang of groomers."

"Groomers?" Ryan asked, his memory tweaking some reports he'd heard on the news.

"Middle Eastern men, coaxing young girls into sex. They were rife throughout the midlands. More notably in towns like Rochdale and Rotherham. When Admiral found out Hannah was being approached, he asked Connor to pay them a visit."

"What happened to them?" Ryan asked, intrigued.

"Well, Hannah was never bothered again... and they never groomed again," Harper answered.

"That's why she came after me so hard? Because of what I did to the man that saved her?"

"No doubt."

Ryan absorbed the information and disconnected the call, then flicked his cigarette on the car park gravel, letting it sizzle before extinguishing it in the pathetic snow. He turned to head back inside as Drinker walked out to meet him.

"The new people coming here will have to get used to staying inside if this snow actually gets worse. It's gonna be colder than step-dads heart." Drinker joked, zipping up his parka-jacket.

"No doubt," Ryan grinned, not just at the joke, but because he couldn't get used to the fact that Drinker had shaved his head to a fine stubble. "We've got about ten days before they start arriving."

"Aye, fucking great idea. Bringing everyone here all at once. What could possibly go wrong?"

"If they give us the armed support for the integration process like they promised, nothing." Ryan slapped him on the shoulder and started to head inside. "Enjoy your lunch break."

It had been years since the last, harsh winter, and everyone was fully prepared for it. The cafeteria was a sea of beanie-hats and coats as everyone sat for lunch, and none of them had been working outside. The production of soap and detergent was increased for the new arrivals, along with beds and other furniture which would transferred into the last remaining function room to serve as sleeping space for the families. They didn't have any time build anymore rooms, and with the fast approaching winter, they couldn't afford to adapt the water system to fit more showers or sinks.

"I've drawn up the shower rota." Cassy announced, tugging the hood of Ryan's coat.

"That was quick," he said as took the piece of paper and scanned it over. "How many families coming in the first two months?"

"Harper said twenty two families between four different sets of survivors."

"We only have seven spare rooms with toilets and showers," Ryan rubbed his chin.

"Leave it to me. I'll make sure it's sorted." She kissed his cheek and headed back towards the water corridor. "Love you."

"Love you too." He watched disappear, happy that she had volun-tarily stepped up and started taking responsibility for the jobs he didn't know how to do. *Just like when Steph stepped up,* his mind wondered, knowing that his sister used the extra work as a coping mechanism.

He grabbed a bowl of sweetcorn soup from the hot counter and headed down to the cold basement. His breath misted in front of his face as he walked through the void, leaving the bowl in front of the cage door.

Hannah's dirty hands reached out and grabbed it. "No spoon again?" she teased dryly.

"Not today," Ryan replied, sitting on the chair opposite the door and staring at her. Hannah titled the bowl to her mouth slowly, took a mouthful then slowly lowered it to the tiled floor, smiling all the while.

Cold winds rattled against the second receptions' outer door, causing the slightly damaged, iron bars to rattle. Ryan ignored it all, keeping his eyes locked on her.

Hannah stayed in a sitting position on the mattress, pulling the blanket up and covering her from the shoulders below, "You know," she picked up the bowl again, "You're not the only person who stares at me like that."

Like me, whoever is staring at you is probably thinking about killing you.

Hannah finished her soup and slid the bowl towards the small opening. "Your pretty, little girlfriend," she said with a malicious smile. "Just in case you were wondering who the other starer is."

Cassy? Ryan tried to hide his surprise.

"If looks could kill..." Hannah continued, "How many lives has she taken since the war?"

"None of your fucking business," He snapped back, though he guessed that Hannah knew the answer was none.

"Well, if I do become her first, I'd be happy knowing that I died staining your *happy-little-family* image."

You leave Cassy out of this, bitch. Ryan wanted to open the door and beat her with the soup bowl. He couldn't. He had to keep it together, and couldn't let Cassy join the dark world he lived in. She'd been through enough. "You get pleasure out of knowing what you do to people, don't you?"

"At least I would have had the stones to murder whoever killed a family member of mine," Hannah taunted, the corner of her mouth twitched. She saw no change in Ryan's glare. "Are you going to tell me why you didn't kill me now?"

It was Ryan's turn to slowly smile. "I didn't kill you because your dad and Connor are eventually going to come here for revenge. We both know that. When they see you're alive and with a gun to your head, I want to know if they meant what they said about turning themselves in, in place for your freedom."

"You think they'll make a trade?" She laughed.

"I saw the looks on their faces." Ryan nodded coldly. "I have no doubt about it..." he stood and folded the chair, placing it against the foundational pillar. "But there won't be a trade. None of you will be leaving alive." He looked back. "What was it you said before you pulled the trigger on my nephew?"

Hannah's face dropped, even her hair seemed to turn pale. "Two birds..."

"One stone." Ryan walked off, leaving her on her own.

ACKNOWLEDGMENTS

Considering this part hasn't been run past my editors, it's probably going to read really badly compared to the story that they worked on. So i'll start with them!

Ericka, C.J, and Abby. Thank you for being involved in the second chapter of this story. I'm still new to this world, but I'm learning at a hell of rate, and it's all thanks to you. Looking forward to working on the next three books with you.

Team Penbrook! Nastassia, Lucy, Chava, Sarah, and Tanya. Thank you for the needed advice and direction during the beta stage. You helped shape this story and kept me going. My ARC readers- thank your for volunteering and being part of this.

Dean Gaida. Your work with the paintbrush is almost as sexy as that pass I made to you in the last match. Glad to have you onboard and bringing it all to life.

Edita. None of this happens without you. None of it. I hope you know that. We can do even more, and we are already.

My family and friends. I don't need to say much more than that.

And finally, and probably most importantly: The fans. It still boggles my mind that I have fans, I can't lie. Your support. Your encouragement. Your feedback. Your reviews... It means the world to me.

Thank you all.
I truly hope you enjoyed this book.
Daniel Munro.

ABOUT THE AUTHOR

In my first book, I used this page as a message to try and help people. and I'm not going to change now. If you want to know more about me personally, my website and Instagram links are below.

For anyone out there who feels like they don't belong, or are struggling within themselves: You're not alone.

I said my first book was proof that you can do more than you believe, and this book should solidify that statement more.

Whatever you are facing right now is temporary. I won't try and claim I know how you feel, because I haven't walked in your shoes. All I can tell you is that with the right help and support, you can find your way out of whatever is trying to pull you down.

You have it in you. You are stronger than you could ever know, and you can do more than you could ever believe. When you do start kicking ass, promise me one thing: Be you. Authentically you. Only you have the right to define who you are.

Much love.

Daniel.

www.authordanielmunro.co.uk

Lightning Source UK Ltd.
Milton Keynes UK
UKHW010234200223
417301UK00004B/6